HONEYMOON FOR ONE

Also by Keira Andrews

Contemporary

The Spy and the Mobster's Son
Honeymoon for One
Beyond the Sea
Ends of the Earth
Arctic Fire

Lifeguards of Barking Beach
Flash Rip
Free Wind

Holiday
The Christmas Deal
The Christmas Leap
The Christmas Veto
A Baby for Christmas
Only One Bed
Merry Cherry Christmas
Santa Daddy
In Case of Emergency
Eight Nights in December
If Only in My Dreams
Where the Lovelight Gleams
Gay Romance Holiday Collection

Sports
Kiss and Cry
Reading the Signs
Cold War
The Next Competitor
Love Match
Synchronicity (free read!)

Gay Amish Romance Series
A Forbidden Rumspringa
A Clean Break
A Way Home

A Very English Christmas

Valor Duology
Valor on the Move
Test of Valor
Complete Valor Duology

Historical

Kidnapped by the Pirate
Semper Fi
The Station
Voyageurs (free read!)

Paranormal

Kick at the Darkness Trilogy
Kick at the Darkness
Fight the Tide
Defy the Future

Fantasy

Barbarian Duet
Wed to the Barbarian
The Barbarian's Vow

HONEYMOON FOR ONE

KEIRA ANDREWS

Honeymoon for One
Written and published by Keira Andrews
Cover by Dar Albert
Formatting by BB eBooks

ISBN: 978-1-988260-36-5

Acknowledgments

Along with the wonderful usual suspects—Anara, Becky, Jules, and Mary—who provided beta reading and support, I must thank Aussies Karen and Pat for lending me their expertise on Australian lingo in making sure I got it right. Clay is a tribute to the "blokey blokes" I met when I worked as a bartender in an outback pub near Cloncurry. These guys really did sound like Crocodile Dundee and said things like "fair dinkum" without irony. It was glorious!

Thank you to DJ Jamison for her eagle-eyed final proofread, and as always to Leta Blake for her invaluable developmental edits and treasured friendship.

Author's Note

My dad was late-deafened as an adult, and I based Ethan's experiences on his. Everyone's journey with hearing loss is unique, and I also want to thank Connor K. for reading the book and sharing his perspective as a late-deafened adult to help make the story as authentic as possible. Much appreciated!

Chapter One

AS THE YOUNG woman took a step onto the almost-empty A train and asked Ethan what was probably a simple question, his heart skipped, stomach instantly knotting. He answered, "I'm sorry, what?"

Her eyebrows drew close, and she repeated herself, but she was turning her head as she spoke, looking up above the subway car doors—probably for a map of stops, which was in vain on the A train—and the words were lost in a mumble of indistinguishable sound.

She still had one foot on the platform, unwilling to commit. She held out her hands in frustration, thin eyebrows raised. Again, she said, "*Mumble*," but this time he also heard "Fulton."

"Yes, it stops at Fulton!" he said.

As the doors closed, she skipped aboard, just as a guy approached from farther down the car, saying something Ethan missed in the roar of metal as the train picked up speed.

The woman gave Ethan a quizzical smile, shaking her head, like, *Why did you have to make that so difficult?* Then she said something to the other man, nodding and smiling at him before taking a seat, the guy retreating back to the end of the car.

Face hot, Ethan slouched on the orange plastic. At least she hadn't gotten too mad. Metal screeched and crashed again, and he winced, the noise amplified by his hearing aids. Hearing someone talk could sometimes be impossible, but trains rattling and banging, jackhammering and construction, engines roaring, busking mariachi bands droning—all that Ethan could hear at a painfully loud volume on his daily commute.

When he got off at Times Square to transfer to the Q train, the station somehow always full of people even midday in January, he hurried past a group of young men dancing, their music throbbing in his ears.

When an accordion player got on the train, along with a group of teenagers shouting and jostling each other, Ethan couldn't take it anymore. Seriously, what fresh hell was this? Since when did people give money to hear the freaking *accordion*?

He just wanted to fantasize about his wedding and honeymoon in peace. And maybe play a little pseudo Scrabble on his phone to calm his nerves.

Why should I be nervous anyway? It's all going to be perfect. Michael and I are finally on the same page again. Even though—

No. He wasn't going to let the doubts creep in. Everything was going to be *perfect*.

His left hearing aid was bugging his ear anyway, so as the bastard accordion player neared, Ethan turned both his aids off and eased them out of his ears and into the little case he carried, which he zipped into the pocket of his puffy winter coat.

Ahhh. The volume of the world was turned way down when he went "off the air," as his boss put it. Ethan wasn't what the docs called "profoundly deaf" without his hearing aids, but sounds were muffled—especially speaking and noises of a higher frequency. His current diagnosis was still in the moderate hearing loss range, but leaning toward severe rather than mild.

Being out in the world without his hearing aids on made his stomach acidy, but New York City was just So. Fucking. Loud. At least with his aids out the music and shouting kids faded into a hum of distant white noise, and he was grateful.

The flash of gratitude was of course immediately followed by a long gnaw of guilt since the more he turned off his aids, the less stimulation his hearing nerves received, which could affect his ability to recognize the nuances of speech.

He could still hear that someone was speaking without his aids, but it was only a vowel-filled murmur, the clarity of the words frustratingly out of reach. His devices helped a lot, but most people talked way too fast and he regularly had to ask people to repeat themselves. Day after day, it was exhausting.

That was part of why he hadn't wanted to plan a big wedding. The thought of trying to hear and talk to all those caterers, reception hall folks, and guests would take all the joy out of the day.

In college, doctors had assured him there was nothing he could have done differently, and that a genetic anomaly was to blame for him losing his hearing. They insisted the one time his ears had rung after a Jay-Z concert hadn't been the culprit. Still, Ethan wondered sometimes, and he obviously wanted to do everything he could to keep the quality of the hearing he still had.

But he'd spent all morning struggling to follow along during a video conference call, and it would just be a wall of noise on the train anyway. Shouldn't the kids have been in school?

He snorted to himself at the thought. Michael sometimes said—with varying degrees of affection depending on his mood— that Ethan had become a grumpy old man when he lost his hearing. Maybe he had. Most twenty-seven-year-olds seemed to still like partying and goofing around, but he was glad to ignore the kids and the accordion's wailing as the train rattled across the Manhattan Bridge. He played the word "kumquat" for twenty-five points in his game, vaulting him into the lead against his best friend, Todd.

Ethan's boss in accounting at Anderson/Fromm Investments

had sent him home early as a wedding gift since she'd blanked on organizing a shower for him. He'd actually been relieved to avoid a party, although he appreciated the sentiment.

He really did—the people he worked with were nice, and he liked them. But he'd honestly rather skip gathering with them in a boardroom to open a card of well wishes as he smiled awkwardly, followed by small talk he struggled to hear while they all ate overly sweet grocery-store cake.

One of the reasons he'd gone into environmental accounting was to be left alone with his spreadsheets and numbers and international government regulations. He created reports on the most cost-efficient ways for the company's offices around the world to use energy and reduce overhead. Ethan had to admit he wasn't much of a people person now that he was hard of hearing, and he'd never really made *friends* at work the way he probably should have.

Michael, always plugged in socially between work, his extended, tight-knit Chinese family, and a seemingly endless parade of casual and intimate friends, said Ethan should simply try harder, like he used to. He still didn't understand how much of an *effort* social situations were now.

As the train rumbled through Brooklyn, Ethan breathed through the flare of resentment. Michael tried, he did. They'd both been extroverts when they'd met, and it was hard for him now that Ethan found socializing so much more exhausting. But Ethan was trying to go out more, and Michael was trying to get used to staying in sometimes. Compromise was what a relationship was all about, right? That's why they were so good together. That's why they were so in love.

His insides went all gooey remembering how Michael had woken him with a blow job that morning. Ethan had wanted to skip work and kiss him all day, but at least now he'd be home early and they could get back to it. After all, they were going to be newlyweds soon. Plus they were still making up for lost time.

Ethan breathed through another pang of guilt. The past was the past, and he couldn't change it. He was finally through the tunnel of his depression, and their relationship the past year had been completely rejuvenated. Even if socially they didn't have as much in common as they used to, their sex life was better than ever. That went to show that they *were* right together.

A shiver of lust ran through him as he glanced up to check which station the train was pulling into. Maybe he and Michael could spend the afternoon in bed before the pre-wedding party that night. Ethan would have preferred no party at all, but compromise and all that. They definitely had plenty of time to get naked first unless Michael had too much work on his plate. But it was the Friday afternoon before their wedding and honeymoon trip, and he was a freelancer, so hopefully he could knock off early.

Closing his eyes, Ethan imagined Michael's glossy black hair between his fingers, the metal stud of the piercing in his tongue, smooth and exciting against Ethan's tongue…and his skin, and his long cock…

Before he popped a boner, Ethan opened his eyes and went back to his phone, where the countdown clock app on his home screen announced:

00001 DAYS UNTIL WEDDING AND HONEYMOON

It was actually happening. His stomach swooped, and his smile must have appeared lunatic to anyone watching him. Not only was he marrying the boy of his dreams, like his mom had wanted him to, but he had three glorious weeks off work for their Australian honeymoon.

They were doing a ten-night bus tour down the eastern coast of Australia from Cairns to Sydney, and then a week in Sydney in an Airbnb condo. They'd do some sightseeing and have lots of sex. Life had given Ethan plenty of lemons, but he and Michael were finally making some goddamn lemonade.

As the train neared Prospect Park, he pulled on his hat and gloves, still grinning to himself. He should put his hearing aids back in, but it was only a few blocks to the apartment. Exiting to the street, he was careful to look both ways, swearing as he splashed into a deep puddle by the curb, his black leather Oxfords instantly soaked. The slush blocked the sewer grates, creating gutter lakes. Ugh, Ethan was so over winter, and it was only mid-January.

But it didn't matter because soon—*tomorrow!*—he and Michael would be married and heading down under for sun and sand and koala bears. Adrenaline fizzing through him, Ethan crossed the street and took a flying jump onto the curb to avoid soaking his shoes again.

Some people thought January was a weird time to get married, but he and Michael had agreed to a courthouse ceremony followed by a late lunch. Ethan's mom had always said it's not the wedding that matters, it's the marriage. This way they could spend most of their money on the honeymoon.

Ethan had actually been shocked when Michael agreed to a small wedding, considering a seven-course gourmet meal and massive reception was more Michael's speed. But then he'd been surprised when Michael had accepted his proposal in the first place. Michael had always sneered at the heteronormativity of marriage in the past, but with love came compromise, and he knew marriage was important to Ethan.

It made him feel so safe and loved to know that Michael would go outside his comfort zone to make Ethan happy. Honestly, most guys would have dumped Ethan's sorry ass a long time ago, but not Michael. Despite the frigid air, Ethan's chest warmed with gratitude and affection.

I'm marrying the boy of my dreams.

After the ceremony, they were going to a trendy little fondue place in Park Slope called Dip as a nod to Ethan's mom and grandmother, who'd come from Switzerland. Since they were renting the whole restaurant for a couple of hours, the owner had agreed to turn off the background music. Aside from Todd, the guests would pretty much just be Michael's friends and immediate family.

It had taken some convincing to get the Wongs on board with a low-key ceremony and lunch before Ethan and Michael headed to the airport for their evening flight. But once he and Michael compromised and agreed to an additional wedding reception in the spring with Michael's extended family and the Wongs' family friends, which was somehow *hundreds* of people and required renting out a banquet hall in Buffalo, they'd stopped shouting and started smiling.

Ethan probably wouldn't be able to have a conversation at the banquet hall without saying, "Pardon?" or "I'm sorry, can you please repeat that?" about a hundred times, but he was used to nodding and smiling and pretending. He usually just laughed agreeably and hoped no one was asking him a question.

But he'd do whatever it took to make the Wongs happy. While they hadn't been exactly ecstatic when he and Michael first moved in together, they'd come around and were good people. Besides, they'd be his family now too, and he wanted them to have the wedding reception they'd dreamed of for their son.

Ethan missed his parents with a familiar pang. Not for the first time, he wondered what they'd think. Not about him being gay or getting married—they'd been a hundred percent supportive of that. Just what they'd think of *him*. When he thought back to being a kid and teenager, he'd been so outgoing. He'd had so many friends.

Even after his parents died, his friends had been a massive comfort. He'd thrown himself into dating and partying, going to concerts, and playing soccer. Now he had to take out his hearing aids if he exercised so the sweat wouldn't damage them, and loud music was torture.

Maybe he wasn't as much fun as he used to be, but surely his parents would like the man he'd become? Especially now that he'd emerged from the depression he'd sunk into for so long after his hearing started to go. All his parents ever wanted was for him to be happy. And he was! He and Michael had stayed together through everything, and now they were about to start the rest of their lives.

He waited for a streetlight, anticipation bubbling up. The ceremony and receptions didn't matter. What mattered was that he and Michael were committing to each other. It hadn't been an easy road, but they'd managed it together. And if Michael didn't seem *quite* as excited about the honeymoon—even though it had been his idea since he knew Ethan had always wanted to go to Australia—that was totally okay.

Since college, Michael had often talked about going to Ibiza for the ultimate party vacay. Staying up all night dancing, and sleeping half the day with a hangover, then doing it all again. Ethan would have done it to make Michael happy, but Michael had insisted on Australia for their honeymoon, saying if it was what Ethan wanted then it was what he wanted too.

And if Ethan didn't quite believe him, that was *fine*. It was good to be loved by a man who was putting him first. He smiled to himself again, doing a giddy little skip despite the wind gusting, the temperature dropping as the day continued.

But what if we have a shitty honeymoon because Michael hates the trip? Is that a bad omen for our marriage? But then why did he insist on it? Why—

He was just being paranoid. Michael regularly told him to stop overthinking things and just *be*. So Ethan would, goddamn it.

The one-bedroom apartment he and Michael shared in Prospect Park was of course nowhere near the actual park, but the area was relatively peaceful compared to midtown. Not that they could afford midtown anyway. The three-story building desperate-ly needed fresh paint and stairwell lights that didn't operate on independent whims, but the apartment itself was roomy (by NYC standards) and gorgeous.

Michael was a graphic designer and had amazing taste. Even though Ethan didn't love the cool color palette of gray and black with an icy touch of blue, it was very stylish. Everyone who came over remarked on how their apartment looked like it came out of a magazine.

There was no elevator, and Ethan hummed to himself as he climbed the three flights, briefly scowling at the flickering light on the second-floor landing that would apparently never be fixed. Often it went out completely, which was definitely a fire code violation.

Inside the apartment, he tossed his coat on a hook, unlaced his shoes, and left them on the mat to dry, shoving over a couple pairs of sneakers. Grimacing, he peeled off his damp, clammy socks and spread them over the heating grate. He took off his hat and ran a hand through his hair, which he kept trimmed at the back but a little longer over his forehead and the tops of his ears to disguise the plastic casings of his hearing aids.

Rubbing at his sore left ear, he went through the little foyer into the living room, surprised that Michael wasn't at his desk. Michael worked from home, and the far end of the main room held his sleek desk and design boards. He'd left a sketchbook open, and Ethan paused to admire the clean lines of the design for a new brand of Chardonnay.

Maybe Michael had run out to get lunch from the Mexican place at the corner. Shit, Ethan should have texted him and picked it up on his way home. He'd just change quickly out of his suit and text to meet up with him. Waking up his phone, Ethan was faintly aware of a low noise as he pushed open the bedroom door, which had been left a few inches ajar.

He stopped dead, staring into the room.

Michael hadn't gone out to grab fish tacos and the amazing guac and plantain chips from Pepe's.

No, Michael was in bed on his back, and he wasn't napping. He wasn't alone. Someone else was there—riding him, spine arched and lips parted on sounds too soft for Ethan to hear. Michael's eyes were closed, his mouth open with faint moans. They both appeared unaware of Ethan's presence, and Ethan stood there like the biggest loser ever, blood gone to ice in his veins, as he watched his fiancé fucking someone else.

Michael gripped the meaty buttocks of the muscular blond man taking his cock. That the man in question was Todd, Ethan's best friend since they'd met in Psych 101 at Buffalo State, sank in a few horrifying, soul-obliterating moments later.

"What?"

Ethan wasn't sure if he'd said it aloud or not, but apparently he had, because Michael and Todd seized up and jerked their eyes to him in the doorway. Ethan didn't need to hear Todd's exclamation—he could read his lips clearly: *"Holy fuck!"*

Todd scrambled off Michael, and now they were talking too fast and frantically for him to understand a word even if he'd had his hearing aids in. Michael's face was flushed crimson, his high cheekbones accentuated more than usual. He reached out his hands pleadingly, like Ethan was a wild dog he was begging not to attack.

As if he could ask for *anything*, splayed out on *their* bed with a condom still on his hard dick. His dick that had just been inside Ethan's *best fucking friend.*

A drum of fury and hurt pounded through him along with a hissing sound in his mind, and Ethan wished he could wake up from whatever fucking nightmare he'd stumbled into. This couldn't be real. This couldn't be happening. He stood there useless as they implored him, his cheeks going hot with shame.

He shouted, "I can't hear you!" and hated himself.

Ethan had to retreat into the hall to fish his fucking hearing aids out of his coat. An awful, sticky mess of humiliation made his eyes burn with tears. For a moment, as he jammed the ear molds back in and hooked the beige plastic housing behind his ears, he considered leaving all together, his legs shaking with the urge to run as hard and fast as he could.

No.

He whirled around and stormed back into the bedroom to find Michael and Todd now on either side of the bed tugging on their clothes. Michael's dark hair, which he wore shaved on the sides and gelled up on top, was spiky. Ethan shouted, "What the fuck is this?"

After zipping his jeans, Michael reached out. Ethan jerked back and thwacked the back of his head on the door frame. Face creasing with apparent concern—which made Ethan's blood pressure fly even higher—Michael stretched out his hand again.

"No!" Ethan's chest rose and fell as he struggled to catch his breath. "Don't touch me. You're never touching me again." A spasm of grief gripped him as the truth of his own words set in. *This can't be real.*

The concern on Michael's face morphed into hurt, his eyes welling. "Please. Let us explain."

Ethan had to laugh or else he might wail or scream. He stared at Todd, who stood on the far side of the bed, his pale face beet red and his blond hair sticking up. His black shirt was buttoned wrong, one side hanging lower than the other.

"*How?*" Ethan looked between them. "You were going to spend the afternoon fucking in our bed, then show up tonight at Rollertown, like—like *nothing*? Like *this* was *nothing*?"

Since Michael had gone along with a quiet little wedding, Ethan had suggested they do a party the night before with all Michael's friends. Even though the music would be too loud,

Ethan had figured that with ironic hipster roller skating, at least he wouldn't have to worry much about being part of conversations.

"We never meant to…" Michael shook his head, and then words burst out. "We didn't *mumble*, but *mumble* have to *mumble*!"

"What?" Ethan clenched his fists. "Talk. Slower. I can't fucking understand you. You always talk too fast! No matter how many times I tell you!"

A flash of irritation passed over Michael's face before his Adam's apple bobbed and he visibly took a breath. He was a few inches shorter than Ethan's six feet, and he had to look up at Ethan. "Sorry. I said we didn't plan this. And you have to understand how much we both love you."

Ethan could only laugh again, his chest hollow. "Do I? Is that what I have to understand?" Bile rose in his throat. "We're supposed to be getting married tomorrow. Tomorrow! How could you?" A sickening realization slammed him like a sucker punch. "This…" He shook his head. "This isn't the first time, is it?" He knew it in his bones as they stammered and glanced at each other, Todd's face turning so red Ethan would have been worried in other circumstances. You know, if he hadn't just walked in on Todd *fucking his fiancé*. "How long?"

Michael mumbled something, then caught himself and enunciated. "About a year and a half. Well… Closer to two years, I guess."

Ethan slumped against the door frame, knees weak, the air whooshing from his lungs as if he'd just been kicked in the gut. "Before I proposed?" He'd asked Michael to marry him on a warm July night six months earlier as they'd strolled along the High Line hand in hand. "Oh my God, I'm such an idiot."

"You're not!" Michael insisted. He said something Ethan didn't pick up, and then, "You were finally getting happy again. I just… I didn't want to…"

The humiliation ran even hotter. "Is that why you said yes? Because you felt sorry for me?"

"No! It was because I love you!" Michael insisted. "I do. We both love you." He looked at Todd. "And, *mumble*."

Todd nodded eagerly. "We never wanted to hurt you. We fought our feelings for so long—"

"How long?" Ethan asked, dreading the answer, his jaw so tight he thought it might snap. Todd and Michael shared another glance, and Ethan wanted to smash their faces.

He'd never hit anyone before, but he could imagine his fists crashing into them and blood spurting out of their noses. No matter if he was scrawny and not as strong as either of them. He wanted them to *hurt*.

Michael answered, "After college, when we all moved to the city... You were so miserable. And obviously we understood why. Losing your hearing sucked. It took you a long time to get a job, and you really shut yourself off. Shut yourself up. You didn't want to go out, you didn't want to make new friends. You were angry all the time."

Ethan couldn't deny it. He'd been depressed as hell after his diagnosis, not to mention surly. He couldn't afford therapy, and it had taken a good four years for him to come to terms with it. He waited for Michael to go on.

"We both wanted to support you and hang in there, but it was hard, Eth." Michael's eyes shone with tears. "It was really, really hard. I leaned on Todd a lot back then. We leaned on each other. You were so distant."

"So it's my fault?" Ethan croaked, his stomach churning. "You know, I wouldn't have blamed you for breaking up with me. I told you that you should!"

"I couldn't!" Michael glanced at Todd. "*We* couldn't. You would have been alone. We couldn't do that to you." He dropped his head. "But *mumble*."

Ethan spat, "I can't hear you when you don't look at me."

Rolling his shoulders back and exhaling a long breath, Michael met Ethan's gaze. "Todd and I fell in love."

Fuck, Ethan was going to vomit. "You want to be with him and not me?"

That imploring expression returned, and Michael motioned with his hands as he talked. "I want to be with both of you. I love you both so much." He looked at Todd, who nodded. "We've been talking about how it could work—how it could actually be really amazing."

"Amazing?" Ethan wasn't sure he'd heard correctly. "How *what* could be amazing?"

Michael's face lit up with hopeful excitement. "How we could be a family together."

"Together," Ethan echoed. "Is that what you said?"

"A lot of *mumble* these days," Todd said.

"What?"

Todd repeated more carefully, "A lot of people are poly these days."

"Poly?" Ethan stared at them. "You want…a threesome?" He and Todd had never been anything but friends, and it would be like fucking his brother. His brother who had betrayed him.

"No, not like that." Todd laughed awkwardly, his gaze skittering around. "Like, we could both be with Michael, and we could be a family together. You're my best friend. It could be great!"

Ethan stared some more. Finally, he said, "Together. So, we'd both fuck Michael, and you and I would be what? Like sister wives in some cult?" He felt so hollow he couldn't even laugh.

"A lot of people are really happy in polyamorous relationships," Michael snapped. "There's nothing wrong with it. Our society is so judgey and heteronormative, and if you can open your mind—"

"I'm not judging other people!" Ethan's rage exploded again, shattering the numbness that had crept in. "If being poly makes other people happy and everyone is on board, great! But that's the catch, right? Everyone being on board? Everyone fucking *knowing* about it? When were you going to tell me? You were waiting until we got *married* to spring it on me?"

Michael flushed and at least looked ashamed. "You've just been so much happier this past year. And you were excited about Australia and *mumble.*"

"So it's my fault again for being happy? For being excited about our fucking *honeymoon*? Right. Seriously, why did you even say yes when I proposed?"

"Because I love you!" Michael reached out before letting his hand drop. "I truly love you. We were babies when we got together. We were twenty, and we didn't know shit. I didn't know shit about myself. I've realized I can't do monogamy. But I do want to marry you! I mean, why shouldn't we get all the perks straight people do? And it meant so much to you."

Ethan wasn't sure he'd heard right. "All the…perks?" A memory surfaced, and a brick dropped in his stomach. "You were really excited about getting on my health benefit plan at work. Is that…" Another sting as the humiliation sank in with bigger hooks. "Did you fucking say yes to get my *benefits*?"

"No!" Michael insisted, but he rubbed his face, averting his gaze. "But you know, I worked two jobs when we moved here. I supported you."

"That's true," Ethan agreed dully. "So this is…payback?"

"*No.* I love you, but I need more than just you. I love Todd too. I want to be with both of you. I know it's important to you to get married because of your mom—"

"Don't talk about my mom! Jesus, you were, what?" Ethan's throat ached. "Doing me a *favor* by marrying me? I thought we loved each other."

"We do!" Michael's dark eyes were wet again. "We *do.* We can still be together. It could be amazing. We can have a different kind of family. I know we should have talked to you about it—"

"Before I walked in on you fucking? Yeah, THAT would have been nice." He looked between the two people he'd relied on most in the whole world. He barely had any family left, and it had been Todd and Michael he'd trusted with his soul when his world came crashing around him.

Todd apparently couldn't look at him now, his head down. Ethan wanted to scream at him to be a man and face him, but another part was glad the fall of Todd's floppy blond hair was obscuring his lowered face. That face had always meant safety and dependability, and the betrayal was too much to process.

Ethan spat, "You both lied to me. For months. Years! I know I wasn't easy to be with." His throat thickened, his voice cracking as he fought tears. "I know I was messed up for a long time, but how could you do this to me?"

"*Mumble mumble!*" Michael exclaimed. "Please. I know this is a shock—"

Ethan backed out, stumbling through the living room to the front door. He grabbed his coat and jammed his bare feet into the sodden Oxfords. Michael and Todd followed behind him, both of them talking, the words lost in a slurry of sound Ethan couldn't distinguish.

As he opened the front door, Michael grabbed his arm. Ethan tore himself loose so violently he careened into the wood with a painful thud. "You two were everything I had!" he screamed, his throat aching. Turning, he lurched for the stairwell down the hall.

They didn't follow. He wasn't sure if he was glad, or if that hurt even more.

His fingers and toes were soon numb as he walked aimlessly. He hadn't grabbed his hat or gloves, and the wind whipped across the park. His hood kept being blown down, so he gave up on it. His hearing aids were zipped in his pocket again, the world dulled and distant. People rushed by, some walking dogs.

Ethan wasn't sure how long he'd been standing there on one of the slushy paths staring into space when someone touched his arm. He jerked away, almost falling on his ass. He opened his mouth to scream at Michael and/or Todd to leave him the fuck alone when Clara came into view, her red lips forming his name and the sound of her high voice only an indistinct murmur.

Her thick, dark eyebrows drew together, and she said his name again with obvious concern. Looking at his ears, she tapped her own—currently covered by Mickey Mouse earmuffs—questioningly. Ethan wanted to simply shake his head and walk away rather than talk to Michael's sister, but she'd only ever been kind.

She'd helped calm the family down when Michael had come out, and had been a steadfast friend when Ethan had withdrawn from the world. Clara was supposed to be his new sister.

He'd really been looking forward to having a sister.

With icy fingers, he managed to put his hearing aids back on, flicking the little switches to activate them. He said, "Sorry."

Clara smiled tentatively. "It's okay. I thought that was you over here. Didn't mean to startle you." She glanced around. "What are you doing?"

"Shouldn't you be at work?"

"It's my study afternoon." She motioned to her backpack. "Figured I'd get in a few hours of MBA crap at your place and dump my books before the party. I'm *so* ready to roll to some classic rock." She grinned at her roller skating pun.

Fuck, the party. "I…"

Her smile vanished. "What is it?"

He tried to laugh. "Does Michael know you're coming over? Because he's been a little busy this afternoon."

Clara stared in obvious confusion. "What's going on?"

Saying it out loud made the pain intensify like an electric

shock. He still couldn't believe this was real life. "I walked in on Michael and Todd in bed." He wished he didn't have to hear his own words.

Her jaw dropped. "I… What? Oh my God!" She opened and closed her mouth a couple more times, and then her shoulders sagged, her eyes going soft. She said something else, but a bus roared by and her words were lost in the rush of sound.

He had to ask, "Can you repeat that?"

"Never mind." Two words Ethan absolutely hated with every fiber of his being. She shook her head, her face creased in sadness. "I'm so sorry."

That her shock was so short-lived sent an awful suspicion screaming through him. He stepped back. "Did you know?"

"No, I swear!" She sighed miserably. "But I suspected."

"Wow." He shook his head. "I really am the world's biggest moron."

"No, you're not! My brother is." Clara reached a gloved hand for his arm. "Let's go somewhere and talk. Okay?"

Ethan let her pilot him out of the park and into the nearest coffee shop. He shuffled to the corner in his puffy coat, his bare hands tingling now that he was inside. The tips of his ears and toes stung as they defrosted, his left ear still aching from his hearing aid.

The jarringly upbeat pop music playing in the background filled his ears, but at least the place was half empty. Packed restaurants and cafes were so noisy Ethan usually only heard half of what people were saying. On autopilot, he sat with his back to the cafe and switched the mode on his hearing aids so the noise behind him was filtered out. It didn't work perfectly, but it helped.

Clara came to the table and put a cup of coffee down in front of him. After taking off her coat and sitting on the padded seat along the wall, she stirred one creamer and half a sugar packet into the cup. The fact that she knew how he liked his coffee thickened Ethan's throat, and he fought not to burst into pathetic tears.

She was still wearing her Mickey Mouse earmuffs, and when she realized, she took them off with a self-conscious chuckle. "I know, I'm too old for Disney at thirty-one, but I've always had cheesy taste. According to—" She broke off.

"Michael's a snob," Ethan said. It was true, but Ethan had always found it endearing. Well, sometimes. "I like your Disney stuff."

"Thanks." She toyed with the teabag string hanging out of her cup, tucking her bobbed black hair behind an ear with her other hand. She was still wearing her office clothes, a pink blouse and brown slacks. Her lip gloss matched her shirt. "Wow. I can't believe this is happening. I'm sorry. You don't deserve this."

"I guess I'm not open-minded enough. Michael wants to be polyamorous, he said." Ethan unzipped his coat enough to tug at his tie and loosen it.

"And he never mentioned it before now?" she asked incredulously, her jaw tightening. "I'm going to slap him upside the head. For fuck's sake."

"You saw it coming, though. Right? I didn't." Ethan picked up his paper cup but didn't drink. The heat made his thawing fingers tingle painfully. "I should have. Todd's all buff and hot. I'm just…meh. Beanpole." *I should have known this was coming. Why would Michael want* me *when there are guys that look like Todd?*

It was easier to think about the ways he'd failed to physically measure up than to consider the ways he might have failed as a person. Because Michael *had* supported him while he'd been depressed. And even after Ethan had come to terms with his hearing loss enough to use his hearing aids and get a job, he still hadn't been the guy he was before.

Fine, I'm different now, but is that so bad? Why the fuck didn't he just break up with me? How could they go behind my back? For two whole years?

Ethan blinked back to attention, realizing Clara was speaking. "I'm sorry, can you say that again?"

She briefly squeezed his hand. "Ethan, you're totally hot. You have amazingly thick, like, *chestnut* hair, your smile is to die for with those dimples, and you're not a beanpole! You're lean, like a swimmer. Todd can keep his bulging muscles. Also his lack of *mumble mumble*. God, I really wanted to be wrong. I *mumble* Michael *mumble*. I love my brother, but *mumble*."

The chatter from a group of girls who'd just sat at a nearby table had Ethan straining to hear. She must have recognized it on his face because she said, careful to enunciate, "He's a coward."

Michael—a coward. Ethan had never once thought of him that way. He was a snob about fashion yet a geek about video games, a terrible cook and a generous tipper. He was so many things, and "coward" had never flickered across Ethan's mind.

He thought of how Michael had held him for hours after he'd stumbled home from the audiologist after his diagnosis in complete shock. Shit, he was going to cry.

He took a few breaths before whispering, "How did I not know? How was I so blind? He and Todd—they... They were...everything to me. Always there for me when things were so bad. I was going to marry him. Tomorrow. I..." The reality settled onto him, the weight of it making it hard to breathe. "I'm not getting married to the boy of my dreams. Like my mom..." He rubbed his face, missing the comfort of his parents so desperately he was afraid he'd weep. When he had a grip on himself, he said, "It's not happening. It's over."

"But... Maybe after some time, you guys could work it out. I know you're in shock right now, but..."

He could see Todd and Michael in his mind—sweaty and passionate, Michael's dick inside Ethan's best friend. They'd have showered and Todd would have left, coming back that night to head over for the pre-wedding celebration.

In fact, now Ethan remembered that the roller rink party had been Todd's suggestion. He'd said how much Michael would appreciate it, and they'd laughed about how hipster it was to roller skate to the Eagles and Steve Miller Band, and surely some Lynyrd Skynyrd and Zeppelin. Todd tended bar at a place where the drink menu came in a cassette case, so he certainly knew hipster.

Ethan's breath stuttered, a pang of grief filling the hollow shock inside him, pressing into every pore. Michael and Todd were *in love* with each other. "I can't believe how good they are at lying. How they could deceive me like that for so long. I trusted them." It was almost worse that they'd kept their secret because they felt sorry for Ethan and didn't want to hurt him. How pathetic was that?

Clara's eyes swam. "I don't know how they could do it either." She muttered something, shaking her head. Ethan didn't bother to ask her to repeat it. It didn't matter.

"I'm not getting married tomorrow. It's not happening." Ethan pressed his palms against his eyes. "And fuck! All the money we spent on the honeymoon." He scrubbed his hands through his hair. "I didn't get cancellation insurance. God, I really am an idiot. Everything's canceled. My wedding, my honeymoon. My life."

"No, not your life. Eth, I know you're hurting, but nothing's canceled, hon."

"The wedding is. I can't marry him. Not now. Not ever."

"Yeah, okay." She swiped at tears. "The wedding's definitely canceled. I don't blame you. But your life isn't over, okay?"

"You're right. I know." Ethan hung his head, even if he didn't quite believe his own words, he knew he couldn't say things like that without scaring people. After he'd spiraled into depression, he'd learned that much. And he didn't want to scare Clara. "But fuck me, I need to actually cancel everything for tomorrow. And where am I going to stay tonight? Shit, where am I going to live? Is Michael going to move in with Todd? Is Todd enough for him? Do they fuck other guys together?"

Humiliation overwhelmed him, so hot he had to unzip his coat. "I bet they do. They've had this whole other life. And I've never been a part of it. I encouraged them to go out clubbing with each other since I hate it now. I was so glad they were friends independently of me." He barked out a laugh, his throat raw. "One big happy family, huh?"

Clara said something, and when he stared at her blankly, she sniffed, her eyes brimming with fresh tears. "I'm so sorry. If you need a place tonight, you can come stay with me, okay? I don't want you to be alone."

He loved her for offering, but he knew her parents were staying with her for the wedding and that would be insanely awkward. "Thank you. I'll be okay. I'll figure out tonight, and tomorrow night—" A fresh wave of horror washed over him as reality sank in bit by bit.

So many times he'd imagined snuggling with Michael on the long flight to Sydney, both of them taking their first trip overseas. Doing it together as a married couple. Starting the first day of the rest of their lives with a grand adventure, their bellies still full of fondue.

"I'm not going to Australia after all." Saying it aloud didn't make it hurt any less, and it still didn't seem real. None of it did. Did he have to call the airline to cancel, or did they just not show up? Did people do that?

"You should still go!" Clara leaned across the table with bright eyes, taking hold of his hand. "That's your dream trip, right? Don't let Michael take that away from you with his selfish bullshit."

"What, go by myself?"

She spoke too fast for Ethan to pick it up. When he jutted out his chin and squinted quizzically—one of his nonverbal cues that he hadn't heard something—she said, "Why not?"

"Because it's pathetic?"

Clara gripped his fingers. "Why? Michael cheating on you was pathetic. People go away by themselves all the time."

"I can't just go *alone*." How was this happening? How was this his freaking life?

"But you—" She broke off and shook her head. "I'm sorry. You're still in shock. I don't know what I'm saying. I'm trying to salvage something good out of this and that's probably not what you need right now. Sorry."

"It's okay. I know you're trying to help." He clung to her hand. She'd been so good to him all these years. At least he'd been able to talk to her. His chest tightened. "I'm really going to miss you, Clara."

Tears spilled down her cheeks, and she stifled a sob. "Don't say that. Maybe we can still…" But apparently she couldn't finish her thought, because the reality was that no matter how much of a cowardly asshole he was, Michael was her brother. They sat in awkward silence until Ethan hugged her and escaped outside as the bitter cold set in.

Chapter Two

THE STAIRWELL WAS dark. Because of course it was. Ethan was apparently the only one who gave a shit about fire codes.

His stupidly bare feet were numb and sore. He'd walked around Prospect Park in his wet leather shoes and then holed up in another coffee shop, sitting there for hours, his mind spinning and hearing aids off.

He'd turned off his phone, and as he swiped it on now to use the flashlight, his screen lit up with a wall of texts. Mostly Todd and Michael. One from Clara. A couple from other confused friends asking about the roller-skating party and where Ethan and Michael were—people who were really *Michael's* friend's, not his.

Ethan trudged up the stairs. When he reached the top, he walked to his apartment and stood in front of it with the key in hand. Then he put in his hearing aids and switched them on. Holding his breath, he leaned in and listened. Was Michael there? Was *Todd?*

A fresh wave of pain knifed through him. How could Todd do this? Todd, who had gone to Ethan's classes and taken notes for him when his hearing had sharply declined, on top of his own course load. Who'd skipped numerous parties to hole up with Ethan and play video games without asking a million questions and always waiting for Ethan to want to talk.

That same person had had Michael's dick inside him that afternoon. And who knew how many afternoons before. And mornings and evenings and nights—all the possible times they'd been together now ticking through Ethan's head uncontrollably. And Todd had probably had his dick inside Michael too, an image which now filled Ethan's mind, competing with the litany of times they could have cheated.

When Ethan had gone to his uncle's for this past Thanksgiving, Todd said he had to work, and Michael had claimed he had to work overtime on the mock-ups for a new ad campaign. Had that all just been excuses to spend the weekend fucking?

Ethan thought of every time the three of them had laughed together, eaten together, played together, or just…been. All tainted now. Years of memories. Ethan wanted to crack open his skull and reach into his brain to scoop them out. Dump them into the toilet and flush them away in a swirl of rushing water.

There was nothing else to do, so Ethan turned the key in the lock. The light was on, and he could tell Michael was there. He wasn't sure how—he just sensed it. After he took off his shoes and hung up his coat, he passed through into the living room, his bare feet tingling as they thawed.

Michael stood by the edge of the black leather couch, which was stylishly sharp-angled and ridiculously uncomfortable, his hands jammed into the pockets of his skinny jeans. It was after midnight, and he'd evidently been waiting. He shifted anxiously from foot to foot, dropping his face, his gelled hair still a mess. He said something about Clara.

"What?" Ethan asked. He just wanted to get in a hot shower and defrost. And wake up from this nightmare.

Michael glanced up at him. "I said Clara ripped me a new one."

Good. Ethan shrugged, waiting. Was he supposed to feel sorry for poor Michael?

"*Mumble mumble* uncle's."

Like he was playing *Wheel of Fortune*, Ethan guessed and filled in the blanks. "The drive to Cheektowaga is, like, six and a half hours, and that's with okay traffic."

Good thing Ethan's aunt was due to pop with their fifth kid any minute, and Uncle Chuck had been afraid if they came to New York for the wedding she might go into labor too far away from their doctor. Ethan would have hated them to make the trip for nothing. He and his dad's younger brother weren't super close, but Chuck was the only family he had left. He was a good guy, and he'd find room in his cramped house if Ethan needed to crash, but Ethan couldn't deal with anyone right now.

"And I don't have a car anyway, so."

Michael nodded. "And you hate the Greyhound."

Resentment bubbled up, bitter on Ethan's tongue as he spat, "Yeah, I do. You know me so well, right? Guess what else I hate? Cheating liars. Somehow you missed that over the years?"

Michael muttered something, hanging his head.

"I can't hear when you don't look at me!" Ethan shouted.

Michael straightened up. "Sorry. I said I deserved that."

"Gosh, thanks for the validation."

Michael's jaw clenched briefly. "Can we please talk about this like adults?"

"Oh, am I being immature here? My bad."

"I know what we did was wrong, okay? But everything's been so good, and we didn't want to mess that up. You were finally living again. You were so depressed before. For years." He ran a hand through his hair, the ends sticking up. "*Years*, Eth. But I hung in there."

"You didn't need to do me any favors." Ethan's cheeks were hot, and he fought the urge to squirm. Shame rushed through him. "You should never have said yes when I proposed."

"I couldn't say no. You were finally back in the land of the living. And I do want to marry you!" Michael lifted his hands, beseeching. "I know how important it is to you because of that stuff with your mom. I wanted to be your family. I wanted to give you what you need."

"I needed you to not be fucking my best friend behind my back!" *Don't cry. Do not fucking cry.*

Michael sighed, dropping his arms to his sides. "I know. But I really do love you. I just don't love *only* you. There was no good way to tell you. We were going to bring it up before the wedding was planned, but then the holidays were coming, and… It was never the right time." He said something else, but Ethan couldn't make it out since Michael was rubbing his face.

"God, would you keep your hands away from your mouth when you're talking? I can't fucking understand you when you do that! How many times do I have to tell you?"

Michael yelled back, "I'm sorry! I try my best! But it's never good enough for you!"

Ethan winced, his hearing aids amplifying the shouting uncomfortably. "It's not that complicated to speak slowly and clearly!"

"I try! But it gets really old repeating myself over and over!"

"Fuck, if it was so hard, why didn't you just dump me ages ago? And gee, sorry you couldn't find a good time to tell me about your cheating. I can imagine it's hard to find the right moment to tell your boyfriend—no, your fiancé!—that you're also fucking his best friend and we're supposed to share you now or some shit. Be some big, open happy family."

Michael crossed his arms. "It works really well for a lot of people, okay? Just think about it for a minute. I mean, haven't you been so much happier the past year? I've been trying to give you everything you want."

"Fuck." Ethan shook his head. "That's why you suggested Australia. Why you've been agreeing with just about everything I say. Everything I want to do you've said yes, when in the past you wouldn't have. Jesus. I thought it was finally coming together for me—for us—that we were working at compromise, but it was all a lie."

And deep down, I knew it.

That was possibly the worst part. That amid his depression, he'd known he was losing Michael. That something fundamental had changed. But when Ethan had started initiating sex again, he'd thought things had gotten better. Michael had seemed as eager as always, hadn't he? Maybe they'd both been trying too hard.

I thought getting married would fix it all somehow.

Ethan's fingers tingled, shock waving through him as true understanding settled in and made a home. As he'd come out of the fugue state he'd been in for too long, he'd been desperate to be happy again. For everything to be perfect. He'd ignored the warning bells that told him there was something off. The doubts about Michael and whether they should really spend the rest of their lives together.

Michael had stayed with him when he'd been depressed, and Ethan had convinced himself that meant everything, even though they didn't really have much in common now aside from their shared history.

Michael watched him warily. He cleared his throat and said, "Eth, maybe you should sit down."

"Oh my God, I was such a fool. I knew we weren't right anymore, and I thought getting married would somehow be a magic fix. And you were…humoring me. For how long? How many other guys have there been? Fuck, we'd talked about not using condoms anymore!" They always had since they'd gotten together during school, a habit they hadn't broken since Ethan in particular had always been a rule follower. "We got tested last month and everything. And you didn't say a word."

"And we're both uninfected!" Michael's eyes were wide with hurt. "I would never have unprotected sex and risk you. Or myself. And there hasn't been anyone else but Todd. We always use condoms."

"Should I be grateful for that? You've lied to me for two years! Or maybe longer—how can I trust anything you say? Not that it matters. I can't..." He shook his head. "I can't believe you did this. For what? Sex?"

Now Michael's eyes flashed. "Well it's not like you had much interest in fucking me! For *years*. Yeah, you know what?" He inhaled sharply, lifting his head, standing straighter with right-eousness. "Sex *is* important to me. I needed more than you wanted to give. A lot more. You were so depressed for so long, and you barely let me touch you. It always felt like you were doing *me* the favor if you deigned to let me fuck you, or if you gave me a half-hearted blow job."

Ethan wanted to deny it, but he couldn't, the simmering guilt bubbling up. During his depression, he hadn't had any interest in sex, and after a while, it became infrequent at best. But the past year when Ethan had tried so hard to fix everything, it had been better!

Too little, too late.

Still, he had to say it. "But hasn't it been really good lately? I... I thought it was." He also thought he might throw up from the humiliation. He'd been so certain their sex life was better than ever, but it hadn't been good enough. What a fucking fool he'd been.

Michael's dark eyes went tender. "It's been so amazing con-necting with you again. But..." He shook his head. "It's still not enough for me. And it's not you. I wouldn't be satisfied with just one man, no matter who he is. And I don't mean that just sexually. I need a lot of interaction and intimacy. That's who I am."

Swallowing thickly, Ethan muttered, "That doesn't give you the right to cheat on me. To lie to my face for so long."

"No, it doesn't. I was wrong." Michael nodded, but he was still holding his head high, that righteousness remaining. "When we first got together, I hadn't really figured out what I was into. It was always pretty vanilla with us, and I want more than that—kinkier things that you aren't into. I shouldn't have to apologize for who I am."

"No, not for wanting it—for lying and going behind my back. You never talked to me about it! If I'm not *kinky* enough for you, you should have said something." Now it was his turn for righteous indignation. "And I can be kinky! You don't know what I want! You've just had this *idea* of me."

His mind raced, running through memories, trying to pinpoint when he should have known. Then a wave of sadness washed over him, sapping his energy. "We've lived together for years, and I don't think we really knew each other deep down."

Michael seemed to deflate as well, and his eyes glistened. "I guess not."

They stood and stared at one another, the truth of it all oppressive and heavy in the air. Ethan cleared his throat. "I think you should go. There's nothing left to say."

There was nothing left, period.

Michael said something too softly. As Ethan stared at him questioningly, he asked again, "What about the wedding?"

"Call everyone and cancel. I'm not marrying you, Michael. Not tomorrow. Not ever. I can never trust you again. It's over."

"Fuck, Ethan." He swiped the fresh tears from his eyes. "Look, I know I screwed up. I was afraid. I know it was wrong, but... *Mumble.*"

"There's no but. You and Todd cheated on me and lied to my face for two *years*. You didn't tell me because you knew I wouldn't want this. So instead of just manning up and coming clean, you guys lied and lied and lied. You were going to *marry* me and get my health benefits and keep on fucking my best friend behind my back. Right?"

Michael sighed. "We wanted to tell you. We were going to tell you."

"In another couple years?" Ethan laughed humorlessly. "Get. Out. Go stay with Todd, or Clara, or whoever—I don't fucking care. I'll pack all my stuff this weekend."

"And go where?" Michael said something Ethan couldn't pick up, and then apparently realized, saying more slowly, "It could take months to get a new place."

Fuck, it was true. The thought of finding another apartment in New York was the final nut-crushing cherry on top of this shit sundae. Ethan wanted to curl into a ball and sleep. Make it all go away. "I don't know."

"You should stay here." Michael nodded resolutely. "I'll move out."

"You think I can live here after this? No. I never liked this furniture anyway. This is all your taste. I just went along with it because I was too depressed to care. You can keep it. Fuck, I never even wanted to move to the city." Living in New York had been Michael's dream—and Todd's. Ethan had followed along because where else would he have gone? Michael and Todd were his everything. Of course he'd gone with them.

Michael tensed, his voice raising, the words coming quickly. "Oh, so that's my fault now? I *mumble* you *mumble*?" He paused, then spoke more clearly. "I made you come here after college? No. You had no clue what you wanted to do. Aside from feeling sorry for yourself. You had hardly any family, and you never tried to make new friends, but I stuck by you."

"Lucky me! And yeah, on top of both my parents dying before I was twenty, losing my hearing was really fucking depressing! It sucked. It still sucks. It'll continue to suck. It is a struggle. Every.

Single. Day. You don't understand how draining it is. How something little like buying a pack of gum or ordering lunch can be exhausting. This city is so *loud,* and it drowns out the words."

Michael's shoulders slumped. "I know. I'm sorry." He scrubbed at his hair, then dropped his hand, defeated. He motioned to the angular coffee table. "What about the rings?"

The blue velvet box was sitting there, the hammered titanium rings inside. Michael loved the dark, non-traditional rings, and Ethan had gone along since he'd simply been thrilled Michael had agreed to marriage in the first place.

Ethan shrugged, little more than a jerk of his shoulder. "Pawn them. Whatever. Marry Todd instead and use them."

"That's not—" Michael sighed, apparently thinking better of what he was going to say. "I never wanted this to happen. I wanted to tell you the truth right after the first time with Todd, but we kept digging ourselves deeper. We kept saying we'd tell you soon."

Ethan had nothing more to add. He waited, wanting Michael out of his sight. Out of his life—although the idea also sent shivery terror through him like ice water down his spine. *What is my life without Michael and Todd? Who* am *I without them?*

Michael held out his hands again. "Maybe—maybe once some time passes, you can think about giving it a try. You know Grace and Sarah and Lina? They have an amazing poly relationship. Baby, if you can open your mind to it—"

"I'm not your baby." The fury seemed to have burned itself out for the moment, and now there was only sorrow. Michael was right that Grace, Sarah, and Lina seemed to have an awesome poly relationship. But Ethan was pretty sure they'd all gone into it with consent.

Reality pressed down around him, making it hard to breathe. This was actually happening. When he'd woken that morning, he'd had a completely different life. A life that was a massive lie.

The earth was scorched and there was no going back.

He repeated, "I'm not your baby, and you're not mine. Not now. Not ever again. I trusted you both. More than anyone. In a hundred years, I could never forgive you. And maybe that makes me immature or petty, but that's the way it is." His empty stomach roiled. "There's nothing else to say. I'll put my shit in storage and stay at a hotel until…"

Fuck, until what?

All he knew was that he wanted to get as far away from Michael and Todd as humanly possible. He had the three weeks off work for the honeymoon, so at least he could apartment hunt…

The idea that Clara had planted bloomed in his mind. Wait, why did he have to stay in New York? The trip was paid for. He had the time off. And he couldn't get much farther way than the other side of the world.

Ethan cleared his throat, a tiny light flickering beyond the hurt and shock and fear—a kernel of hope he could barely recognize as he grasped for it. "Until I figure out where I'm going to live after I get back from Australia."

Chapter Three

THE ONE MORNING he could sleep in, his bloody phone started buzzing.

Clay groaned, his irritation giving way to a jolt of worry. He stretched out on the hotel bed and grabbed at his phone, squinting at the screen as he sat up and leaned against the wall.

Relief flooded him, but his heart sank as he read the text messages that had come in one after the other with more urgency, irritation returning full strength. "Strewth," he muttered. What time was it in Norway? He attempted the mental math before grumbling, "To hell with it."

Besides, what did it matter? Pete needed more money no matter what time it was. He threw off the covers, shivering in the air con and scratching his bare arse as he made his way to the coffee maker and put in a pod. Tapping the microphone on his phone he spoke a message into WhatsApp. "Hold your horses. Got to talk to your mum first."

Of course it came out: *All the horses go talk to Emma first.*

He erased the gibberish and typed out the proper message. Almost instantly came the reply that Pete had already cleared it with his mother. "Uh-huh," Clay muttered. "She never says no to you."

He'd much rather not call his ex-missus until he had at least a coffee in him, if not brekkie, but he went for a piss and then opened his contacts and hit the number. It rang a few times before Barry answered, and Clay put on his most affable voice, as if he was greeting tour guests.

"G'day, Baz. It's Clay here. Is Barb around?"

"Hello. Yes, she's in the garden. The lilies are really stealing the show. Although I must say the Dianthus—"

"Too right, I'm sure it all looks a ripper." Once the Latin words came out, Barry tended to go on and on. "Can I just have a word with Barb? It's about Pete." Not that he needed an excuse to speak to his ex-wife, but it tended to speed up the process. She and her new husband lived in Christchurch, New Zealand. Apparently the gardening was far superior than in their dusty outback hometown, and flowers had become Barb's new obsession.

When she came on, she said, "Little bugger keeps running out of money."

"That he does. How much more are we gonna send before we say enough is enough?"

She sighed. "He promises he's got a job lined up at one of the ski resorts next week."

"All right, transfer a few more hundred. But we've got to put our foot down. This is meant to be a working holiday, not just partying. He's twenty-four now. At his age—"

"Don't remind me. We had two kids and a mortgage. Look how that turned out."

It was nonsense to feel a stab of hurt, and Clay put on a smile even though she couldn't see him. "Yeah, well, we didn't have too bad a time of it."

"'Course not. Just teasing. Where are you today? Sam said you're up the coast again? She actually answered when I rang yesterday. It was a bloody miracle."

Clay winced. Sam had been furious with her mother when Barb had left with Barry. She was a daddy's girl and had been fiercely protective of him. Hadn't spoken to her mum for months until Clay had put his foot down. It could still be prickly between Sam and Barb, but their relationship had slowly thawed, thank goodness.

Still, the urge to defend Sam rose up. "You know her days are chockers with summer classes and work at the pub. Not to mention Jase."

Barb sighed. "Yes, I know. I'm not criticizing. Much. Oh, did she tell you she scored well on that exam?"

"She did. It's brilliant." At least one of their kids had a head for uni. Pete had barely graduated with his QCE before doing a runner and bumming around Thailand and Vietnam as soon as he was eighteen. "And I'm in Cairns. Went to Port Douglas yesterday morning with the Sydney group. Back up there this arvo with the new bunch. We head back down the coast in a couple days."

"No rest for the wicked. Anyway, I'll send the bugger the money so he leaves us in peace."

"Ta. Happy gardening."

"Bye for now, Mr. Kelly."

Even though Barb was Mrs. Wallingford now, she still always said goodbye with her traditional farewell. It was strangely comforting, even if it made Clay fidgety at the same time. But he was proud of how amicable the split had been. That was the word the lawyer had used over and over: *amicable*.

Clay needed to shower and trim his beard, but he pulled on shorts and a tank top and headed down the sleepy street to Macca's for a hash brown and a sausage McMuffin. Sam would lecture him on healthy eating and try to push some vegan thing with nuts and seeds and tofu on him if he was home with her, but what she didn't know wouldn't hurt.

With a patch of grease seeping through his paper bag as he returned to the hotel, he sidestepped a gaggle of tourists staring up in wonder at the flying foxes that lived in the massive fig tree on the library grounds.

"Good lord, they're *bats*!" a fellow exclaimed in a very proper English accent, his children yelping in response.

Even though the bats were meant to be sleeping in the day, they still managed to make a hell of a row, drawing constant attention. Clay glanced up at the black shapes hanging from dense branches. They were a sight to see when they took flight at dusk to go foraging. Beautiful in a strange way, even with the shrieking racket they made.

The ringer on his phone was still off, but the buzzing started in again just as he got back to his room. First was a text from Pete:

Thanks heaps, Dad.

Clay wanted to tell him to pull his socks up and stop getting pissed every night and drinking away his money, and to take something seriously for once like his sister, but Pete knew it all anyway. Instead Clay responded:

Get a job, mate. Soon. Love ya.

Then Clay tapped on Sam's name, her wide smiling face in the little picture making him smile. She had her mother's soft golden curls instead of Clay's wiry, brownish-red mop that he kept trimmed short. He'd always been softer on Sam than her brother, it was true. But she'd always been a good girl, and Pete had never listened to a word. Not that Clay didn't love Pete just as much. 'Course he did. It was that Pete had him exasperated more often than not.

But this morning, Sam was bucking the trend, and Clay groaned as he eyed the pictures she'd sent. One after the other, seven smiling women filled the screen. They were either in their thirties, or forties like him, all surely very nice, but… A brunette was posed at the beach with a retriever at her feet. Sam wrote:

This one has a dog! Open your app and send her a message. I added them all to your faves list. You're too young and hot to still be single. Jase agrees, for the record. His parents are ancient.

Clay laughed, shaking his head. He was glad to know his

daughter's boyfriend approved of his hotness. Why he'd ever agreed to set up the profile on OzLove.com, he'd never know. Actually, he knew exactly why—Sam had given him an ear-bashing about it so many times he finally gave in so he could enjoy the cricket in peace and quiet.

He'd promised to do it the next day, but she'd insisted on opening the account right then and there on her laptop before making him install the app on his phone. She'd chosen his profile pic and lectured him on the importance of making the right first impression so he had the chance to make a second.

Clay had protested that he was a bit slimmer in the shirtless picture—which Sam had taken a few years earlier on their trip to Bali before she started uni. It had turned out to be the last family vacation they'd all taken together before things with Barb had gone pear-shaped. Well, not so much pear-shaped as it'd just…ended.

He caught his reflection in the long mirror by the closet as he went to toss the food receipt in the bin. He was still fit even if he was a little softer around the middle than in his prime. He swam most nights on the tour before bed, or lifted weights in the hotel gyms. Too many freckles on his arms and shoulders, but he was tall and strong. Barb had always said he was a catch. Although she hadn't stuck around, so maybe he shouldn't take her word for it.

As if it would make up for the fast food, he dropped to the carpet and did twenty pushups, laughing at himself when he finished. Sam was right—he was still young. Only forty-four, although with two grown kids sometimes he felt older than perhaps he should have. But in the outback it hadn't been out of the ordinary at all to get hitched and start a family straight out of school. Now he definitely felt like the odd one out on the dating apps.

He shuddered to think of the painfully awkward speed dating event he'd reluctantly attended a few months before. He didn't seem to have anything in common with single women in Sydney. They were perfectly pleasant, but it felt so forced. Maybe he needed to move back to a small town to find another wife. Go back to basics.

Clay snorted to himself now as he turned off the phone and unwrapped his breakfast before it got any colder. At least he was happy with his own company, and with Sam's, and their dog Gilly's. Romance and sex had never been all they were cracked up to be from where he was sitting.

Perhaps there was a yearning for *more* that he couldn't quite explain. It should have made him eager to date and find the right woman, but scrolling through the smiling photos only left him feeling empty.

He turned on the telly and looked for the sports or news, grimacing at the crap picture. It never ceased to amaze him that the fancier hotels on the tour didn't have digital cable while the motel-style ones did. Sitting on the bed, he ate and sipped his coffee, which wasn't as strong as he would've liked, but it did the job.

The greasy brekkie hit the spot, even though he knew he shouldn't have it because of cholesterol and saturated fat and lots of other nasty stuff that Sam lectured him on. She was smart as a whip and knew what she was on about, but sometimes a man just needed Macca's. Not to mention a holiday, but he'd have another ten nights going back down the coast to Sydney with the tour before he had a real break.

He'd already cleaned the coach, so he had a couple more hours to himself before he met Shiv, the tour guide, downstairs to greet the new lot. It would be a long day with the welcome dinner out at the aboriginal center, but they'd be in Cairns two more nights, so at least he'd been able to unpack a bit. Not that he had much gear with him. Still, he could settle in more than at the one-night stops.

Clay finished watching the international cricket report and had a shower. He trimmed his beard and was just settling back down for more morning telly when there was a knock. He slung a towel around his hips and opened the door to find Shiv there, all shaved and looking smart in a white linen shirt that complemented his dark skin. His short black hair was slicked back neatly.

Shiv grinned. "'Morning! Did you see India lost the test?"

"Yep. Kiwis flogged them."

"It was glorious. My auntie in Pakistan is gloating all over Facebook."

Clay chuckled. Cricket rivalries brought out the competitive streaks in everyone. "As long as we can beat India in a few weeks."

"Mate, we'd better. I don't even want to think about losing."

"Me either." Clay raised an eyebrow. "Did you just come to talk about cricket, or can I get dressed?"

Shiv laughed, and there was something in his tone that put Clay on guard. "Sorry, mate. Just have a tiny favor to ask."

Clay ushered him inside as he heard people coming down the hall. He crossed his arms. "All right, spit it out."

"Remember Jane and Sharon? From the trip up here?"

"Two Irish sheilas. Nice girls."

"Very nice. In fact, we have a lunch date with them."

Groaning, Clay shook his head. "I sure as hell do not. They're too young for me."

Shiv scoffed. "They're my age. You're only ten years older. You need to live a little. I know you got married practically out of the womb, but you're still young and now you're single. Sow some wild oats!"

Clay snorted. "Are you about to tell me how hot I am?"

Shiv gave him a contemplative look. "Will it help convince you to come to lunch? Because you're smokin' hot, mate."

"Ta," Clay replied drily.

"Come on! Jane's into me, and if we can just have a nice little meal with them, I know I can lock her down for later tonight. Besides, aren't you in need of some relaxation? We're two single blokes, and you've got that outback man of mystery thing going on."

"I do?" It was Clay's turn to scoff.

"Totally! You're a throwback with all your old-fashioned slang and square jaw. A man's man. Chicks dig it. Trust me." He dropped the cajoling tone. "Honestly, I really need this. Lori's swanning about Italy with that Tuscan arsehole, and…" He trailed off and sighed miserably.

Shiv's wife had been doing coach tours in Italy for the same company they worked for, and had sent Shiv a text message several months earlier, leaving him after ten years of marriage without even a phone call. It had hit him hard.

Shiv added, "Did I show you the picture of them in Amalfi? I mean, does that bogan ever wear a shirt?"

"You really need to stay off Facebook. Or at least stop stalking Lori's account." Hell, he hated seeing Shiv so beat down. At least if he was trying to pick up another woman, maybe he'd stop moping about Lori. "We have to be ready by just after one to make sure we're there for the early birds."

Face lighting up, Shiv nodded. "Absolutely. It's the perfect arrangement. Short little lunch with a deadline. Nice and casual, and you and her friend will be there for buffers. Hey, Sharon's not bad looking either. Maybe we'll both get lucky. You've been single too long."

"All right, all right, you sound like my daughter. Let me know where and when and leave me in peace unless you want to see me without the towel."

"Nah, nah, I'm good." Grinning, Shiv backed out of the room. "In the hotel restaurant at noon. Thanks, mate. You're a star."

"A sucker's more like it," Clay muttered to himself. He

flopped back on the bed.

It wasn't that he had anything against Jane and Sharon, who'd been lovely tour guests. And sure, they were attractive and younger than the usual seniors. Not a thing wrong with them. But Christ almighty did he hate small talk.

It wasn't as though he was *lonely* or some rubbish.

The split with Barb had been two years ago now, and maybe it *was* strange that he hadn't been chomping at the bit to date around and sow some belated wild oats. He and Barb had had a fine time in the bedroom over the years. Perfectly fine. He'd never been sex-mad the way his mates had been when they were younger. He enjoyed a kiss and a cuddle and a bit between the sheets, but could live without it.

He was tired of stressing about his lacking love life. Or, more to the point, he was tired of other people stressing about it for him. Maybe the right woman would come along, but he wasn't going to knock himself out trying to find her.

He'd found a second career he enjoyed driving coaches, and when he was in Sydney he got to see lots of Sam and their dog. Give him cricket or footie on the telly, and an ice-cold stubby of beer, and he wasn't missing a thing.

Chapter Four

"WHY DID I think this was a good idea?" Ethan muttered to himself as he stepped off the elevator into the lobby of the hotel. A couple gave him a strange look, which likely meant he was talking too loudly. Another of the awesome perks of being hard of hearing was not realizing when he was talking louder than he thought. He tried to smile at them, his stomach churning.

At least he'd been able to check in early and have a quick shower and shave. He was exhausted, but knew he had to stay awake the rest of the day to fight jet lag. The flights from New York to LA, then to Brisbane, and finally up to Cairns—which Aussies seemed to pronounce "Cans"—hadn't had any major delays, but he felt as though he'd been traveling for days. Which he probably had? He wasn't sure.

It had been dark for almost all of the flight to Brisbane, an endless night he'd tried to sleep through since the movies didn't have captions. If his phone had enough storage, he could have preloaded a few movies and watched them with the sound going right to his hearing aids via Bluetooth, but he only had less than a gig left. In the end, he'd dozed fitfully, and with his hearing aids off, he barely heard the baby wailing in the row behind.

They'd hit a few spots of turbulence, and Ethan had read the emergency card repeatedly and reminded himself that the closest emergency exit was six rows behind him. He'd counted the seat backs when he boarded, knowing that if the cabin was dark or filled with smoke, he'd theoretically be able to grope for the seats and count his way to the exit.

Theoretically.

Of course when they were over the ocean, the odds of surviving a water landing were about nil, but it didn't hurt to be prepared. He imagined Michael's eye-roll, telling him he shouldn't have watched that plane crash investigation show.

There was another slice of pain, so sharp he had to catch his breath. He could get distracted and blissfully forget about Michael and Todd for small snatches of time, and then he'd remember and experience it all again in a rush—hurt, humiliation, fury, despair.

Along with the stark, undeniable truth underneath it all, that he'd only proposed to Michael out of some misguided attempt to fix what was wrong in their relationship. In his life. This little cycle had played out repeatedly, the momentary relief of distraction followed by the crushing return of his new reality.

Are they thinking about me? Or are they too busy fucking?

Now here he was—alone in Australia. He thought he might puke. It was humid AF, and sweat already dampened his palms as he scanned the lobby for the tour group, his nerves not helping. He kept a bandanna folded in his pocket to dab at the sweat around his ears, making sure his aids didn't get too wet. He had to sweat a lot for it to really be a concern, but the tropical humidity had him on guard.

His itinerary had said to meet in the lobby at one-thirty, but as Ethan gazed around, he didn't see any groups or someone holding up a sign. When he poked his head outside and was hit by a fresh wall of humidity, he realized the DL Tours bus was there, the door standing open. Ethan's heart skipped. Shit, was he late? He peered in tentatively.

Sitting behind the wheel on the right side of the bus was a

man probably in his early forties. Sexy in that rough kind of manly way, with short brownish hair and a neat beard and mustache, wearing navy uniform pants and a short-sleeved white button-up shirt bearing the boxy DL Tours logo over the breast pocket.

"Ah, *mumble*," the driver said.

A man Ethan assumed was the tour guide appeared atop a few steps that led up to the bus. Early thirties or so and stocky, he had brown skin and short dark hair, and his teeth gleamed in a wide smile. "G'day! Come on in."

"Hi. I'm Ethan Robinson." He gave the driver and guide a little wave. "I'm so sorry I'm late. I thought it said one-thirty?"

"Nah, *mumble mumble*," the guide said, moving back a few feet into the bus and handing him a DL Tours tote bag with stuff in it.

Ethan joined him in the narrow aisle, aware of dozens of eyes on him. "I'm sorry? I didn't catch that." Ethan turned his head, motioning to one ear. "I'm hard of hearing." Ugh. He hated giving this spiel. "If you could speak slowly and clearly and look straight at me while you do, I'd really appreciate it."

"Sorry! *Mumble mumble.*"

Ethan shifted uneasily. He was tempted to just nod and smile and pretend he'd understood. He was used to Michael or Todd being there to help fill in the blanks, and he felt flayed open as everyone watched. "Sorry, that was still too fast. It's hard with the accent."

The guide leaned closer, his demeanor shifting to that of a person talking to a child. His eyebrows went up, and he put a hand on Ethan's shoulder. "Can you. Understand me. Now?"

Wishing the ground—or bus floor—would open, Ethan nodded, his skin crawling with the stares of everyone else on board.

"Great!" Now the guide yelled as well as talked down to him. "I said everyone else were early birds. You're not late."

Ethan wanted to tell him that shouting wasn't necessary—and

in fact could be painful because of the amplification in his hearing aids—but he already squirmed under the scrutiny of his fellow tourists. At a glance they all looked at least forty years older than he was, and it hit him like a ton of bricks.

Oh my God, I'm on a seniors' tour. Not that I have anything against old people, but…

The guide leaned to the side and peered out the door. "Is Michael coming along in a minute?"

Ethan's heart plummeted into his gut with an acidy thud. He'd emailed the tour company and told them it was only going to be him, but apparently that memo had been lost. Before he could formulate an answer, the guide gave him a grin and joked, "No wonder that the honeymooners are the last on board!"

The murmur of laughter from everyone and a few probably good-natured comments swirled into a mess of sound. Ethan's cheeks were hot, and he contemplated turning around and escaping back to his room to hide. "I… We…" *Fuck.* "There's no honeymoon!" he blurted. "We broke up right before the wedding. I'm here alone." *Like a pathetic loser.*

In the sudden silence, the guide's jaw dropped. "Sorry, *mumble*. Didn't realize."

Ethan's face was so hot his head might explode. "It's okay. It's fine. I'm fine!"

"Of course you are!" the guide agreed, and the other passengers nodded vigorously. "Here, take the front seat. Best view as we *mumble mumble*!"

Eager to not have to see all the expressions of pity, Ethan dropped into the seat. His gaze locked with the driver's, and the driver gave him a sympathetic half-smile before turning back to the wheel. Ethan slid to the window seat and debated again whether or not he should abort and run back to his room.

He'd been a complete fucking idiot to think coming on this trip alone was a good idea.

The guide picked up a microphone and said, "Now that we're all here, let me do a quick introduction. I'm Shiv Chatterjee. I grew up in Melbourne, and defected for uni and became a Sydneysider. I love working in tourism. It's great meeting new people and showing you this beautiful country." He seemed to be making an effort to speak clearly, so at least that was something.

Shiv went on, "And that's Clayton Kelly behind the wheel. He's from what we call the back of beyond—in his case, the Queensland outback. Used to work in the mines as a mechanic, and that has come in handy once or twice, although these buses are top of the line, don't worry. Clayton doesn't say much, but still waters run deep. You're in good hands."

Still holding the mic, Shiv took the seat across the aisle and continued his welcome speech. It was easier to hear the lower tones of a man's voice, but with an Aussie accent, the different, broader vowel sounds were already proving a challenge. Consonants were always the hardest for Ethan to hear, and Shiv seemed to drop them altogether on some words, especially the letter "r," although he couldn't be sure since he didn't have Michael to ask.

Are he and Todd together? Todd's probably moved in already. Do they miss me? Do they even care that I'm on the other side of the world? Or are they glad I'm gone? Did they just really want me out of the picture for years? Was that poly stuff only an excuse?

Unbidden, a memory of his mom crowded in. It was when she'd been moved to a hospice. He'd been fourteen, and she'd tried to reassure him about her own impending death, even though he was the one who should have been comforting her. Her hand had seemed so thin as she squeezed his, her skin papery in his sweaty grasp.

"It won't always hurt this much. All things fade. It doesn't mean you forget, but the pain won't be there in every breath, sweetie."

Eyes burning, Ethan cursed himself. Like he wasn't upset enough already, he had to go thinking about his mom too? God, if only she was there with him. She'd wanted to come to Australia so much, and he'd planned to enjoy the fuck out of it for her as well as himself. So far he only wanted to crawl into a hole.

The tours in Australia had seemed to be either for backpackers or seniors, although since this one hadn't had "senior" or "golden" in the title, Ethan had hoped it might attract more of an in-between crowd. The backpackers would have been more his age, but Ethan didn't want to party and stay at youth hostels in dorm rooms. He could imagine the wall of sound and how he'd fight to hear any conversation. At least the seniors wouldn't be blasting music.

Through the large windshield, Ethan looked out at the white plumes of surf where the ocean met the rocks at the bottom of the cliffs, the road curving north as they left Cairns. He realized Shiv was talking and that he'd tuned it out without having to turn off his hearing aids.

Be in the now. Listen to the tour guide. Fuck everything else.

Ethan watched Shiv speaking in the seat across the aisle, talking about the geography of the area and the wet season. Apparently they'd lucked out by arriving on a day when the sun was peeking out from the clouds, shining on the blue-green water of the Pacific. It really was amazingly beautiful. After being on planes for what felt like days, it was surreal.

After a few minutes, Shiv gave him a nervous smile, and Ethan turned away, heart skipping. It could make people uncomfortable, the way he'd watch them intently when he was trying to hear every word. He opened the tote bag and pulled out a welcome package with the itinerary and two name tags that attached with a magnet instead of a pin. His hands shook ridiculously as he attached his to his T-shirt. He tossed Michael's back into the bag. Maybe he'd burn it later.

And I'd probably start a fire and burn down the hotel because I'm cursed. Or maybe—

Trying to clamp down on his thoughts before he spiraled into an anxious litany of what-ifs, he looked out the window and hoped he caught most of the commentary as they drove the winding road north to Port Douglas. Ethan had never been on such a fancy bus. Much better than Greyhounds, the windows taking up the whole upper half of the vehicle so everyone had a good view.

I'm really here.

He wanted to be thrilled. He was finally in Australia, living his dream—really his mom's dream, but something they'd shared. Maybe his mom was watching in heaven and seeing it all with him. He wasn't sure if he believed that, but it was a nice thought. She'd made him promise to go to Australia for her one day, and at least he was fulfilling his vow. That was something.

Fuck, seriously, DO NOT START CRYING.

It was bad enough everyone else on the bus probably thought he was not only late and therefore irresponsible, but that he was a pathetic loser going on his honeymoon alone. Fuck, did they all assume he'd been dumped?

Ethan tamped down on his brain sternly before he could spiral too far down that road and experience the anger and hurt and humiliation and fear again. Regardless of what they thought, he didn't need to start freaking *crying* on top of it. He already stuck out like a sore thumb.

Fortunately, they stopped at a lookout and Ethan was able to get out of his head for at least a few minutes as he took in the view. The oppressive heat was more bearable up on the cliff road than it had been in the city, although Cairns was tiny. Must have been the breeze, which caused one lady's hat to go flying.

Ethan dove for it, snagging the floppy brim just before it sailed over the ledge of the stone wall along the lookout. "Here you go." He handed it back to her.

The woman exclaimed something he couldn't hear over the rush of wind and another tour bus rumbling by on the road. She was small and white-haired, and her husband wasn't much bigger. They wore fanny packs and running shoes and wide smiles. Their accents were English, Ethan thought.

"Good man," the husband said, clapping Ethan on the shoulder with a surprisingly strong grip. His name tag said he was Clive, and his wife was Sylvia according to hers.

Ethan nodded and smiled, then went back to the view. He hadn't gone near his Instagram or Facebook, but maybe he should post a pic. Show Michael and Todd and their friends that he was having a GREAT TIME without them. The *best* time! He didn't need them.

Turning his back to the glimmering ocean, he took out his phone and tapped the icon to flip the camera toward him. Holding out his right arm, he cursed himself for not getting one of those Pop Socket things that were supposed to make it easier to take selfies. At least he'd gotten a new SIM card at the airport so he wasn't paying astronomical roaming fees.

With the different SIM, his phone number had temporarily changed, so Michael and Todd wouldn't be able to reach him even if they wanted to. Maybe there were dozens of texts floating out there in the cloud. Maybe they were sorry, and begging him to forgive them.

Ethan wasn't even sure if he wanted that. And suddenly the thought of posting on social media—of the confused and sympathetic comments that would likely follow since word had surely spread about the non-wedding—was way too much.

Ethan dropped his arm. The wind was causing a whistling in his hearing aids, and he fiddled with them impatiently as someone said something. He looked up and blinked at the driver, who stood a few feet away.

Turning his head a couple inches and jutting his chin forward, Ethan put his hand behind his ear. "Sorry?"

The driver stepped closer. They were about the same height,

just over six feet, but Clayton was more muscular, his shoulders broad. His hair had looked mostly brown inside the bus, but in the sun his beard gleamed ginger. "Asked if you'd like me to take a snap for you. Unless you want to do it yourself." His voice was a low rumble.

Even if he didn't post on Insta, Ethan should still take a few pictures, right? Might regret it later if he didn't. He held out his phone tentatively. "If you're sure you don't mind?"

Clayton said something that was probably "Not a bit" or words along those lines since he took the phone. Ethan tried to tame his hair, then smiled. But Clayton gave him a dubious look, eyebrows drawing close.

"Try to look like you're on holiday, not lining up for the firing squad." Then he seemed to think better of what he'd said. "Sorry, mate. Imagine things are tough at the moment." He quickly added, "Unless they're not. Look, I'll just shut up and take the pic."

Ethan smiled, genuinely this time, a little burst of warmth flowing through him. "It's okay. I've never been on a honeymoon alone. Or with anyone else, for that matter. So I've definitely had better days." *Shut up, the guy is just being nice by taking your picture. He doesn't want your sob story!*

Ethan squared his shoulders and tried again to smile. This time he was able to as Clayton lined up the shot, very serious about his photo-taking duties as he tapped the screen. Then he handed the phone back, his rough fingers brushing Ethan's.

Ethan smiled again. "Thanks. I really appreciate it." He glanced around at the rest of the group, broken off into twos along the lookout area. There seemed around twenty other people. "Might have to get you to take more pictures as we go. I think I'm the only one by myself." *Also the only one without an AARP membership.*

"No worries. We have single people taking the tour all the

time."

As they all filed back onto the bus, Ethan wondered if that was true. The word "single" also echoed in his mind.

Single.

He was probably a dumbass, but it was really the first time he'd actually thought about the fact that he was *single* again. He'd been part of a couple for so long he could barely remember not having a boyfriend. He'd had a couple of flings in high school, but those years were also clouded with grief for his mom. He'd kept everything casual, going to parties and not getting too close.

Then his dad had died suddenly from a heart attack in Ethan's freshman year of college, and grief had taken over again. It wasn't until Ethan was a sophomore and Michael had burst into his life—so fashionable and hip and different from everyone Ethan had grown up with—that he'd ever gotten serious about a guy.

And now here I am. Single.

They stopped in the little nearby town, where there wasn't much to do and Ethan walked around by himself looking in stores and pretending to be interested in discount golf wear and tourist souvenirs. Eventually, the bus headed back to Cairns. Shiv said a few more things about the rain forest or something, and Ethan caught some of it, not really listening as he looked out his window at the sea, grayer now that dark clouds were moving back in.

He was finally in Australia, and he'd never felt so *single* in his life.

Chapter Five

"GUYS, I SWEAR it's not a hangover," Shiv joked.

They were all gathered in front of the hotel, the bus idling nearby with doors closed and AC presumably on. Ethan had missed a bit of what else Shiv had said, but the dude looked like crap, his eyes bloodshot and hair sweaty in a way that didn't seem to be from the actual heat.

The upshot was apparently that only Clayton was accompanying them on their first full day of the tour—a boat trip out to the Great Barrier Reef. Apparently Clayton usually only dropped them off and picked them up at the end of the day trip, and as Shiv waved them off and disappeared back into the hotel, a little bubble of excitement filled Ethan's chest. Which was stupid, but Clayton was hot, and Ethan was fucking desperate for distraction.

He took a seat in the middle of the bus, which he'd noticed held forty-eight according to a little strip of regulations up on the wall at the front. He counted nineteen guests including himself, so at least there was lots of room to spread out.

At the welcome dinner the night before at an aboriginal cultural center, Ethan had discovered everyone else was either from the UK or Canada, and he guessed that the youngest were new retirees in their sixties. They were all friendly and kind, no one seeming to care that he'd been set to marry another guy.

A Canadian man named Stan in his seventies wore hearing aids as well, although his were the smaller, inside-the-ear variety. Ethan had found he needed more power than that style could give. Still, Stan's wife, Violet, was nice to talk to because she was used to dealing with hearing loss and enunciated crisply.

The others sitting near Ethan hadn't seemed to mind repeating themselves as they'd eaten gamey kangaroo meat and other Australian dishes at a buffet following a show of dancing and cultural stories. Still, Ethan hadn't often asked them to repeat anything, usually just trying to fill in the blanks himself, staying quiet and hoping that if anyone asked him a question he didn't make a fool of himself by talking about something completely different. Restaurants were the worst. If he was talking one-on-one with someone in a quiet place, it was way less stressful.

Clayton only drove them a couple of blocks down to the pier before they were filing out again, using the door at the front and the one in the middle, which was handy. Ethan waited until the older people were off, so he fell into step with Clayton as they brought up the rear and ambled along the pier toward one of the big ferry-type boats.

"I'm surprised we didn't just walk down," Ethan said.

"Better to keep everyone together. And it can be harder for the older folks. Especially in this heat."

"Oh, of course. Didn't even think of that." *Stupid. Just keep your mouth shut.* He was suddenly desperate to say something smart, or ask something smart, or—well, anything that wasn't stupid. "Clayton, I was wondering—"

"*Mumble* fine."

"Sorry?"

Clayton turned his face toward Ethan. "Said Clay's fine. Shiv likes to stand on ceremony and call me Clayton since he once called me 'Clinton' all day until one of the guests spoke up. I was just waiting to see how long it would take him to get his head out of his arse." He glanced around, but the others were several paces ahead.

Ethan felt a little beat of pleasure at the conspiratorial tone. "Okay. Clay."

Clay smiled at him, his beautiful blue eyes crinkling around the corners and teeth flashing white. "You had a question?"

"Oh!" Ethan scrambled to think of a single intelligent thing to say. "Um… Is Shiv sick? I didn't hear everything he said, but he looks terrible."

"Yeah, claims it's food poisoning, but I dunno. He might be chucking a sickie."

Ethan wasn't sure he heard properly and tried to make sense of the words. "You think he's faking?"

Clay blinked in surprise, frowning. "No. I was only joking, mate. Shiv wouldn't do that. He's very good at his job. He's definitely crook." He sounded a bit offended.

"Oh, no! I'm sure he's sick! I just wasn't sure I understood what you were saying." Ethan shoved his hands in the pockets of his khaki shorts. *Great, now he thinks I'm an asshole.* He tried to laugh off the sudden awkwardness while simultaneously wishing the endless wooden pier would open up and drop him into the depths below. Clay was being so nice, and Ethan had to ruin it.

Clay murmured something, and Ethan looked up from his feet and said, "Sorry, can you repeat that?"

"I just didn't want you to think DL hires guides who aren't committed to the work. This is actually the first time I've seen him miss a day."

"Poor guy. Food poisoning's the worst. Did you say… Does 'crook' mean sick?"

Clay smiled. "It does. Sorry, I forget there can be a bit of a learning curve. Especially for Americans. Canadians seem to understand our slang a bit more for whatever reason, and obviously the Brits do. We've got a lot in common." His eyes twinkled. "Except during the Ashes."

"Oh, right." Ethan tried to guess from the context and came up blank. Had he heard the right words?

"You've got no bloody idea what I'm talking about, do ya?"

Ethan had to laugh, even as his face went hot. "Nope. Sorry, my hearing is crap."

The rumble of Clay's good-natured laughter was a comforting sound. "Nah, it's not your fault at all, mate. I'm talking about cricket. Don't think it's very popular in America. I'll fill you in later if you like." They'd apparently reached the boat, and Clay clapped a big hand on Ethan's shoulder. "But I can talk cricket all day, and I doubt you want to be bored shitless."

He gave Ethan a smile before waving to a boat staff member and heading over to talk to him. Ethan watched as they looked intently at a clipboard, having a conversation about something, Clay pointing and shaking his head.

And for a moment, Ethan let himself enjoy the little thrill he'd felt from the weight of Clay's hand touching him. Then the guilt rushed in. He was supposed to be *married* now. He shouldn't be attracted to another guy, even if it was totally one-sided.

Why the hell not? Michael's been fucking my best friend for two years. It's over between us. Forever. Maybe a rebound fling is exactly what I need.

He laughed at himself. The dude had been nice to him for, like, five minutes, and Ethan had built it into a fling in his head already. He really was pathetic.

Soon they were boarding, and Ethan headed straight up for the top deck, along with a few others from the group and other passengers. The ferry held a few hundred, Ethan guessed, so there were quite a few other tours and individual travelers on board. He sat by the railing, putting on his sunglasses. It was mostly overcast, but still bright.

Clay noticed him and came over to sit, and fuck it. Why

shouldn't Ethan be happy about that? Clay was gorgeous, and looked nothing like Michael or Todd—Ethan braced as the images cartwheeled through his head—and what was wrong with enjoying the view? Besides, it distracted him from the exhausting cycle of hurt-fury-humiliation-despair, and it was nice to not feel completely alone.

"Did you bring a hat?" Clay asked, settling his own wide-brimmed brown leather hat on his head. It almost looked like a cowboy hat, and Ethan imagined Clay riding a horse through the outback, red dirt flying up.

"Hmm?" Ethan said, trying to refocus.

"Even when it's overcast, the sun's fiercer down here than in your hemisphere." He squinted up at the sky, and Ethan followed his gaze. The sun was peeking through thick clouds that at least weren't gray. Yet. Clay added, "Really have to watch myself being a bluey. Especially on the water. Oh, sorry. 'Bluey' means redhead."

Ethan laughed. "I love how there's a weird name for everything here. I mean, not *weird*, just different."

"Oh, we Aussies are a strange lot. No offense taken. So, no hat?"

"Shit, no. I meant to buy one yesterday and I totally forgot."

Clay ribbed him good-naturedly. "How do you come to Oz without a hat?"

Instead of doing what any normal person would do and joking back, Ethan blurted, "I had one, but my boyfriend got it for me for Christmas. Fiancé, I mean. Ex-fiancé. Ex-boyfriend. Ex-everything." *Shoot me now.* He finished lamely, "I just didn't want to bring anything associated with him."

Clay nodded, his smile gone. He said something Ethan missed as a young couple laughed nearby. Ethan tried to think of something else to say. Clay seemed okay with the gay thing, which was a little surprising given the stereotypes of outback men, but he probably didn't want to sit around talking about Ethan's ex-boyfriend. Fiancé. Whatever. Then Ethan felt guilty for being surprised.

Why am I buying into stereotypes in the first place? If he's not a homophobe, that shouldn't be surprising! I guess he could be hiding it because this is his job, dealing with guests of all backgrounds and—no! Why am I being so suspicious? Why am I thinking the worst of him? Fuck, why am I overthinking this like EVERYTHING EVER? And why didn't I overthink the thing that really mattered most? My relationship with Michael and our fucking doomed wedding?

Clay cleared his throat and said, "When we get back to the mainland later this arvo, I'll show you where you can buy a good hat. *Mumble mumble.*"

Ethan didn't ask him to repeat himself since he was pretty sure he'd gotten the important part. He hoped so, at least. "Thanks. That would be awesome." Clay was surely only being friendly—only doing his job—but Ethan couldn't help but smile. It was comforting to feel like at least one person cared about him here on the other side of the world. And if that person was sexy AF, a little fantasy never hurt anyone.

Like I haven't been living in a fantasy world thinking me and Michael were going to live happily ever after when we should have broken up years ago.

"How did you enjoy the aboriginal center last night?"

Ethan jumped on the subject change. "It was really interesting! It's cool that all the people working there are from the same tribe and they make the souvenirs instead of selling stuff made in China or wherever. I wish there was more written info, though. It was hard to hear some of the presentation, especially since it was dark. But the dancing and the fire stuff was really cool." *Am I saying "cool" too much?* He added, "It helps if I can see people's mouths when they're talking."

"Do you read lips, then?" Clay asked slowly, obviously making an effort to make sure Ethan could hear him.

"Not the way someone in the Deaf community would. But I've picked it up a bit with some words. Swear words especially. People tend to be more emphatic when they say those."

Clay chuckled. "Makes sense."

"It can fill in some gaps, but the thing that helps the most is if people speak clearly while they look at me—so the sound comes straight at me, you know what I mean? And not too fast."

"Can you understand me all right?"

"Yeah, you're awesome. Your voice is deep, so that helps. And you don't get pissed when I ask you to repeat yourself. Well, so far," he joked, laughing lamely. Memories of arguments with Michael flickered through his mind, familiar dread in his stomach. Followed by vibrant images of Michael and Todd fucking, so that was FUN.

Clay's eyebrows shot up. "People get aggro with you?"

"Sometimes. I get it—it's frustrating to have to repeat stuff. The worst is when people treat me like I'm stupid."

"Huh." He seemed to be pondering it. "They're the drongos. Not you." He smiled sheepishly. "Idiots, I mean. My dad used to call nearly everyone a 'drongo.' Not many people use that word anymore, but I can't help it sometimes."

Ethan smiled. "Thanks for explaining. And thanks for saying they're the idiots."

"Right idiots, I reckon. Wankers, wallys, dickheads. I could go on."

The boat's engines thrummed to life, and once they cleared the harbor and picked up speed, the vessel rocked on the choppy waves, and some people went back downstairs. One young woman standing near the bow almost went flying as she tried to take a selfie, the guy she was with barely catching her as the boat pitched side to side.

A pimply faced crew member in a red shirt and shorts came to the bow and yelled something Ethan couldn't catch with the noise of the wind. Presumably it was that they'd have to go downstairs now that the sea had gotten too rough, and sure enough, other red-shirted crew arrived and helped people off the long benches and toward the exit.

The ferry really rocked in the waves, and a ripple of fear snaked down Ethan's spine as he waited for the rows closer to the stairs to go. The young crew were walking the older people down and taking no chances, which was wise. As Ethan stood, the boat pitched, and he stumbled into Clay, who'd also gotten to his feet.

Spreading his legs, Clay stabilized them, his big, rough hands on Ethan's shoulders. Although they were almost the same height—with Clay only an inch taller—where Ethan was lean, he was brawny. Ethan had flattened his hands on Clay's chest, and through the cotton of his undershirt and DL uniform shirt, he could feel the muscle of his pecs. The ferry rocked violently again, but Clay kept them steady, his strong hands warm through Ethan's tee.

There was a murmur of speaking, and Ethan turned to see a teenage boy standing a few feet away, his mouth pressed into an impatient line.

Ethan let go of Clay's chest and was about to apologize, but Clay—keeping one hand firmly on Ethan's shoulder—said, "Just catching our balance, mate." He urged Ethan to go first, staying behind him, guiding him with his hand. He kept it there the whole way down the narrow stairs as they wobbled and pitched.

When they reached the enclosed lower deck, Clay let go and took off his hat. He said something Ethan didn't hear, then walked away. Ethan watched as Clay went around the big room, checking on the rest of the group. The deck had tables for four people around the outside and two rows in the middle as well.

Some people were looking positively green, and crew members were passing out paper bags. Ethan realized with a sinking sensation that they were barf bags just as a woman hurled all over the floor nearby. He was just able to dance out of the way. He waited to make sure someone would look after her before finding an empty table on the far side.

As more and more people started being violently ill, Ethan turned off his hearing aids, the sounds of retching setting his own stomach churning. An old woman at the next table was sweating profusely, and before he could look away, she puked into her bag. Ethan squeezed his eyes shut.

Oh my God, how long is this boat ride?

It turned out it was really, really fucking long.

Ethan had never given it a ton of thought, but he'd imagined the Great Barrier Reef as being just off the coast in Cairns. In reality, it was a ninety-minute trip out, and in the rough seas, the cabin reeking of acrid puke, Ethan thought it would never end. He'd always had a strong stomach, but a low-grade nausea had settled in by the time they reached the massive concrete platform that was a permanent addition to the reef.

There were other sightseeing platforms in the distance as well, presumably owned by different companies. At least the platform was rock solid and drilled into the ocean floor, so it was wonderfully stable and not moving.

The weather had sadly not improved, the sky overcast and drizzly, no hint of sunshine remaining. There were different activities they could do, including scuba diving, snorkeling, a submarine ride, or a trip in a glass-bottomed boat. Scuba was out because Ethan was afraid of what the pressure might do to his ears. He'd planned on trying the snorkeling, although Michael had teased him, saying he'd chicken out because of his slightly irrational fear of sharks.

To be fair, Ethan thought it was a *completely* rational fear. Also, *fuck Michael.* He winced as the hurt and humiliation and fear whipped through him in sequence, landing on anger and clinging to that before he could spiral.

The main area of the covered rectangular platform was open on one long side, the ferry moored to the opposite side. On one end was the kitchen where the buffet lunch would be served, along with clusters of long tables.

With the rain, everyone from the ferry was now crowded on the platform instead of immediately going into the water to explore. Some people looked horribly sick, and Clive shouted to Ethan that there were even tourist helicopters coming to evacuate some of them—at a steep cost to the seasick.

The worst part was that they had a good five hours before the boat would take them back to the mainland. Ethan went down to a glass-sided underwater viewing room, which was cool. He checked his phone. He'd managed to kill about ten minutes.

He could still hear the annoying echoes of Michael's teasing about how he'd punk out of snorkeling when the time came, and he wished he could shut off his stupid brain.

Fuck it. What do I have to lose? Aside from my life if a shark eats me.

Ethan laughed to himself a little hysterically, garnering side-eye from a nearby family who'd been watching purple fish swim by the glass wall.

Fuck it. Fuck Michael. I can do this.

He went back upstairs, determined. It had said in the brochure of activities that there were snorkeling lessons, and he figured it was a good idea. If nothing else, there'd be a few other people around for the sharks to eat first. But then the other shoe dropped.

Michael wasn't with him to help translate.

Ethan's hearing aids weren't waterproof, so he'd be pretty fucking deaf out in the water without them. Maybe the instructors wouldn't even want to take him. Humiliation trickled down his spine as his mind spun out a bunch of scenarios, each more crappy than the last.

Why did I even come on this trip? What was I thinking?

The nausea spiked, and he felt so small and ridiculous, standing there on the crowded platform by himself. A middle-aged woman with curly hair who was wearing a wetsuit stopped in front of him and said something. Of course he couldn't make it out, and he hated himself as he had to ask, "Pardon?" He turned his head a bit, cupping his hand behind one ear.

She smiled and spoke louder and slower, thank God. "Just wondering if you're doing okay? Look a bit lost, mate."

"I…" What the hell. "I wanted to do a snorkeling lesson, but I'm not sure if I even can. I'd have to take off my hearing aids."

"No worries! You're talking to the right woman. I'm Steph, and I'm going to do a little lesson in ten. Let me tell you the basics now while you can hear me, and I'll try to use gestures you can understand while we're in the water. Sound good?"

It really did, and he nodded gratefully.

Ten minutes later in a narrow changing stall made of corrugated metal, Ethan strained to get his hand to the right angle behind him to zip up the wetsuit, but he managed. He felt like a bony idiot in the skintight material, but whatever.

It's not like there's anyone you know here to give a shit what you look like.

After tucking his hearing aids in their case, he zipped them into his backpack's inner pocket, along with his phone and wallet. He exited the stall and looked around, suddenly realizing he needed a place to keep his bag—and since he was pathetically alone on this trip instead of with his new husband, there was no one to watch his shit.

He stood there gripping the backpack. Peering around the crowded platform, he tried to find someone from the group, but there were so many other tours there as well that he couldn't spot anyone. Maybe they'd all gone out on the submersible tour.

Steph tapped him and motioned toward the side of the platform. Ethan looked at his bag, and she said something and pointed toward a bin where other bags were piled. Ethan stared at it in horror. Perhaps those people were more trusting than he was, but no one seemed to be guarding the purses and bags there, and sure, they were on a platform in the ocean and all had to go back on the same boat, but would that stop a thief from trying?

His throat went dry. As much as it would blow to lose his wallet and phone, the thought of losing his hearing aids made his knees actually tremble. He shook his head at Steph, who said something likely meant to be cajoling, smiling at him.

Suddenly Clay was there, his brows drawn together. Relief flooded Ethan. He was probably talking too loud, but he said, "I'm sorry to bug you, but could you just keep an eye on my bag? My hearing aids are in there. I really cannot lose them."

Clay started to say something, but then seemed to think better of it and nodded. He took hold of one of the straps and clapped a big hand on Ethan's shoulder, giving him a squeeze. Ethan forced his fingers to uncurl from the other strap, and he smiled his gratitude as Clay slung the pack over one shoulder and patted it, giving the silent reassurance that he'd keep it safe.

Ethan could finally exhale, and he smiled at Clay again, knowing he could trust him. Which was probably stupid since he barely knew the dude, but Clay just seemed so…capable. Maybe it was because he was older, but it was sexy in a whole different way than Ethan was used to.

On the side of the platform, there were metal steps leading down into the choppy water. Steph fitted Ethan with a mask, life vest, and flippers, and then took him and two old ladies into the water only a few feet from the side of the platform. There was a ring several feet in diameter that they held onto, their feet floating up behind them. Now in a circle, they could practice putting their faces in the water and breathing through the snorkels.

It was amazing how peaceful it looked underwater even though the ocean was rough. The blues and greens were shockingly vivid given how gray the day was, and Ethan watched in wonder as coral swayed and fish darted in and out. With his ears underwater, he could actually hear better than he could in the air, the sounds of movement louder. It was something about the sound going through bone rather than the nerves in his ears, but he rarely went swimming in New York.

Maybe I should join the Y when I get back. But I need to find an apartment and—

Ethan clamped down on his thoughts before they spun out of control. He was snorkeling on the Great Barrier Reef. He was going to be in the now if it freaking killed him.

Steph moved them a bit farther away from the platform, and Ethan kicked with his flippers, enjoying the sensation through the water as he watched some more colorful fish, now orange and yellow, swimming through the endless blue-green.

Then he saw a motherfucking jellyfish—no, three jellyfish!—and seized up, splashing his head up.

He said—okay, probably screamed—"Jellyfish!" but Steph only smiled. She pointed in the jellyfish's amorphous direction and gave Ethan the universal "okay" symbol.

Right, they'd said something about the jellyfish around the area not being anything to worry about. Pulse still thrumming, Ethan gave her a weak smile and put his face back in, gripping the ring. He saw more jellyfish floating, their white bodies lit on the inside. As they pulsed and sailed gracefully through the water, Ethan decided they were actually beautiful. He was still avoiding the fuckers just in case, but they were cool to watch.

The lesson was over too quickly, and he decided he was good to stay out by himself, giving Steph a nod and smile. There were other people in the water now, all sticking close to the platform, and he kept accidentally kicking people with his flippers. After getting someone else's flipper in the face, Ethan headed out farther, marveling at all the colors and shapes of the coral and plants that waved gently in the current.

When he surfaced, he realized with a seize of panic that he'd gotten farther away from the platform than he'd intended when he'd broken free from the cluster of others. Somehow, with his face in the water, it had seemed calmer, and he'd followed the bright schools of fish all the way near the edge of the snorkeling area, marked by lines of buoys. Here, the ocean swells were larger. A wave washed over his face, and he sputtered, kicking with his flippers and trying not to swallow the salt water.

Do the lifeguards know I'm here? What if they call to me and I can't hear? I have my life vest. I can't drown in that, can I? Will they come get me? That's their job, isn't it?

He squinted back at the platform, struggling to catch his breath, an iron band around his lungs. But then he spotted a man standing on the side of the platform by the railing. He wore navy uniform shorts, a white short-sleeved shirt, and a brown hat. Over his shoulder he carried a backpack with a distinctive red starburst on the rear pocket.

Clay lifted his arm in a wave, and Ethan looked behind him. But there was no one else there, just the buoys and open sea, another sightseeing platform rising in the distance, hazy and small. Ethan pivoted and waved back to Clay, who lifted his arm again. It looked like… A thumbs-up.

More swells rolled in, but with Clay watching, Ethan cleared his mask, secured his mouthpiece, and went back to the underwater world with impossibly vibrant colors, looking right and left at the coral and schools of fish. He saw a few other people from time to time, but none close by. For the most part he was alone with the sea—

And a motherfucking giant-ass sea turtle.

He'd been turning his head slowly when the large shape appeared in his right peripheral vision, sending a jolt of pure terror screaming through him. But after a moment he realized it wasn't a shark or a stingray or anything terrible, but a huge sea turtle, which seemed completely unfazed by Ethan's presence as it swam, moving at a steady, not particularly fast pace.

Ethan glanced around, but he was the only person there. Heart soaring, he kicked his flippers and followed along with the turtle, not getting *too* close, but still probably within six or seven feet. The turtle seemed fixated on a jellyfish that was pulsing by, getting closer and closer until—

Holy shitballs. It's eating the jellyfish!

With a big *chomp*, the turtle went right for the jellyfish's middle. He swallowed down the main part of the creature, the rest of it left to drift in the water, fish zooming in from out of nowhere to snap up the jellyfish crumbs. Now Ethan really regretted not buying one of the stupidly expensive underwater cameras as he watched the turtle go for another poor dumb jellyfish, who never saw it coming, what with having no eyes and no brain.

It was freaking *awesome*.

Ethan followed the turtle for a bit, but when he got water in his mask again and lifted his head to clear it, a wave hit him square in the face and he got a little freaked. Spitting out salt water, he paddled back to the platform. Really, nothing was going to top a sea turtle eating a jellyfish, so he might as well put an end to his snorkeling adventure before he got in over his head.

After depositing his flippers and mask in the right boxes, Ethan turned to find Clay there with a towel, Ethan's sandals, and of course his backpack. "Thank you!" Ethan exclaimed, grinning like an idiot but feeling happier than he had in what seemed like a long time, even if it had only been days.

"I saw a sea turtle eat a jellyfish!" he told Clay, trying to modulate so he wasn't yelling. Clay's eyebrows shot up, and a grin spread over his handsome face, his cheeks creasing above his beard. He gave Ethan another thumbs-up.

Ethan was dripping and needed to change out of the wetsuit, and he took his pack from Clay gratefully. Ethan jerked his thumb behind him toward the changing stalls, and Clay nodded.

Ethan wasn't really expecting him to be waiting, but when he came back out with his hearing aids in, the hum of activity and voices all around the platform jarring after the peace of the sea, Clay was still there, ready to listen as Ethan told him all about his adventure.

"OKAY, EVERYONE. WE cannot leave until every person has reported back and had their name checked off the list. This is a safety issue. We're looking for a Michael Wong, Lu Lee, Wenjing Han, Audrey Steinberg—"

Ethan stopped listening to the other names being announced on the boat's loudspeaker, his heart thumping dully, Michael's name repeating on a loop in his head. The announcement was then apparently read in Mandarin, and Ethan gazed around uneasily, as if Michael—and Todd—were suddenly going to appear.

Obviously they weren't, and "Michael Wong" was not an uncommon name. Apparently there was another one on the boat who hadn't followed the instructions to check in when they re-boarded.

Ethan flipped through a brochure, killing time as they all waited for the irresponsible passengers to get their names checked off so the boat could leave, safe in the knowledge they hadn't abandoned anyone out in the middle of nowhere to be eaten by sharks. Although the platform was there, so it wasn't like anyone would actually be left at sea.

Then the announcement came again with fewer names, but "Michael Wong" was repeated. Hearing the words aloud again was like salt in his wounds, but Ethan refused to take out his hearing aids. He could hear Michael's stupid name and survive. He couldn't let the terrorists win. Or something.

To distract himself, he watched Clay doing a round of the deck, checking in on all the tour members. Sure, Ethan was on his honeymoon alone, but at least he had eye candy. Clay was way hotter than the dude who'd played Crocodile Dundee, but he had a similar laid-back, confident vibe. Like he could manfully wrestle a crocodile no prob, but he had a sensitive side too.

As the minutes ticked by slowly, Clay talked to the other tour guests, smiling affably, his uniform shirt stretching across his broad shoulders as he leaned over to say something to Gwen, a nice Welsh lady in her seventies who'd been one of the people violently ill earlier. Clay spoke to her for a few minutes, and she beamed at him even though she still looked a little green.

When Clay reached Ethan, he took the seat across from him, and Ethan tried not to grin. He reminded himself Clay was only being kind, but he hadn't sat with anyone else and Ethan couldn't help but feel special.

I'm delusional, but fuck it. Fantasy FTW.

Clay asked, "Holding up all right, mate? I know today wasn't as much fun as we'd have hoped with this weather."

For some reason, Ethan wanted to reassure him. "Yeah. I'm good. It was great. I mean, I saw a sea turtle eat a jellyfish. No complaints here."

Clay grinned. "I'm still jealous."

A young staff member in red appeared in the middle of the deck and spoke into a bullhorn, making Ethan wince. "We are still looking for Michael Wong. Michael Wong, you must check in! We cannot leave until you do!"

As she repeated the message in Mandarin, Clay bolted straighter in his seat, saying something Ethan missed. He shook his head and sprang up, hurrying over to the young woman with the megaphone. They spoke for a minute, Clay's expression serious. A few other staff members came over, including one with a clipboard. Clay turned to him, his jaw tightening. He seemed to speak sternly to the guy, who nodded a few times and then rubbed his face.

The other staff looked annoyed, and the girl with the megaphone seemed barely able to resist rolling her eyes as she stared daggers at the guy with the clipboard. They dispersed, and Clay came back to the table. As he sat, he met Ethan's gaze. He seemed…sheepish?

Clay leaned forward across the table and carefully said, "I told them Michael wasn't on this tour after all, and to take his name *off the list*. The wally with the clipboard apparently forgot." He shook his head and said something else Ethan didn't pick up, looking miserable, his mouth turning down.

In that moment, Ethan didn't care about anything else but seeing Clay smile confidently again. "Oh, it's okay. It's not your fault!" A bolt of anger at goddamn Michael flashed through him, as irrational as it might have been.

Clay shook his head. "I should have clocked it as soon as they said his name."

"How were you supposed to know? I didn't figure it out either. It's a common name."

Clay rubbed his beard and muttered something. Ethan hesitated, but then tentatively asked, "Can you please say that again? When your hand's near your mouth, it can distort the sound."

Clay dropped his hand to the table between them like a rock. "Sorry. Should have realized."

"It's okay. I know it's a huge pain."

Clay frowned. "It's not. If I forget, please remind me."

Gratitude warmed Ethan's chest. "Okay. Thanks. Um, anyway, hearing his name sucked, but it's not like I'm not aware almost every second that he's not here with me. I'm trying to distract myself, but…" He didn't say how, his cheeks getting hot now as he thought of his growing crush. Good thing Clay couldn't read his mind. "I need to get used to it. Him not being with me."

Clay studied him carefully. "You will. Believe me. I've been there, and you get used to it. Life goes on. It even gets better, I think." He quickly added, "Depending on the situation, of course."

Ethan smiled softly. "That's good to hear. Thank you." He stared into Clay's eyes, and he was probably imagining things, but he felt as though understanding passed between them. Ethan tried to think of something else to say, his heart thumping as the moment stretched out.

The boat finally started moving with a loud rumble of the engines, and Ethan and Clay both jumped a little before laughing awkwardly. Clay peered around. "You know, there's a little deck out the back. Some fresh air might be good, and it shouldn't be as bumpy as it was earlier given the tides."

Nodding, Ethan followed his lead. Indeed, there was a little outside space at the rear of the main deck. The crew still wasn't letting anyone up on the top deck, and there were no official seats, but Clay and Ethan were able to perch on a box containing life jackets, high enough that their feet dangled.

It was loud outside with the hum of the engine and the wind, but Clay seemed content to sit in silence. The sun reappeared, and they both put on their sunglasses, Clay's sexy aviators making Ethan's mouth go dry.

Maybe it should have been weird to hang out with a virtual stranger, but Clay seemed…different. Ethan stole glances at him as Clay leaned back against the wall behind them. Ethan could glimpse that his eyes were closed, and he admired the gleam of red in Clay's beard, and the way faint freckles sprinkled his skin, even on the tip of his ear.

Ethan was probably losing it after what had happened, but Clay's solid presence made him feel safe. Maybe it was that he was older and so completely unlike Michael. He probably didn't give a shit about fashion or clubbing or what hashtags were trending.

Clay was a man—adult and solid. And *hot*, but it was the

dependability and strength emanating from him that attracted Ethan the most. Someone to lean on, and you wouldn't have to worry that it would be too much or that he'd flit off to some noisy fucking party to escape your neediness.

Okay, so maybe Ethan was really indulging in fantasy now, but it still felt good to be next to a man like Clay. Something to aspire to when he was healed from this shit with Michael. Because he *would* heal from it. He wasn't going to let them win.

The ferry swayed on the waves, but it was definitely calmer now in the waning afternoon. As they rolled on a bigger swell, Ethan's knee bumped into Clay's muscular thigh, their legs pressing together. Ethan was about to apologize, but Clay had his eyes closed and didn't seem bothered by it a bit.

They swayed back and forth, their arms brushing now too, the wiry hair on Clay's sending goosebumps over Ethan's skin. He'd never been with an older man, and hadn't thought much about it aside from maybe lusting over Hugh Jackman and George Clooney sometimes, because who didn't?

But Clay was very much flesh and blood next to him and not in a movie, and as Ethan leaned into him again as the boat rolled, he imagined what it would be like to feel the touch of his whole body. Naked, with Clay on top of him, that solid weight pressing him down, Clay between his legs…

Well, Ethan's dick was certainly interested in the idea, and he bit his lip, inching away before he humiliated himself, grinning like an idiot as he looked out at the waves, shimmering blue in the snatches of sunlight. Shit, he'd forgotten how *fun* a crush could be.

Of course thoughts of Michael and Todd smashed back through his head, drenching him in virtual ice water. He inhaled the briny air deeply, reminded himself to be in the now. And if the boat kept nudging him and Clay against each other, it didn't hurt anyone.

When they reached the hotel later, Ethan loitered as the other guests left and said goodnight to Clay, who stood by the bus and reminded them to have their suitcases outside their room door by six-fifteen in the morning for porterage.

Ethan pretended to look through his backpack for something, even though the other people on the tour wouldn't think anything of him hanging back to talk to Clay. There was nothing to think about.

Still, he waited until they were gone to say, "What's the name of that store? With the hats? I'm sure I can find it if you point me in the right direction."

"I've got to go that way to grab some tucker anyway. If you wait while I park the bus, won't *mumble mumble*." He paused as Ethan squinted at him. Clay repeated, speaking more slowly, "Won't take more than ten minutes."

"Oh, sure. Yeah. Cool."

So Ethan waited, pacing in the shade of the hotel's entry, which had a high roof over the curved drive. The low-grade nausea he'd felt most of the day at sea had faded, but his stomach was jittery again. He was strangely excited to go hat shopping with Clay, which proved he was a dumbass, because Clay was only being nice to him.

He feels sorry for me because I'm alone. Not to mention a loser, not even bringing a hat to Australia for fuck's sake. He'd take Violet to the hat store too if she needed one. But Violet planned ahead way better than I did. He's just being generous. Of course he is, because what else would he be? It's his job to be nice to dumbass tourists.

Clay appeared, and Ethan almost jumped out of his skin, suddenly full of nerves. He tried to laugh it off. "Hey. I was daydreaming."

Clay's lips hitched in a little smile, not like he was laughing at him, but with a sweetness and understanding that was probably completely fabricated in Ethan's mess of a mind. Still, it felt as if he'd found a friend, and he realized Clay was the first new person he'd connected with in years. *Years.*

As Clay led the way down the street, he said, "We should just make it before they close."

Ethan had checked his phone, and it wasn't even five. "So early?"

"Yeah, most shops close by six at the latest. Except Thursdays. That's late shopping. Open until nine."

"Huh. I guess I'm used to a lot of stuff being twenty-four hours. You're a little more laid-back down here. Understatement of the year."

Clay laughed. "You'll find more of that in Sydney, but Cairns is really a glorified small town."

They quickly reached the shopping area. On each side of the wide street, the sidewalk was covered by a roof, and there were a variety of shops from jewelry to Ugg boots to a drugstore, grocery store, clothing stores, and even designer stuff in a fancy building across the way.

Clay led the way into a store selling surf gear and said to the girl inside, "Won't take much of your time. *Mumble mumble.*"

She pointed them to a rack of what Ethan thought of as fishing hats, round with a brim and fitting close to the head. She said something Ethan missed, and then, "Fifty UPF."

Ethan thanked her and picked a navy hat. He put it on, suddenly self-conscious of Clay watching, and checked it out in the mirror. It seemed to fit, and he looked super dorky, but when didn't he? He'd look dorkier with a lobster burn. "I guess it's good?"

"Looks great," Clay said.

He said it with such confidence that Ethan wore it out of the store, the girl cutting off the tags for him after he bought it. "Thanks for your help," Ethan said to Clay. "I feel like this is probably way above your pay grade."

Clay only laughed with that low rumble. Ethan's stomach flip-flopped, and it definitely wasn't lingering seasickness.

Chapter Six

IT WASN'T EVEN seven a.m., but Clay already had to swipe sweat from his brow as he loaded the luggage into the coach, the humidity thick in the air and on his skin, heavy clouds gathered overhead. One of the porters was good enough to help, and Clay shook his hand before heading into the restaurant. It wouldn't be their longest day of driving on the tour, but it would be long enough, and he needed a coffee and a good helping of brekkie to get him started.

Like at all the hotels the tour used, the breakfast was a buffet. This one had some delicious mango yogurt Clay always looked forward to, as well as a good fry-up. Since a large number of Chinese tourists visited Cairns, there was also fried rice, congee, dumplings, and other foods Clay didn't reckon many Aussies were used to eating for breakfast. It was good to cater to everyone, though, and he'd discovered the dumplings were nice with a bit of scrambled egg.

After loading his plate, he tucked one of the complimentary newspapers under his arm and went into the open-area dining room at the front of the hotel just off the buffet. Shiv waved to him from a table by the massive windows. Clay wove around the other tables, nodding to some of the tour guests he recognized. He sat and said good morning to Shiv, who looked a damn sight better than he did the day before.

"Not so crook today?" Clay asked.

"Heaps better." Still, he only had a piece of toast and a boiled egg on his plate. "Thanks again for taking over."

"No worries. The way you were feeling, being tossed around on that boat sure wouldn't have helped."

Shiv grimaced. "Lots of sick passengers?"

"Yep. I didn't feel so great myself. Some of ours were a little off, but no one was too bad. Well, the Welsh lady didn't have a good time of it, but she perked up later."

Shiv poked at his phone and took a little bite of toast and Vegemite. After a minute of silence as they ate, he asked, "Wonder what happened with that Ethan's fiancé? Probably quite a story."

"It's none of our business, is it?" Clay said—more sharply than he intended.

Frowning, Shiv glanced up. "Suppose not. Just curious is all." He went back to his phone.

They ate in peace, Clay skipping to the sports pages. But he soon found himself glancing around, wondering where Ethan was. Maybe he'd slept in or didn't like breakfast. Not that it mattered one way or the other, and Clay wasn't sure why he was even pondering the bloke's brekkie preferences.

He didn't typically get so involved with the guests. Not that he was *involved*—he'd shown him where to buy a hat and chatted a bit. Tried to cheer him up a little since he was down in the dumps. Ethan had seemed so mortified when he'd first come on the bus and there'd been the misunderstanding. Clay had been afraid the lad would burst into tears, but he'd rallied.

And though it truly wasn't any of their business, Clay had wondered more than once what the story was with Ethan and the absent Michael Wong. They had single guests from time to time, but it wasn't the norm, and rarely one as young as Ethan who wasn't traveling with a parent. They sometimes had mother/daughter duos onboard, but a younger guy in his twenties usually chose the backpacker tours. How did Ethan end up coming alone on what was meant to be his honeymoon? Took guts, that did.

Glancing around, there was still no sign of him, and Clay wasn't sure why he was even thinking about it. He supposed there was something about Ethan that intrigued him. Perhaps it was the puzzle of his breakup, or that he seemed so very lonely. The vulnerability in Ethan made Clay want to take care of him, but of course he would worry for anyone who'd been through such a trauma.

He admired Ethan's courage in coming on the trip. He'd looked sick with nerves going into the water alone and unable to hear, but once he was out there he'd gone farther than anyone else in the rough conditions. It had been lovely to see him smiling so much afterward, showing the dimples in his cheeks.

Shiv's phone beeped, and his face lit up. "It's Jane," he said, although Clay hadn't asked. "She's going to be in Alice in a couple weeks. Wants me to fly up when we get back to Sydney and have a holiday weekend with her."

"Great. And before you ask, her friend was lovely, but I ain't going to Alice Springs to help you get another root." It had been bad enough making small talk at lunch and trying to be friendly enough but not *too* friendly.

Shiv laughed. "No worries, mate. Your duty is done. Sharon was nice, though. Not a bad bod on her. If you change your mind…"

Clay pointedly turned the page on the newspaper and got stuck into an article about a teenage girl who'd been murdered down in Brisbane. Of course reading it was a mistake, and his stomach tightened as he thought about Sam. She'd known not to go off with strangers since she was a little girl, but often it seemed these killers weren't strangers at all.

Pulling out his phone, he typed out a quick message to her.

Morning. Everything ok?

He waited, tense and gulping his coffee until he saw the little bubble of dots appear. A few moments later, her reply was there.

Of course. Why wouldn't it be? On my way to class. xo

Clay was surprised she was up and out so early for uni, but then he remembered New South Wales was an hour ahead this time of year. Queensland refused to get on board with daylight savings, which of course led to confusion with two time zones in the east. It was a pain in the arse.

He typed:

Just checking in. Be careful, love.

Clay could imagine her eye roll as she sent back:

If this is about the dead girl in the news, stop worrying. I'm right as rain. Love you, Dad.

He had to chuckle. Sam had always been able to see through him, even in a damn text message. As he debated writing more, he caught sight of Ethan coming into the dining room with a coffee and full plate.

Clay smiled to himself as he watched him weaving between tables, his long legs clad in skinny jeans and his green T-shirt reading:

"Please insert witty slogan here."

Clay chuckled again, and when Ethan caught sight of him, he gave Clay a little wave, his cheeks dimpling. If Clay and Shiv had been at a bigger table, perhaps Clay would have beckoned Ethan over, but generally they left the guests to mingle together or eat alone. Probably for the best. Clay had a job to do, after all.

When he and Shiv left to get ready for the day, Clay glanced at Ethan's table. To his surprise, Ethan was looking right at him, and for a moment they just stared at each other, Clay's step faltering as he followed Shiv. Clay nodded, and Ethan smiled nervously and dropped his head.

That morning was spent waiting after driving the group a bit north to Kuranda, where they took a ride on the cable car over the rain forest and saw Barron Falls. It was pouring rain, and visibility wasn't the best, but the falls were a corker during the wet season.

As Ethan climbed on board last, Clay asked, "Enjoy yourself?"

Ethan grinned, the smile transforming his face. He looked so serious much of the time, with those big, solemn brown eyes. A young man with an old soul, Clay thought. But when he really smiled, it was like a light came on.

It made Clay smile as well as Ethan said, "It was awesome! Pretty foggy, so we couldn't really see much going up, but the waterfall was incredible. Just…so much water!" His cheeks went a charming pink. "I mean, obviously, since it's a waterfall and everything."

"Ah, but this is the best time of year for it."

Shiv was waiting, and Ethan hurried on after giving Clay another smile. Clay found himself whistling softly as he got them on the road down toward the Atherton Tablelands. They stopped at a smaller waterfall and the truly massive Cathedral Fig Tree, an ancient strangler tree stories high—and wide—that never failed to impress.

He strolled along the boardwalk path that looped around the tree, offering to take photos as Shiv gave them a little talk. Clay's gaze found Ethan reading an information plaque, and he wandered over and asked, "Did you hear everything all right?"

"Pardon?"

Clay smiled and enunciated more slowly. "Wondered if you heard everything all right."

Ethan laughed ruefully. "Not all of it, but this helps." He motioned to the plaque. "It's really cool."

"It is. I think this is one of the nicest days on the tour. Mission Beach tonight is quite relaxing. The little resort's not overly fancy, but it's right by the water." He hesitated, then said, "And if you're an early bird, the sunrises tend to be real rippers. I usually go out around five this time of year."

One of Clay's favorite things about doing the East Coast tour was peaceful morning sunrises at sleepy Mission Beach, where he was often the only one about now that the kids were back in school and the resorts weren't so crowded.

"I'm assuming 'ripper' is good." Ethan grinned. "It sounds good."

Shiv had wandered close, and he laughed, giving Clay a playful slap on the back. "I think Clayton should come with a translator sometimes. These outback blokes can be walking Aussie stereotypes. Has he called anyone a 'drongo' yet? Or said 'fair dinkum'? Oh, and 'strewth!' is my favorite. He keeps it old-school."

Ethan's smile dimmed a bit as he said, "I can understand him just fine. And didn't you say you were 'chockers' after breakfast?"

Shiv laughed. "Guilty as charged. We certainly do have our own unique spin on the English language. I'm just teasin' him. He loves it." He grinned at Clay. "Right?"

He didn't really mind, but Clay still gave him an exaggerated glower and muttered, "Piss off."

Ethan burst out laughing, and as Shiv moved on with a smile to go talk to an old couple from Alberta, Clay chuckled. "Didn't think you'd be able to hear that."

"I could read your lips on that one."

They shared a grin before Ethan went back to reading. Clay lingered with Ethan as the others moved on. It had rained, and fat drops of water clung to leaves and branches, the air moist and rich with the smell of moss, wood, and earth. Aside from the chirping of birds, it was wonderfully quiet.

As Ethan finished reading about the root system of the strangler figs, Clay hesitated, wondering if it was rude to ask. "Do you ever use sign language?"

"Sign language?" At Clay's nod, Ethan said, "No. I think if it had happened when I was a kid, I would have learned. But I was finishing college when my hearing started to go."

"Why did it? If you don't mind me asking." He was being damn nosy, but curiosity tugged at him. He rarely spoke to guests this much, but he found himself wanting to know more about Ethan. Likely because he was so different from a typical senior guest on the tour.

Ethan shrugged. "I don't mind. I can talk about it now." He was silent for a moment, staring up at the massive fig's gnarled branches. "For a while, I noticed everything was getting muffled. I thought maybe I had some ear infection, or maybe one of those gross balls of wax stuck in there. The kind you see on YouTube?"

"Like the pimple popping? I only watch the cricket and footie highlights, mate."

Ethan chuckled. "Fair enough. Anyway, I got referred to an ENT, and I was just expecting her to give me some antibiotics or pull out the wax. I dunno, I figured it was just something routine. Instead she did a hearing test. I sat in a little booth that was completely soundproof. She was on the other side of the glass, and I was supposed to repeat the words and sounds she made through the intercom."

"Right. Makes sense."

Looking up again, Ethan's shoulders hitched before he exhaled with a sigh. "So at first I could hear okay, even though it was faint. Then I couldn't really hear anything. I was sitting there waiting for her to keep talking and making sounds, wondering why she wasn't. I started to get claustrophobic, and when she finally opened the door to let me out, there was this look in her eyes I'll never forget." He shivered. "It was so horribly sympathetic, you know?" At Clay's nod, he added, "I knew something bad was happening, but I didn't want to believe it."

They'd stopped on the boardwalk around the tree, a faint drizzle beginning, the others almost out of sight around a bend in the forest. Chest tight, Clay almost didn't want to ask. "Then what happened?"

"She sent me to an audiologist, who did more tests and told me it was nonsyndromic hearing loss. Meaning there weren't any other signs or symptoms. Like, I didn't have a disease where deafness was just a symptom of it."

Clay nodded. "Then what caused it?"

"A gene mutation. My mom was probably a carrier and didn't know it. So I have bilateral sensorineural hearing loss. It's still technically a moderate loss, but eventually it'll likely be severe. Maybe even profound. I was almost twenty-two when it started, so I'm what they call a 'late-deafened adult.' I've never been part of the capital-D Deaf community."

Clay frowned. "What's the distinction?"

"That's a whole cultural thing with ASL and stuff. Being Deaf is part of their identity and culture."

"Ah, I see. Well, could you be part of that community? If you wanted?" The drizzle continued, a fine mist that felt lovely in the heat of the humid day. They had to catch up with the rest of the group, but at the moment Clay didn't care about a thing except hearing more from Ethan.

"I don't know. I think it's really different if you're born without hearing, or it happens when you're young. A lot of people don't see it as a disability. It's just who they are. You know what I mean? They're happy and comfortable being Deaf, and I totally respect that. It's awesome. I envy them sometimes. But for me..."

"Damn hard to accept, I reckon."

A ghost of a smile tugged at Ethan's full lips as he met Clay's gaze. "Yeah. Damn hard. I feel like some people think I should be over it by now or something. And I *have* accepted it, but... It still sucks. Especially if I'm by myself, and I can't understand something." He shrugged tensely. "It can be unnerving. And the frustration doesn't go away. At least not for me. Other people get frustrated with me too, and it's stressful."

"I can imagine." It really was a frightening thought, to have a vital sense diminished as an adult. Clay would have liked a word with whoever thought Ethan should simply get over it.

Ethan shoved his hands in his pockets. "It can be so isolating. It's like… I'm not deaf enough to use ASL, but I'm not a hearing person anymore either. Still, I live in the hearing world—the only world I've ever known. I'm not part of Deaf culture. I don't know where I fit. Who I am." He tipped his head back to look up at the fig towering over them.

As Ethan gazed up with those big eyes that seemed so sad, Clay ached to say the right thing to make it better. Damned if he knew what that was, though. He cleared his throat. "Don't they have those implants now?"

Ethan dropped his head to meet Clay's gaze. "Sorry, I missed that."

"What about those high-tech implants that help you hear?"

"Oh, yeah. Cochlear implants. I've thought about it, of course. But they're really expensive. My health benefits at work have shitty coverage for hearing. Barely covers the cost of one visit a year to the audiologist, and nothing for my hearing aids. And the thing is, with a CI, you can lose what natural hearing you still have. The sound through an implant is apparently flatter. More digital-like, instead of natural sounds being amplified with my hearing aids. But my doctor doesn't think I'm a good candidate at this point anyway. I dunno. There are pros and cons."

Clay nodded, again wishing he could think of the right thing to say. They stood there looking at each other, the drizzle forming little drops on the ends of Ethan's thick hair.

Ethan was practically whispering when he said, "The thought of losing *all* my hearing—the world being truly silent—it's just…" He shivered, speaking louder as he added, "Anyway. They're making improvements all the time, so I'll just see what happens."

Clay could see the fear in Ethan's eyes—in his tight smile and the way his fingers twitched into fists. He was struck by the urge to comfort, and he almost reached out before jamming his hands into his pockets. "It's scary though, mate."

"Oi! Get a move on back there," Shiv called out good-naturedly, appearing in Clay's peripheral vision from farther along the boardwalk, which looped back to where the coach was parked.

Clay waved. "Coming!"

Ethan smiled at Clay as he started walking. "Sorry. I'm slowing us down with my drama." He barely glanced at the next information plaque.

Clay did reach out then, giving Ethan's shoulder a quick squeeze. "No worries. We have plenty of time. They can't go anywhere without me."

Ethan's dimples creased his face. "Thanks."

So they ambled along, and Clay made sure Ethan got the chance to read every last plaque.

Chapter Seven

AT FIVE O'CLOCK in the gray light of predawn, Clay made his way across the dewy strip of grass between the resort and the little path that cut through the ridge of palm trees that stood before the sand. There were pebbles and stray leaves and sticks on the path, but his feet had been hardened by the dry earth of the outback long ago.

He'd pulled on shorts and a T-shirt, and the breeze off the water was cool and perfect. Sipping from his thermos of coffee, he headed south down the narrow, deserted strip of beach. The foliage to the right grew from just palm trees, thickening into dense bush as he passed the resort's border. To the left, gentle waves met the beach and some rocks scattered just offshore with a low, rhythmic drone.

There wasn't another soul in sight. Just the way he liked it.

Yet when a figure appeared a minute later back down the sand where he'd come from, Clay found himself smiling. He recognized Ethan's slim build and long legs, and gave him a wave when he got closer. Wearing khakis and a T-shirt, Ethan waved back, carrying what tourists often called "flip-flops" instead of thongs in his other hand. Clay supposed the name was apt.

It took a couple minutes for Ethan to reach him, and when he did, he said, "Morning. Wow, this is amazing." He dropped his thongs on the sand and looked out over the water. "It's getting pink."

"Just wait." Clay poured some coffee into the lid of his thermos and offered it to Ethan. "It's only black, so if you like anything fancy you're out of luck."

"If I what? Sorry, didn't catch that." Ethan fiddled with his hearing aids. "Might be better if I keep my back to the water. I can put on a different setting and it'll block that noise out."

Clay raised his voice a bit and was careful to enunciate more slowly. "You'll miss the sunrise facing the trees. I said the coffee's just black."

"Oh! Um… I like it this way, actually. It's perfect." Their fingers brushed as Ethan took the lid and sipped before passing it back. He glanced around, then peered out to sea. "What's that island?" Ethan pointed to the shadowy humps in the distance.

"Main one's Dunk Island. Can't remember what the others are called."

"They kind of look like volcanoes out there. It's cool."

They stood there in peaceful silence as the pale yellow sky became both more blue and more pink. Light clouds covered much of the sky, turning a warm blush with patches of vibrant blue between them. The pink reflected on the ocean with a rosy glow, and Ethan made little sighing noises and took a bunch of pictures with his phone. He had long fingers, and Clay wondered if he played the piano, although for all he knew, finger length had nothing to do with it.

Ethan exclaimed, "It's like the whole world is pink." He watched with wonder, a smile playing at his lips, and the sunrise reflected in his eyes and across his pale, smooth skin. Clay was glad he'd told Ethan his secret. Ethan put his phone with his thongs and rolled his trousers to his knees before grinning at Clay and splashing into the surf.

"Watch the current!" Clay shouted. "It's stronger down here

than in the swimming area."

Ethan didn't acknowledge him, and Clay realized he probably hadn't heard. It wasn't like Ethan would go swimming since he had his clothes on and hearing aids in, but there were no nets this far down the beach.

As Ethan went in farther, the pink-lit water swirling almost to his knees, Clay had visions of a croc coming along for its brekkie. It wasn't too likely in this area, but not impossible, especially during the wet.

And the next bloody moment, Ethan staggered back, wind-milling his arms before tumbling onto his arse. Clay was already racing toward him as the next swell neared, and he grabbed under Ethan's arms from behind and scooped him up as the water flowed harmlessly around their knees, no crocs or jellyfish in sight. Still, Clay backed them up onto the sand, practically carrying Ethan.

Ethan's back was pressed to Clay's chest, and Clay had his arms locked around him. He shivered and let go, stepping back as Ethan turned. Ethan's Adam's apple bobbed. "Shit, I cannot get my hearing aids wet. Thank you. I tripped on a rock."

Clay nodded, his heart thudding. "Right. Also there aren't any nets down this end. Crocs and jellyfish could be around."

Eyes bugging out, Ethan whirled back to the water, then spun to face Clay. "Are you fucking with me?"

"No, mate." Clay shook his head in case his words were lost. He tried to speak clearly. "Wouldn't joke about that. The known croc habitats are all sign-posted, and it's much more likely to come across one in the swamps and rivers a bit inland. But they do take people on beaches sometimes in Far North Queensland."

Mouth open, Ethan stared. "Wow. I knew there were salt-water crocodiles, I just didn't think…" He glanced back at the sea. "It's so peaceful." Then he looked down and backed up away from the water. "Are we safe here?"

"Yeah, no worries. It's being in the water that's the danger. Even knee-deep isn't safe. They can take folks quite shallow."

Ethan huffed out a laugh. "Are you saying 'take'? You mean eat, right?"

Clay had to laugh too. "Yep. I guess it's our polite way of saying it. Sharks and crocs 'take' people. Anyway, no harm done. Maybe just to your pride."

"What's that saying? That it goeth before a fall?" Ethan swiped at his arse, his face red in the fading pink sunrise, blue and yellow beginning to surge across the clouds. "Thanks for being there." He smiled, but it didn't hold. "Shit, I have to be careful. If my hearing aids got damaged…" He exhaled shakily. "Or, you know, if I got *eaten by a freaking crocodile*, it would kind of put a damper on things. Like my life, for starters."

"And the paperwork would be a nightmare if I let a croc take a guest on my watch," Clay deadpanned.

Ethan laughed genuinely, and Clay almost wanted to call him pretty when he smiled like that. Strange to think of a bloke that way.

Clay said, "Come on, let's finish the coffee." He mimed drinking when Ethan briefly furrowed his brow.

They walked a bit farther away from the water near the foliage, where he hoped the sound of the waves wasn't so troublesome for Ethan. Ethan sat in his wet trousers, grimacing. Clay said, "Hang 'em up in the sun while you're at brekkie and they'll dry in no time."

Minute by minute, the pink sunrise slipped away, and they watched in silence, passing the thermos lid back and forth. After a time, Ethan said, "This really was incredible. Best sunrise I've ever seen."

"Fair dinkum? Well, I'm glad." A little warm swell of pride filled Clay.

Ethan laughed delightedly. "You said it! Fair dinkum!"

Clay chuckled. "Suppose I did. You can take the boy out of the outback, but…"

"I feel like I'm so far away from home. I mean, I am. I've never been farther than Canada before, and this is a whole new world. New York in winter—it's so gray and cold and, I don't know. Blah. This is like paradise. With crocodiles and jellyfish, but still. Paradise. It's been, I don't know? What day is it even? New York almost feels like another lifetime."

"Guess that's a good thing. You can enjoy your holiday, despite everything."

Ethan looked at the horizon, where the last vestiges of pink and yellow faded into blue. "Yeah. It's strange, being here. It's like I'm on the moon, and they're on a distant planet."

"They?" Clay asked, being nosy. In the silence that stretched out, Ethan sitting like a statue, he suddenly felt foolish and blurted, "You probably mean your family."

Ethan's throat worked as he swallowed forcefully. "No, actually. My Mom died when I was fourteen, and my dad a few years later. I'm an only child, and there's not really anyone except my uncle and his family left. They're cool, but we're not super close or anything. And I have cousins, but they're all spread out and no one really keeps in touch."

Clay cursed himself for bringing it up. "Sorry to hear that."

Shrugging, Ethan looked at his feet and dug his toes into the sand. "S'okay." He didn't clarify who he'd meant by "they," and Clay sure as hell didn't ask. "It was actually my mom who made me want to come to Australia. You know that old movie, *Crocodile Dundee*?"

Clay had to laugh. "I think I might have heard of it."

Ethan laughed too. "I guess it was a big deal back then."

"Yep, in those ancient times, it was a very big deal. I was still a kid when it came out, for the record."

"Duly noted. Anyway, my mom had just come to the States

from Switzerland with my grandmother. My mom was about nineteen, I think. She didn't know anyone and hardly spoke English, and she became obsessed with that movie. Even, like, ten years later after she had me, she still loved *Crocodile Dundee*. It was like comfort food, you know? It's one of the first movies I ever remember watching. My dad said when he first met her, he wasn't sure where she was from because she had an Australian accent on some words. He was like, "What is this gorgeous Swiss-German-Australian doing in Buffalo? And how is she interested in a nebbishy Jew like me?" Ethan smiled fondly.

Clay chuckled. "Where's Buffalo?"

"Where's Buffalo?" Ethan repeated. When Clay nodded, he said, "Western New York. The state, not the city. Close to Niagara Falls and the Canadian border. I don't even know how she and Oma ended up there. It was one of the coldest places with the most snow they could have picked, but I guess they were used to that. And it was definitely nowhere near Switzerland. They didn't want to be anywhere near Europe."

After sipping more coffee and passing the lid, Clay asked, "Why's that?"

"Oh, my grandfather was an abusive alcoholic asshole. They moved to Germany first, and he followed them there, so they decided an ocean between them was a good idea."

"Ah. Sorry to hear it."

"Yeah." Ethan swallowed some coffee and gazed out at the horizon. "I never met him, or anyone else on that side of the family. Mom was an only child. I guess it didn't go down so well when she and Oma left? They didn't like talking about it. They worked as maids in a hotel, and eventually my mom met my dad and had me. Ran her own private maid service with Oma where they cleaned people's houses. It was really successful, and then Mom got sick." He added with a flat tone, "Cancer. Oma died not long after her."

"That's rough, mate. Sorry to hear it."

"Yeah. Thanks." Ethan shrugged, his shoulders tight. "It is what it is, you know? Can't change it. Anyway. Do you have a big family?"

"Big enough. Dad's gone—killed in an accident out on the back roads. Fifteen years ago now."

"I'm sorry."

Clay nodded in acknowledgment. "Feels a long time ago now. Wasn't always an easy man, but of course I miss him. As you said, it is what it is."

Ethan nodded. "Yeah." They smiled sadly at each other in recognition of their shared losses.

"Auntie Marg still lives here in Queensland; Uncle Eddie and Auntie Susan too. Lots of cousins. My sister Jen lives in Perth with her husband and kids, and our mum lives with her." He breathed through the inevitable swell of guilt, even though with him being away so much, it wasn't feasible for Mum to live with him and Sam. "She has early onset Alzheimer's. She's only sixty-three, but she can't be left on her own."

Ethan's face creased with sympathy. "I'm so sorry to hear that. Wow. She's so young."

"She is. Married as a teenager like my grandparents before her. They only passed on in the last few years. Then I married young too. It seems to be changing a bit now, but in my town it was the norm."

Some emotion flickered across Ethan's face before he nodded and said, "Oh, I see." It had looked like…disappointment? Strange. Ethan asked, "Do you visit Perth a lot? It's pretty far."

"It is, but the airlines have sales fairly regularly. I go over every two months or so. It's a lovely place. Western Australia still has an untouched quality to it. Could imagine myself living there. We'll see what happens."

Ethan smiled softly. "Cool. I'm glad you get to see your mom fairly often."

"Yeah." He swallowed hard over the pang of grief. "Last time I visited, she didn't recognize me at first. It's a hell of a thing, when your own mum doesn't know you. It's like she's already gone even though she's not."

He didn't know why he was talking about this with a bloke who was practically a stranger. But the words had flowed out. There was just something about Ethan he trusted.

"I can't even imagine." Ethan put his warm hand on Clay's forearm, those long fingers wrapping around comfortingly. Although the day was warming, Clay shivered. Ethan whipped his hand back and said, "Sorry. I'm not trying to…" He laughed anxiously. "Sorry if I made you uncomfortable."

Clay shrugged, suddenly feeling awkward as well. "Not at all, mate." He cast about for something else to say. "So that's my family in a nutshell. And I've got the kids, of course." He paused. "Did you get all that?"

Ethan smiled faintly. "I did, thank you. I really appreciate that you make the effort to talk slowly. It helps so much."

Clay shrugged off the praise. "Reckon it's just how I talk."

"So you've got kids? That's awesome!" Ethan glanced down, fiddling with his rolled-up pants and brushing sand from the dark hair on his legs.

Clay waited until Ethan was looking at him to say, "My son Peter's twenty-four and off traveling. Avoiding settling down, but I shouldn't begrudge him. Just wish he was a bit better with money. Samantha's almost twenty-two and finishing uni in Sydney. Always been clever and at the top of her class. When I'm in Sydney we live together in a little rental house in Parramatta—one of the suburbs. We have a dog named Gilly. Part Australian shepherd and maybe Lab. We're not sure. Every time I get back home he treats me like a conquering hero. That's dogs for you, bless 'em."

Ethan smiled, the breeze blowing his thick brown hair back off his forehead. "How old is he?"

"Not sure exactly. We found him abandoned on the side of the road last year with a broken leg. Poor bugger. Vet reckons he's seven or eight. He was in a shocking state when we came across him. Very malnourished. But despite that, he's such a softie; always eager for attention and love. So trusting, even after he'd been practically tortured. Still wish I could find whoever'd owned him. I'm not typically a violent man, but…"

"I don't understand how people can be so cruel. I'm so glad you guys found him." He was quiet a few moments, biting his full bottom lip and making it even redder. "And your wife's in Sydney too?"

Ah, right. Clay'd almost forgotten. Funny how it seemed so long ago that they'd still been together in the Curry. "Divorced a couple years ago. Barb and I had a good run, I reckon. She's remarried now and living in Christchurch. She met him online and decided she didn't want to be married to me anymore."

Again, Clay didn't know why he was telling all this to Ethan. He normally didn't talk to anyone this much. Not about things that mattered, at least. His skin felt too tight. It was embarrassing, that his wife had left him for another man. That Clay wasn't enough.

Ethan's eyes widened, and he looked so pained for a moment that Clay was about to ask if he was all right. Then Ethan asked, "So you were still together when your wife met that guy?"

Clay nodded, trying to laugh. "She'd had enough of me."

"It's not *your* fault," Ethan said fiercely.

The tension eased, Clay's fingers uncurling. He dug them rhythmically into the sand at his sides. "Suppose it's no one's fault, really." That Ethan didn't think poorly of him was an odd relief.

Ethan asked, "Did you see it coming?"

"Nah. We weren't setting the world on fire, but we did all

right. Had the kids and chugged along. I suppose once Pete and then Sam moved out… Well, Barb and I didn't have much left to talk about. She got itchy feet. Wanted more than me or the Curry could give her. Can't really blame her. It was a shock, but we've made the best of it."

Ethan nodded. He opened his mouth, then hesitated. Picking up a pale white shell that was poking out of the sand and keeping his gaze on it, he asked, "Are you dating anyone now?"

Clay squirmed, his cheeks getting hot. His ex was remarried, and here he'd barely been on a date. Would Ethan think him pathetic? He considered making up a fake girlfriend in Sydney, but the notion of lying to Ethan soured his stomach. And why did he care so much about what Ethan thought?

He answered, "Nah. My daughter is always on me to use the dating apps and get out more. But I dunno. I'm busy with my job, and when I'm home I want to relax and spend time with Sam and Gilly." He shrugged. "Reckon if the right woman comes along, it'll be meant to happen."

"Right. And I get why you'd be gun-shy. It hurts like hell to be cheated on." He dropped his head and fiddled with the empty Thermos lid now, his long fingers tracing the round edges.

Ah. Clay didn't ask, but his instincts told him this was at least part of what had happened with Michael Wong. *Wanker.* Granted, Clay had only just met Ethan, but if he were gay—

A sort of manic laugh rose up in him but didn't break free. Of course he wasn't, so he didn't know why he was thinking nonsense. He refocused on his own breakup.

"To be fair, she hadn't actually met Barry in person. But she was taken with him, and even if it hadn't worked out with the two of them, she wanted more from her life."

"Wow. So she just flew to New Zealand to be with him and they hadn't even met?"

"No way. I drove her down to Brissie and made sure he was a

decent fellow first. Brisbane, I mean."

Ethan's jaw dropped. "Did you say you took your wife to meet the guy she was leaving you for?"

Clay shrugged. "Had to make sure he wasn't one of those lunatics you hear about."

"Wow. How long was the drive to Brisbane from the out-back?"

"From the Curry it's about nineteen hours, give or take."

"Holy shit! One way?"

"Yep." Clay shrugged again, feeling self-conscious. "We're used to long distances where I'm from. Maybe I'm a fool, but she was my wife. Had to make sure she'd be all right. Known her all my life, and we'd been together since she set her sights on me in school."

Ethan looked at him like Clay had just hung the moon and stars. "You're amazing."

His face went hot, and he shrugged again, feeling strangely pleased. "I'm no saint, believe me. It hurt when she left, no question. It's a hit to the pride, that's for sure. But it was for the best. Took a while for me to see that, but it truly was." He paused before he added, "It'll get better, mate. I promise."

For a moment, Ethan just looked back at him. His eyes glistened, and his lips trembled. Then he nodded, chest rising with a deep breath as he turned his gaze back to the water.

They sat in silence, the waves rolling in with a calming rhythm, the sun rising in the blue sky, the earlier clouds evaporating. Ethan traced designs in the sand with his finger, his bare arm brushing against Clay's. Clay could have shifted over, but he didn't.

After a time, Ethan turned his head back to Clay and asked, "Do you ever talk to her?"

"Oh yeah, once a week or so. Usually about whatever the kids are up to. Barb and I are still friendly. Like I said, I've known her since I was a boy. Would be strange not to know her at all anymore. I think that would be sad after everything. To have nothing left."

"Where online did she meet him?"

"Wasn't a dating site or anything." Clay didn't know if he was being defensive of Barb or himself. He didn't want Ethan to think she'd been actively looking for someone else, that there'd been something wrong with him. Which was silly, but there it was. "They were chatting about a TV show—*Dark Orphan*."

Ethan frowned for a moment. "Did you say *Orphan Black*?"

He laughed. "Right, that's the one. Sci-fi was never really my cuppa, but Barb always loved it. Spaceships and clones and all that. Vampires and werewolves too."

"What do you like?"

"Cricket, of course. A good footy match—or any footy match, really. And I enjoy shows about coppers."

"Cop shows?" At Clay's nod, Ethan said, "Me too! Have you ever seen *Southland*? It's about cops in LA. I was kind of obsessed with it in college. Maybe partly because I had a raging crush on Ben McKenzie, but also because it was a really excellent show."

"I'll have to see if I can find it on Netflix or wherever." Clay didn't know who Ben McKenzie was, and wondered what he looked like. Not that it mattered. It surprised him how easily and openly Ethan talked about…gay things. It was good, though, that the world had changed.

After a few more quiet moments, Ethan asked, "So how old were you when you got married? You said you were young."

"Didn't seem like it at the time. Nineteen and out of school—getting hitched was usually the next thing you did in the Curry."

Ethan frowned. "I'm sorry, what's the town called?"

"Cloncurry's the proper name. The Curry to locals. It's a mining town—copper and gold. About eight hundred kilometers due west from Townsville, where we'll have a rest stop tomorrow. Not a bad little place. There's a river, so it's not quite as dry as some places in the outback."

"Is it crazy hot?"

Clay laughed. "That's a fair description. In winter, it's about…" He did a rough calculation to Fahrenheit. "Eighty degrees. Hundred in the summer. Or higher."

"Whoa. How many people live there?"

"Around three thousand."

Ethan's eyebrows shot up. "Did you say three thousand?" At Clay's nod, he said, "Wow, that really is small. How far were you from a city?"

"Not too far. A hundred and twenty kilometers east from Mount Isa."

"How many people live there?"

Clay smiled ruefully. "About twenty thousand or so. Far cry from the Big Apple."

Ethan laughed. "You could say that. Although New York is way too big for me. Too crowded. I never really wanted to live there, but…" He seemed to give himself a shake, then asked, "Did you have a lot of culture shock when you moved away from home?"

"Reckon I did, yeah. Only left two years ago, of course. Took my time."

"You what?" Ethan squinted a bit.

Clay realized he'd dropped his face while he was speaking to screw the lid back on the empty Thermos. He looked straight at Ethan and repeated, "Took my time. Late bloomer, I guess."

"It's never too late. I believe that." He nodded and repeated, "I believe that."

"I'm living proof, mate. So's Barb. She does this new-age thing now. Reiki. Bunch of mumbo-jumbo to me, but last time I saw her, she had a light in her eyes I hadn't seen since she was a girl. She'd always dreamed of leaving the Curry, but I reckon she never thought she could. Not back in our time, at least."

"You're not that old."

Clay scoffed. "Tell that to my lower back. But the world's changed heaps since Barb and I were kids and got hitched. The internet barely existed, and we didn't have it at home yet. We could count our telly stations on one hand. The world was so…far away. Forget the world. Bloody Brisbane seemed like the other side of the moon. Let alone Sydney or Melbourne."

"I bet. Shiv said you were a mechanic?"

"Yeah. Worked on mining equipment with my old man most of my life. And utes sometimes."

Ethan frowned. "What was the second thing?"

"Utes."

Ethan's brow was still furrowed. "Can you spell that?"

"U-t-e-s." Then it dawned. "Sorry. You lot call them pickup trucks."

"Ohhh." Ethan laughed. "Gotcha. I'm sorry I interrupted."

"No worries. Are you sure you still want to hear this? It's not very exciting." At Ethan's enthusiastic nod, Clay went on. "Well, Dad had already passed on when Barb decided she was leaving, and Mum was in Perth with Jen. I didn't much fancy the idea of staying by myself. Sam rang up and said she had a plan for me to move down to Sydney. She didn't much fancy the idea of me left in the Curry on my own either."

Ethan smiled. "She sounds like a good daughter."

"Oh, she is. Sam's a super daughter. The best a bloke could ask for."

"You totally light up when you talk about her." Ethan smiled. "It's nice."

"Do I?" He was faintly embarrassed, but what the hell. "We've always been close. Not that I wasn't close with Pete as well. He's a good lad. Not as responsible or clever as his sister, but of course I love the bludger."

"You love…what?" Ethan frowned.

"Pete. He can be a bludger." Ethan's brow was still creased, so Clay added, "Likes partying more than working."

"Right." Ethan nodded. "I know the type. How did you start driving for DL?"

"The mum of one of Sam's mates works in head office and mentioned that they were hiring. I decided since I was changing everything else about my life, might as well give it a whirl. It's been good. The long hauls get tiring, though. Wouldn't mind sticking to day trips in the future. Maybe even run my own little outfit. Get a minibus and take people out for the day. We'll see."

"What was the last part? Did you say you want to have your own tour company?" Ethan grimaced. "Sorry to make you repeat yourself." He sighed heavily. "It's such a fucking pain."

Clay made sure to speak clearly. "It's not a problem. Said I'd like to have my own minibus and do tours. Be my own boss."

"Cool. I work in environmental accounting. Lots of numbers and spreadsheets and researching government regulations on energy and that kind of stuff. I'm stuck in an office, but most of the time I can just do my work without talking to people. That sounds nice, though—being your own boss."

"Yeah. Reckon it could be good. We'll see." He squinted up at the sky. "We should get back for brekkie."

"Right." Ethan's smile this time was small and grateful, a warmth filling his eyes in the rising sun. "Thanks for hanging out." He rested his hand on Clay's shoulder, and tingly gooseflesh spread. "Especially since this is your time off and everything."

"Nah, it's nothing." He pushed to his feet, dislodging Ethan's hand, his skin still feeling strangely warm.

Ethan stood too, laughing and lamenting his wet trousers as they walked back down the narrow stretch of sand. There were some people out now on the resort's beachfront, the morning getting under way.

After a minute, Ethan said, "I'm glad you and your wife are still friends. I don't know if I could do that."

"Well, it's not for everyone, mate. But Barb's doing well with Barry. He's a nice enough bloke. Bit of a prig, but she likes him. Barry hates it when people call him 'Baz,' so I do every time." He grinned slyly. "Can't help myself."

Ethan burst out laughing. "Did you say 'Baz'?"

"Yep. That's what you call someone by the name of Barry. Baz, or Bazza."

"That's awesome." They neared the hotel, and Ethan said, "That really was the best sunrise ever. And we had it all to ourselves."

"It's my little secret this time of year."

A shy little smile tugged on Ethan's mouth. "Thanks for sharing your secret with me."

"No worries, mate. Anytime. I'm glad you liked it." It really wasn't a big deal—it wasn't like he owned the beach. But as he went back to his room to get into uniform, Clay felt rather pleased with himself nonetheless.

Chapter Eight

EVERYONE LAUGHED, AND Ethan felt so incredibly lonely.

It was the worst sound—people around him laughing at a joke or comment that Ethan hadn't heard. He smiled along with the six members of the group he was eating breakfast with in the resort restaurant. It had been kind of them to invite him to sit, and he tried to keep up with the conversation, but the restaurant was tiled and one big room, with no sound breaks or soft materials to deaden noise.

There was background music playing through speakers, and lots of families and other visitors, excited chatter filling the air. Ethan had sat with his back to the main part of the restaurant and switched the settings on his hearing aids so the noise behind him was blocked, but it was still tough to hear half of what was being said at his table.

He didn't bother asking Dale, a retired teacher from Quebec traveling with his wife, to repeat whatever he'd said that had been so funny. It just made things awkward for everyone, and the statements were rarely as funny when they had to be repeated and explained. Ethan had learned long ago to just smile and laugh along, pretending he was in on the joke.

He glanced around, wondering where Clay was. Surely getting the bus ready for another day. After Mission Beach, the tour had stopped for three nights at Hamilton Island in the Whitsundays. After breakfast, they'd be taking a boat back to the mainland.

The Whitsundays, at the tail end of the Great Barrier Reef, were stunningly gorgeous, with white sand and blue-green water. Ethan had enjoyed swimming in the pools and going on organized hikes and trying snorkeling again, this time in much calmer water. He hadn't seen a sea turtle eat a jellyfish, but it had still been cool.

Far less cool was the fact that he didn't see Clay at all the two days before. Not that he'd been *searching* for him, but in-between all the activities he signed up for to keep himself busy and not think about—a flash of Todd and Michael in bed filled his mind, and he cursed himself—to keep busy and not think about *that*, he hadn't spotted Clay anywhere around the resort.

Which made sense—these were Clay and Shiv's days off, and they probably holed up in their rooms for some alone time. They'd been to Hamilton Island a hundred times, probably. And Clay had already gone above and beyond his job by spending time with Ethan when he didn't have to. He wasn't obligated to keep Ethan company.

I chose to come alone. If I'm lonely, that's my fault. Clay isn't my friend, he's just been kind. And he's sure as hell not more than a friend.

Of course then another voice piped up, feeding his anxiety.

Maybe he doesn't like me. Maybe he's avoiding me because I've been too clingy when he was only being nice to the pathetic loser on his honeymoon alone.

Just then, he heard Clay's name and snapped his attention back to the table.

A British woman named Joanna was finishing saying something, and Ethan asked, "I'm sorry, could you repeat that?"

"Never mind." She waved a dismissive hand.

But Ethan was certain he'd heard Clay's name, and he had to know for sure. "Can you please tell me what you said?"

She shouted, "Was just saying poor Clay wasn't feeling very

special yesterday. Hope he's recovered."

Ethan lost all interest in his cheese omelette. "What's wrong with him?"

"Upset tummy, Shiv said. Poor fellow."

Diners at a nearby table were looking, and Ethan wanted to tell Joanna to please just speak slowly and clearly and not shout because it didn't actually help the clarity of the words, but people often took offense, no matter how gently he tried to explain. He simply nodded and said, "Hope he's okay."

Fortunately, when Ethan walked into the lobby a little later to head down to the meeting spot near the dock, there was Clay in his navy uniform pants and white, short-sleeved button-up shirt. Ethan's stomach did a little cartwheel, which he tried to ignore. But it whirled again when Clay spotted him and waved.

"'Morning," Clay said when Ethan was closer. He looked a little paler than usual, his cheeks not as ruddy. In the sun through the lobby's skylight, the hair on Clay's muscular, freckled arms shone copper.

Stop looking at his arms, oh my God. Speak. "Hey. How are you feeling? Joanna said you were sick?"

Clay grimaced and muttered something as he rubbed his face.

"Sorry, I didn't get that." Ethan smiled apologetically. "I know it's a pain."

"No, don't apologize. Get lots of older folks who are hearing impaired on the tours. I should use more care."

Ethan winced internally. "Oh, um… Just FYI, that's considered an offensive term now. It puts the focus on what someone can't do. 'Impaired' is negative. I guess it was politically correct in the nineties or whenever? But now people prefer hard of hearing, or just deaf or deafened. Or capital-D Deaf if that's how they identify."

Clay's cheeks went pink. "I'm sorry, mate! Had no idea."

"Oh, it's okay! I'm not offended. I didn't know either until I lost my hearing. I lurk on some forums for people like me, and they call themselves hard of hearing, or HOH. So I think of myself that way too."

"I really am sorry. Thank you for telling me."

"Of course. I know you didn't mean anything negative." Now he'd made it all awkward, but Ethan would hate for Clay to use the wrong term with someone who *would* be offended. He'd found most hearing people just didn't know. But he'd been one of those people not so long ago—although it felt like a lifetime—so he tried to educate. "Anyway, what were you saying? You're feeling better?"

Clay's cheeks above his beard were still rosy. "Right. Maybe it was something I ate, or that bug Shiv had up in Cairns. Not sure. On the mend today, though. Good thing since we've got a whopper of a drive. But there really isn't much between here and Fraser Island. Used to stop in Rocky for a night to break it up, but there's not much to see."

"Rocky?" Ethan tried to remember his Queensland geography.

"Rockhampton. It's worth it to just power through to Hervey Bay and get to Fraser Island."

"Too bad you're stuck doing all the driving."

Clay laughed. "Well, it's my job, isn't it? Can't complain too much. Still, glad the drive's today and not yesterday or the day before. Would've had to make some extra stops for the dunny, let me tell you."

Ethan laughed too, assuming that was Aussie for bathroom, a word they didn't seem to use much. He'd asked a groundskeeper on the island where the closest bathroom was, and the guy had given him a strange look before saying, "*Well, the* toilet's *around the corner to the left.*"

He asked Clay, "What would happen if you were really too sick to drive?"

"I'd have to be damn hurt to not be able to do my job. One

time the company had to fly me up from Sydney to Brissie since the driver had a fall and buggered up his knee badly. You can imagine they aren't too keen to spend heaps of money like that unless they really have to."

"Yeah, I bet. Well, if you need anything, please let me know."

"I'll be right. But thanks, mate. Oh, that reminds me." Clay was carrying a messenger bag, and he pulled out a sheaf of paper. "I was thinking that if you're farther back in the bus and can only hear Shiv and me over the loudspeaker, it might be harder to pick up what we're saying. So I made a copy of the guide's notes. Just thought it could help if you could read the info as well. It's mostly point form, and Shiv'll elaborate, but there are interesting facts and figures and whatnot."

"I…" Ethan stared at the paper in his hand, at least twenty stapled pages. He looked back up at Clay, who watched him uncertainly. "You made this for me?"

He waved his hand through the air. "Thought it might be useful." Then his face went serious. "But I didn't mean any offense."

"Oh! No, no, I'm not offended!" Ethan wanted to hug him, but that would obviously be crossing a bunch of lines. He repeated, "I'm not offended." *I'm surprised. I'm touched. I'm…happy.*

Clay exhaled in obvious relief, giving a little laugh. "That's good. Wasn't sure there for a minute. I bet people can be real arseholes, and how you said some drongos treat you like you're stupid. Wasn't what I meant to do."

"No, you didn't at all!" Ethan grinned, holding up the papers. "This is awesome. Seriously, thank you. It'll be great to be able to follow along today. So you talk as well? Maybe I didn't hear properly before, but I was sitting near the back last time." The passengers all rotated through the bus so everyone got a chance to sit in different spots. Being only half full, it was nice to be able to stretch out.

"Ah, just the odd story. I let the guides do the talking for the most part. But sometimes I need to make announcements or whatnot."

"Of course. I… Thank you again. This is really great."

Clay waved him off. "It was nothing. Just asked the sheila at the front desk to run off a copy."

"Right. Cool." *Stop making a big deal of this. Don't be a weirdo!* Still, it was a kind thing that Clay had thought of him at all, and as they headed to the docks, other group members falling into step and talking to Clay, Ethan tried not to grin too much.

AS ETHAN WALKED through the resort on Fraser Island the next afternoon after a tour to gorgeous Lake McKenzie, he finally admitted to himself that he was looking for Clay.

Because he's nice! He's fun to talk to. Besides, my harmless crush is just that. Harmless. Why shouldn't I enjoy it? Nothing's going to happen. He's apparently straight, and I'm on the rebound. But we can be friendly. I like his accent, and he's a nice guy.

Of course, Clay wasn't just nice. He was *sexy*. His accent? *Sexy.* The Australian slang he used that made him sound like Crocodile Dundee sometimes? *Sexy.* His broad shoulders and solid build? *Sexy.* That he didn't have chiseled abs and was a little soft around the middle? *Sexy.* Those blue eyes, and how the auburn in his hair gleamed in the sun, especially in his beard and the hair on his arms, and how he had freckles…

Sexy, sexy, sexy.

But the sexiest thing of all was how thoughtful he was. How he made such an effort to make sure Ethan could hear him when he spoke. How he'd told him the secret of the Mission Bay sunrise. How he'd copied the tour guide notes for him. Even back in Cairns, how he'd held Ethan's backpack while Ethan was snorkeling and watched over him, then later took him to buy a hat.

Ethan was wearing the hat now, and it gave him a giddy little thrill.

Is he straight though?

The question had been niggling at him. Clay had been married to a woman for years and had kids, but of course that didn't mean he was straight. He could be bi or pan. Although he'd mentioned the right woman coming along.

Still, when Ethan had touched his arm that morning on Mission Beach and looked into Clay's eyes, he swore there had been a flicker between them. That unnamed frisson of *knowing*.

Wishful thinking. Don't be an idiot.

There were four pools at the resort, and Ethan strolled around the first two. It was sunny, and through his polarized sunglasses, the water, surrounding palm trees, and forest beyond were vibrant. He waved hello to Shiv—who was reading on a lounger since there was nothing planned for the day after that morning's trip to the lake in four-by-four jeeps—and continued on to a smaller, kidney-shaped pool that was more tucked away, and—

Fuck. Clay.

There he was, stretched out on a chaise lounge under the shade of an umbrella and surrounding trees on the deck at the far end of the pool. There were a few adults in the water paddling lazily, others on the more exposed side of the concrete deck sunbathing. Kids seemed to be in the bigger pools, their splashing and shrieks distant noises now.

Oh so casually, Ethan ambled around the pool, stealing glances at Clay from the corner of his eye. The chaises on either side of him were vacant. In fact, that whole shady side of the pool was empty and quiet. There was no music piped in, just the rustle of leaves in the breeze. It was perfect.

Clay wore his sexy-AF aviator sunglasses, navy bathing trunks, and nothing else but his gold-colored watch. It was kind of old-fashioned to wear a watch, and it was *sexy*. He'd apparently taken a dip, since his hair was wet and darker, and drops of water dried on his skin.

His long, muscular legs were crossed at the ankle. There was a newspaper folded over his stomach, his fingers laced on top of it. His nipples were pink amid the reddish hair on his chest, and as Ethan got closer, he imagined licking those nipples.

Heat roaring through him, he swallowed thickly. This was a bad idea, and he should turn back the way he came. But now he was close enough that if Clay saw him, it might seem rude, like Ethan had turned around and left because he was avoiding Clay. So he kept walking slowly around the curve of the shaded deep end, where one woman in a bikini swam a slow side stroke.

Clay's chaise was partly reclined, and it was entirely possible he was napping and didn't have any idea Ethan was even there. Ethan slowed even more so his flip-flops didn't flap on the concrete.

Okay, if I walk by and he doesn't notice me, that's a sign. I'll keep going and stop being ridiculous.

He was still at least ten feet away when Clay called, "Ethan!" and lifted a hand in a wave.

"Oh, hey!" Ethan replied too loudly. *Calm the fuck down.* He smiled as he approached. "You found a good shady spot."

"Yep. Got skin cancer once when I was younger, so I reckoned me and the sun aren't mates."

Ethan gaped. "Oh my God. I'm sorry. You said before that you had to be careful, but I didn't realize."

"Nah, nah. Don't be sorry." He casually motioned to the chaise on his left in invitation. Ethan spread out his striped resort towel and settled in, his heart beating too fast as he took off his hat since they were in the shade. Clay added, "I shouldn't be so dramatic—it wasn't melanoma. Basal cell carcinoma. Quite common in Australia. It can't spread, so it's not dangerous like other cancers. Still, I had to have surgery to remove it, so it's not nothing."

"Wow. I'm glad it wasn't melanoma. Obviously. Where was it?" he asked before realizing how intrusive that was. Even though Clay really felt like a friend now, Ethan had to remember it was probably mostly in his head. "I'm sorry, I'm being totally nosy! You don't have to tell me."

See? This was a bad idea. I'm going to make a fool of myself with this crush. Maybe it's not so harmless after all.

"No worries. It was on the back of my left shoulder." Clay leaned forward, angling so Ethan could see. He reached over that shoulder with his right hand, his fingers finding a pale circle of a scar. Just below it was a tattoo, a green sort of shield with a yellow sun rising over a green horizon and five stars dotting the shield. It was a few inches wide and several inches long.

"Cool tattoo." Ethan had never been compelled to get one, but he enjoyed looking at other people's. Before he could stop himself, he traced it with his fingertip. Clay's back was freckled as well, and *goddamn*, why was that so sexy? The seconds ticked by as he touched Clay, neither of them saying anything.

Finally, Ethan asked, "Does it mean something?" He was still touching, and Clay shivered. Ethan dropped his hand, his mouth dry.

Clay cleared his throat as he sat back. "It's part of the Cricket Australia logo. On their uniforms there's a roo on the left and an emu on the right, and 'Australia' written underneath." He laughed and muttered something Ethan missed.

"What was the last part? Sorry."

"I thought having the full logo was overkill for a tattoo. Didn't want it too big, but I like having a little something."

"You really love cricket, huh?"

Clay laughed. "What gave me away?"

Ethan chuckled. "Oh, you were going to tell me about that thing. The…" He racked his brain for the right word. "Ashes?"

"Ah, yes." Clay tipped his head forward and peered at Ethan over the rims of his aviators with his intensely blue eyes. A thrill of desire shot through Ethan's veins. Clay asked, "Are you sure you really want to know? No need to humor me, mate."

"No, I really do!" He laughed, and it came out shaky, so he faked a cough. "I always loved sports when I was younger, and I want to get back into them. Although the Mets were epically bad last season, so I wasn't very inspired to hop back on the bandwagon."

"What happened to make you lose your interest? I can't imagine."

"Oh. It was…" Ethan motioned to his ears. "I lost interest in basically everything. I was really depressed for, like, four years. But the last year's been a lot better. I've come to terms with it, I guess. But I'm still not the way I was before."

"Ah." Clay nodded sympathetically. "I understand. Still finding your footing. It can take a while. When I first moved down to Sydney, it was quite a culture shock. My entire life was upended. Home, work—the whole bit."

"Yeah." Ethan hesitated, but the way Clay watched him so patiently and without judgment gave him the confidence to say, "And now, being single again, it's just so…weird. Like, who am I if… If I'm not with Michael?" Saying his name aloud was painful, but felt good at the same time, to release some of the pressure inside him.

Clay nodded again. "I was half of Mr. and Mrs. Kelly for so long. It hurt to lose that, no mistake." He smiled sadly. "Hell, I still feel like I'm finding my footing. Thought I should have figured it all out by now, but that's life for ya, I reckon."

Warmth filled Ethan's chest, affection and understanding flowing. "Always full of surprises, right?" *And some that were actually good surprises. Like meeting a sexy older man who somehow likes me. Somehow gets me.*

"Indeed." Clay looked at him for a moment. Then he said, "You know, it's nice to chat about it with someone on the same page. Haven't really made many mates since I moved, and aside from Facebook, I don't see the blokes from the Curry. Not that we'd talk much about this sort of thing."

It made Ethan feel so damn *good* to be in Clay's confidence. He had to stop himself from grinning delightedly. Instead, he joked, "Strong silent types in the outback, huh?"

Clay chuckled. "Something like that." He sipped from a bottle of water. "Glad to have met you." Then he jolted and looked horrified. "Not saying I'm glad at the trauma you've had. It's awful that your wedding was called off." He grimaced. "Maybe it's best for me not to talk about all this after all."

"No, no. It's okay. I know what you meant. No offense taken." He smiled genuinely, relieved when Clay visibly relaxed. But maybe it was time to lighten the subject. Sitting back on his chaise, Ethan said, "All right, tell me all about the mysterious Ashes. Maybe cricket can be my new sport." And since it was something important to Clay, he really did want to know about it.

Clay grinned. "If you insist." He sat back and re-crossed his ankles. "What do you know about cricket?"

"Um…nothing? It's kind of like baseball and takes forever to play?"

Throwing his head back, Clay laughed, exposing his neck. Ethan watched his Adam's apple. Clay said, "I'll start at the beginning."

Ethan nodded and uh-huhed as Clay outlined the basics. Stumps, bats, a wicket, a pitch, creases, bowling—Ethan wasn't sure he really understood all the info, but he kept nodding, loving the rumble of Clay's voice.

"Is this making sense?" Clay asked.

"Yes! I mean, it's a lot to try and take in, but I think I get it."

"We should watch a match. It's really the best way to learn."

Belly somersaulting, Ethan tried to keep his voice casual. "That would be cool, yeah. So what's the thing about ashes?"

"The Ashes is a test series between England and Australia. Test matches can go five days, as opposed to an ODI—" He cut off. "You're going to be bored shitless if I go into the overs and innings and all that. In a nutshell, England and Australia play a series every year or so of five matches. It's very competitive. Lots of patriotic pride tied up in it. The name comes from the late 1800s, when we beat England for the first time over there. Being beaten by the colonies on English soil was quite a shock for the poor pommies, bless their hearts. Our bowler went fourteen wickets for ninety."

"I have no idea what that means, but it sounds good?" Ethan laughed. Clay laughed as well, and God, he was so hot.

"It was very good. So one of the London papers published a mock obit for English cricket after we won. At the end it said, 'The body will be cremated and the ashes taken to Australia.' The Brits were determined to get the ashes back, and over the years, *mumble mumble.*"

A chattering couple walking by made the last part impossible to hear, but Ethan guessed, "Over the years that became the name of the tournament?"

Clay frowned after the couple, who thankfully kept walking. "You've got it. Legend goes that when England came back to Australia to play, a lady gave the captain an urn with the ashes of a burnt cricket bail inside. That urn's in a museum at the MCC in England, but now the winning team gets a crystal version of it to keep until the next series."

"Are you serious?"

"Mate, I never joke about cricket. Ever."

Ethan grinned. "I love that the trophy is an urn. That's awesome. Thanks for explaining all that."

"I'd give you an ear-bashing all day about cricket if you let me."

I'd let you do so many things to me.

Before Ethan's mind could veer too far down the path of wondering what Clay's beard would feel like against his face if they kissed, Clay said, "Tell me about baseball. Your Mets aren't doing so well?"

"Not last season. But there was one year when I was a kid? We didn't make the World Series, but it was still amazing. You know, when everything seems to go right during the season, and the players are all awesome guys and you feel like you *know* them, and you're rooting so hard for them. And when they win, it's just the best feeling in the world."

Clay grinned. "Nothing like it, mate." Then he laughed, his shoulders shaking.

"What?" Ethan laughed too. "You get it, right?"

"Absolutely." Clay looked like he was trying to stop laughing but couldn't manage it.

"*What?*" Ethan nudged Clay's bare arm with his fist, resisting the urge to flatten his palm over the firm, hair-dusted muscles. He groaned as he thought back over what he'd said. "Oh, I see. 'Rooting so hard.' You know I didn't mean it like that. 'Root' doesn't mean sex in the US." He giggled, because he and Clay were apparently twelve.

As they laughed together over the silly joke, Ethan's hearing aid battery beeped in his left ear. That meant the right likely would go soon too. Grimacing at the loud beep, he said, "Sorry, I need to go change my hearing aid batteries. They beep to let me know."

"No worries. I'll try to compose myself. Of course now my mind's full of stupid jokes."

Ethan grinned. "Tell me one before I go."

"Well, did you know Australians don't have sex?"

Hearing the word "sex" come out of Clay's mouth had Ethan's balls tingling and his head going light. His voice sounded too high as he said, "No? What do they do?"

"They mate."

Ethan burst out laughing, and Clay joined in. Sure, it was childish. But he didn't give a shit. It was *fun*. Michael would have rolled his eyes because he was always too snobby for puns. And wow, Ethan realized he and Michael hadn't had goofy fun in a long, long time.

He'd missed feeling so relaxed. Like, he didn't have to worry about what Clay would think if he made a dumb joke or announced, "that's what she said" after a double entendre. Because Clay would laugh along with him.

Because Clay was *awesome*.

Ethan gave him a wave and circled the pool, walking on air. He imagined he could feel the heat of Clay's gaze on his body. *I might have to go jerk off if I don't get my shit together. He's only being friendly. Stop imagining things!*

The eco resort had raised, wooden, covered boardwalks with guest rooms along them and lots of foliage around. He was smiling to himself—okay, grinning—and waved as he passed Stan and Violet. Inside his room, Ethan kept his suitcases neatly packed and closed since he'd read to never put a suitcase on a bed due to the threat of bedbugs.

A few minutes later, Ethan's belongings were strewn across the spare bed, his heart racing and mouth dry. His hearing aid batteries weren't there. "Fuck, fuck, FUCK!"

He pawed through his clothes again. Nothing. Telling himself they had to be somewhere, he tried to be methodical as he searched. Nothing. He ran into the bathroom and looked there again. Nothing. The reminder beeps from his hearing aids as the clock wound down did not freaking help, the right one chiming in now, as he'd expected.

Ethan opened drawers even though he hadn't put anything away. He dug through the trash bins, which hadn't been emptied yet by housekeeping. Finally, after searching three more times, he had to declare defeat. His batteries were not there. Trying to catch a ragged breath, he stood in the middle of his room, which looked like a hurricane had passed through.

Then he remembered the little balcony with a forest view. He unlocked the door and slid it open with a bang, his heart pounding. Nothing. He tried to think of when he'd last seen the pack of little round batteries and came up blank. Had he left them in the Whitsundays? He couldn't imagine doing that, but he'd taken everything out of his big suitcase to reorganize.

And of course he usually kept a couple batteries in his little hearing aid case, but hadn't replaced them since he'd been on one of the flights when his batteries had gone.

"Fuck!"

If he was on the mainland, it would be easy enough to buy more at a drugstore. Heart in his throat, he rushed out of his room and down the walkway back toward reception. Maybe they had a store. He hadn't noticed anything—maybe a gift shop wasn't eco-friendly?—but there had to be somewhere to buy stuff on the island. Right?

Wrong.

The young guy behind the front desk shook his head apologetically. "We only have a few essentials available." He added something else that was lost in the four ominous beeps in Ethan's left ear, signaling that battery would die momentarily. Sure enough, after a few heartbeats, it went quiet. The guy was saying something else, and Ethan strained to understand with only his right hearing aid, turning his head and leaning in.

The guy looked at him like he was waiting for a response, and Ethan said, "I'm sorry?"

He waved a hand dismissively, and Ethan easily read his lips since he was used to these words: "Never mind."

"Can you not fucking—" He caught himself and breathed deeply to choke down the frustration. He lowered his voice, or at least he hoped he did. "Can you please write down what you said?"

Glancing at him warily as if Ethan was a lunatic, the guy scrawled on a piece of hotel notepaper:

I'll ask housekeeping to go through the towels and make sure nothing was accidentally picked up.

Still breathing hard, Ethan nodded. "Thank you." He turned and walked away from the desk, his lungs tight. As he descended the wide stairs leading down to a restaurant on one side and the pool area beyond glass doors, he spotted Stan and Violet sitting in the shade outside in an area with padded wicker furniture and tables. He approached them to ask what kind of batteries Stan used.

Of course not the same kind—Stan's were smaller. He and his wife were very kind and sympathetic, and Ethan was going to fucking *cry* like the loser he was, so he quickly thanked them and escaped back into the lobby. Where he stood as the minutes ticked by, trying not to completely lose his shit. His right aid was going to go soon, the reminder beep making him wince.

Then Clay was there, his face pinched in concern as he said something Ethan didn't hear in the murmur of noise from the restaurant nearby and people through the lobby. Ethan told him about the missing batteries and added, "I guess I left them at the last place? I don't know. Doesn't matter now. They're not here." Clay said something that was probably sympathetic, and Ethan shook his head. "Sorry, it's hard with only one now. And the right one won't last much longer."

Clay nodded and glanced around, then guided Ethan to a little tucked-away corner, his big hand warm and comforting on

Ethan's shoulder before dropping away. Ethan blew out a long breath. "Anyway, I asked Stan, but his hearing aids are different and the batteries won't fit mine."

"Damn it." Clay was clearly trying to speak even more carefully. His sunglasses were perched on his head, and he leaned in, looking at Ethan intently. "Where do you get more batteries? Does it have to be a specialty-type place?"

"No, just a drugstore. But they don't have one here."

"I'll ask the desk when the next boat to the mainland is. If you tell me which batteries, I can fetch them from the chemist and come back as soon as I can."

Clay's kindness made Ethan's eyes burn again with the threat of tears. His right hearing aid beeped, but with Clay's steady presence, he was able to take a deep breath and calm his spiky pulse. "That's really cool of you to offer. But no, it's your day off. I'll be fine."

"It's no bother. I always enjoy a boat ride."

Clay was amazing. It was *entirely* a freaking bother, but he was so comforting and unruffled. *So sexy.* No, no, this wasn't the time to be thinking about *that*, but it loosened the massive knot of tension in Ethan's chest. "I'll be okay." He blew out a long breath, glancing around the high-ceilinged lobby. No one seemed to be watching his meltdown, at least. "I'm okay. I can get batteries in the morning. I'm sorry. Sometimes my anxiety just..." He made an exploding motion with his hands.

Clay smiled, and Ethan really, *really* wanted to kiss him. "No worries. We all have our moments. I can imagine it's a frightening thing, not being able to hear. Would make a bloke feel awfully...bare. If you know what I mean."

Do not think about Clay naked. "Yeah, that's it exactly. Vulnerable, I guess. But it helps—" He broke off. Would it be weird to say it? What the hell. Before he could lose his nerve, he said, "It helps having you here. Thank you."

Of course now he was a hundred percent thinking about Clay naked, and when Clay slung an arm around Ethan's shoulders and gave him a manly half-hug squeezy thing, that did not help.

He spoke quietly and steadily near Ethan's right ear, not shouting like a lot of well-meaning people would. "How about I buy us a couple of tinnies of Four X—they'll allow those by the pool, but no glass. There's a bar over by the main deck, and we can take 'em back to the shade."

Ethan was pressed against the side of Clay's big, strong body, a situation his dick was very interested in pursuing further. Afraid of how high-pitched his voice might come out, he simply nodded. Clay clapped his back and let go, and they made their way outside. Ethan tried to get the beer charged to his room, but of course Clay waved him off, not accepting any arguments.

"This shout's on me."

Ethan's brows drew together. "This what?"

"Shout." He motioned to the cans of beer the bartender put on the counter.

"I thought that's what you said. A shout's like a round of drinks?" At Clay's nod, Ethan grinned. "Cool. Thanks. Then I'll get the one after." His smile faded. "I mean, unless you have other stuff to do. You don't have to hang out with me all day."

Clay shrugged. "Nowhere else to be, mate."

Ethan tried to contain himself, but he knew he was grinning at Clay. Probably mooning at him, but he was grateful, the feeling of safety flowing through him reassuringly.

Back at their loungers with their sunglasses on, Ethan drank the wonderfully cold beer, the can housed in a foamy insulator with the resort logo on the side. Breathing easily again, he said, "Thank you. This is perfect." And despite the impending loss of his hearing aid, he meant it. "We should go swimming. I can hear better under water."

"Yeah?" He said something else that was a mumble.

Ethan guessed that he'd been asking why. "I think because any sound is conducted through the bones in my skull, not the air."

"Huh." Clay sipped his beer, his throat working. There were a few freckles across the hollow of his throat that Ethan wanted to lean over and kiss softly. "Is it like that for all deaf people?"

"I don't know. I think it depends on the degree of hearing loss, and what kind you have." He paused. "Am I talking too loudly?"

"Nope," Clay said. "There's no one nearby anyway."

So he probably was talking too loudly, but Clay was being kind, like always because he was *awesome*. Ethan tried to modulate his volume.

"There are two basic kinds, but lots of variety within those two categories. I think I told you mine's sensorineural? Basically the nerves and sensors in the inner ear are damaged, and it can be caused by lots of different things. Conductive hearing loss is more mechanical. Like a punctured eardrum or build-up of wax or water. Something blocking the sound. Some people have a bit of both. It all depends." His right hearing aid gave the more urgent, faster beep, alerting him that the batteries were about to give out. "Well, these are toast until tomorrow. Going off the air." He winced as he eased out his hearing aids, rubbing at his sore ears.

Then he realized Clay was wincing too, and quickly switched the right one off. He tried not to shout. "Sorry, guess the batteries still had another minute." He couldn't hear it, but if he took out his hearing aids while they were on, or if the ear mold came loose, there was a high-pitched squealing whine that Michael told him was like torture.

A vindictive thought came when he thought of all the times Michael had complained: *Good.* But Ethan was by a pool with Clay, and he didn't want to think about Michael, or Todd, or any of it. New York was the other side of the world, and Ethan was going to be in the now. He was going to be with Clay.

After they finished their beer, they went for a swim, Clay trying to talk under the water and not doing a very good job. They surfaced and laughed, then played a little game, sort of like Marco Polo, with Clay closing his eyes in their empty end of the pool and trying to catch Ethan. When Ethan stood, the water was up to his chest, the perfect height for goofing around.

Ethan tried not to laugh and cry out as he bobbed and dodged Clay's outstretched hands. And maybe after a few minutes, he totally let himself be caught, Clay's big hands wrapping around his arms. Clay's eyes popped open, and water dripped from the end of his nose. They grinned at each other, standing so close that Ethan would only have to move a few inches before their lips met and…

Laughing, he pulled away and made a rolling motion with his hand. "Let's play again!"

They did, and Ethan managed not to kiss Clay and ruin it all.

Chapter Nine

CLAY WOKE TO the faint buzzing of his phone on the side table. Since Pete never seemed to remember time differences when he was overseas, Clay had taken to switching to vibrate mode overnight when he was working. He needed every wink of sleep he could get before the long days behind the wheel. The odd text wouldn't rouse him, but if someone rang with an emergency, the vibrating usually went on long enough to wake him.

Instantly awake as he realized it was indeed a call coming in, he lunged for his phone, heart racing as he blinked at the picture of Sam's smiling face on the screen. With clumsy fingers, he swiped to answer. "Sam? What's wrong, love?"

"Everything's fine now, no worries. Had to take Gilly to the vet, but he's on the mend."

Clay's chest was painfully tight. "What was it?" He missed Gilly when he was on the road, and the thought of something happening to the poor boy while he was so far away made him sick to his stomach.

"Bloody paralysis tick. Was getting ready for bed, and he just seemed a bit crook. Hadn't finished his dinner, and I didn't want to take any chances. We took him straight over to the vet, and sure enough. I checked him earlier, but might have missed the little bastard."

His heart still thumped. "Good girl, not waiting. Gilly not wolfing down every bite's always a cause for concern." God, he wished he was there with them. Gilly was a hairy beast, a mess of brown and reddish-tan fur, and they checked him daily for the ticks that could kill a dog with just one bite. "He's bucking up now?" Clay realized he hadn't even checked the time. There was faint light around the edges of the curtains, and he reached for his watch on the table and saw it was just after six. His alarm would be going off soon.

"Yep. Just spoke to the vet. They got the antiserum in straight away. We only came home for a few hours since they said there was nothing else we could do. Hated leaving him there, but they said we couldn't see him again until this morning. We're going back in a minute."

"All right. Give me a ring once you do. Jase was over, was he?"

Sam sighed loudly. "Yes, Dad. I'm a grown woman, and you know I'm going to sleep with whoever I want to and you don't get a vote."

"Strewth! No need to get the shits. Can't I ask who my daughter's spending time with?" For the past year, it had been Jason, and he wasn't a bad lad. Not a no-hoper like her first boyfriend back in the Curry, and he had a good job at a bank. Clay had to admit he still wasn't keen on the thought of his little girl…well, *being a woman*, but she was grown, like she said.

"Of course it was Jase. Now remember we're supposed to be leaving Friday arvo to drive down to Merimbula for the weekend. Coming back Monday since Jase took an extra day off. He's borrowing his mate's camper van, and we're taking our bikes. But we'll see how Gilly's doing. Since we caught the tick early, the vet says he should be right. Hoping we can bring him home by Friday for sure."

It was Wednesday now, and Clay would be home Saturday morning. He'd actually be back in Sydney on Friday night, but it was such a long slog of driving that day that he stayed in the hotel since Saturday morning he and Shiv took the guests around Sydney before the tour ended at noon. He'd discovered it wasn't worth hauling himself out to Parramatta because he had to drive any guests that didn't want to walk back to the hotel after the farewell dinner.

"All right, love. Let me know how you get on. Looking forward to seeing you on Monday. Poor old Gilly. Give him an extra cuddle from me."

"I will. How're you going? Roads have been all right? Nice guests?"

"Yeah, not too much traffic. Guests are a nice lot." He was about to tell her about Ethan, but then felt strange about it. Would she think it odd that he was being so chummy with someone not much older than her?

It's not strange, is it? Just being friendly.

Before he could say anything else, Sam asked, "Did you look at those profiles?"

Clay groaned. "Not yet. I will, I promise."

Her voice softened. "You don't have to. I just hate to think of you being lonely. Mum has Barry, and it's been a couple years."

"I've got you when I'm in Sydney, haven't I? And Gilly. I'm not lonely." He wasn't sure if it was true or not, but he just wanted to relax in his time off. Or spend the day with a bloke like Ethan. No stress, no mess. "Have you spoken to Pete and your mum this week?"

"Uh-huh. Pete and I send Snapchats most days. He's having fun. You know, the usual Pete stuff."

"Is Snapchat the one where the damn things disappear?"

She laughed. "Yep. I know, I know, you don't see the point of it. And I Skyped with Mum on Tuesday. She took me through her garden. She's obsessed with it. But it makes her happy."

Clay chuckled. "That it does. All right, love. Ring me when

you speak to the vet."

"Will do. Love ya. Drive safe."

After turning off his phone, he scratched his chest and yawned. Clay always slept naked and cuddled up under the blankets, although the air con was a little weak, and he'd pushed the covers down to his waist.

He smiled thinking about what a great day it had been. He was normally content to be by himself on the few off days during the tour, but he was glad Ethan had come across him.

They'd had their fair share of grog, and he knew he should get up and chug some water, although he'd made sure not to get pissed since it wasn't professional. Although he had to admit he hadn't worried too much about professionalism the night before. Not that he'd broken any rules—not really.

Still, he supposed he didn't think of Ethan as a guest at this point, but as a mate. Hell, Ethan was only a few years older than Pete—Clay was just looking out for him. Nothing wrong with that. The bloke was lonely, and he'd had quite a turn when he realized his batteries were gone. Clay certainly wouldn't want to be alone in an unfamiliar place—hell, an unfamiliar continent—and not be able to hear.

Ethan had looked so stricken, and Clay had almost given him a hug right there in the lobby. But that would've been an odd thing to do, so he'd bucked him up, and they'd spent the rest of the day and evening together after playing around in the pool and relaxing. It'd been good to see Ethan's dimples again.

They'd gone for dinner at the island's pizza place, drinking more beer and sharing a meat-lovers pizza. Sitting outside on the torch-lit patio after night fell, it had been peaceful pushing a notepad Clay had gotten off one of the staff back and forth, asking each other questions and answering.

He wasn't sure why he'd kept the pad. It just hadn't seemed right to chuck it in the bin. Now, Clay read through it again, smiling to himself at their notes. The first one was from Ethan.

Do you mind if I write too? I don't like talking when I can't hear myself. It's still hard to modulate the volume and I feel really uncomfortable. Especially in public. Sorry, I know it's a pain that you'll have to read too.

After passing over the pad, Ethan had watched him, biting his lip as if he was afraid Clay was going to throw up his hands in disgust. Clay had given him a smile and written:

No worries, mate. Reading isn't a hardship. Why, have you heard otherwise? I'll have you know I rated a B in school.

When Ethan read the note, he'd looked up at Clay with a smile, and they'd shared a laugh. Clay truly hadn't minded at all. It was a good feeling, to be on a level playing field. He didn't want Ethan to be self-conscious or feel…lesser.

Ethan: *Favorite cop movie?*

Clay: *Always liked* Lethal Weapon, *but Mel Gibson's turned out to be a real dickhead.* Die Hard *is still a good one. Before your time, I reckon.*

Ethan: *It's my fave Xmas movie. A classic.*

Made Clay feel a bit old to think of *Die Hard* as a classic, but he supposed it was nowadays. He flipped the pad, laughing out loud in the stillness of his room. He should get up and shower soon, but he couldn't seem to stop paging through the silly notes.

Clay: *What do you think of the* Bourne Identity *flicks?*

Ethan: *They're awesome. Matt Damon was super hot in those.*

It still made Clay squirm to see those words. When he'd read them the night before, he'd felt his face turn beet red, even though there was no reason for it. He knew Ethan was gay. Why had it been a shock to see proof of it in black and white? He read the next note with lingering embarrassment.

Ethan: *I'm sorry. Didn't mean to make you uncomfortable.*

Clay had shook his head and insisted it was all good before jumping up to fetch a couple more drinks. When he'd returned, Ethan had slid across another note, his eyebrow raised.

Ethan: *What's the most Crocodile Dundee thing you've ever done?*

Clay: *Reckon it was wrestling a croc.*

Ethan had whipped his head up and shouted, "Shut up!" before narrowing his eyes. A few people nearby turned to look at them, but Clay had ignored them, watching Ethan write something and slide the pad back.

Ethan: *I'm 99% sure you're fucking with me.*

Clay hadn't been able to keep a straight face, and he laughed to himself now thinking about it. They'd gone on like that back and forth as the evening had worn on, a breeze lifting Ethan's hair from his forehead from time to time. Goosebumps had tickled Clay's skin even though it was a humid night.

His prick decided to come to life now. He spit into his palm and reached down and gave it a few tugs, teasing his thumb over the head absently. Still looking at the notebook, he flipped the pages, chuckling at his own terrible drawing of a wicket as he'd tried to explain more about cricket. Ethan had seemed genuinely interested, and it pleased Clay even now. He was still idly jerking himself, warmth tingling through his body as he read another page.

Clay: *What kind of music do you listen to?*

He'd slid the pad across the table and realized a moment too late that it might be a stupid question. He'd said, "Sorry, I didn't mean—" before he remembered that of course Ethan couldn't hear him. Ethan had had his head down, writing his answer. He'd glanced up and gave Clay a little smile before writing more.

Ethan: *It's okay. I still do listen to music sometimes. Not as much as I did before, but I can hear music in my hearing aids through Bluetooth if I play it on my phone. It's pretty cool. I like more lyric-driven stuff, I guess. Where I can hear the voices better and it's not just noise. Sam Smith, Ed Sheeran. It's probably lame, but I'm an old man at heart. How about you?*

Clay: *Oldies, I guess. Men at Work, Bruce Springsteen. Melbourne band called Crowded House. Don't really follow the new stuff.*

He remembered Ethan's mischievous smile as he'd asked Clay: *Just how old* are *you?*

It had been a cheeky question, and Clay grinned now to think of it, still tugging on his dick. He'd replied: *Not ready to cark it yet, you ratbag.* He remembered the way Ethan had eagerly read his response, eyes widening and laughter bursting from him. The way his knee had knocked against Clay's under the table when he'd shifted his chair to let a family with a stroller get by—the warm pressure of it, and how neither of them had moved once the family was gone…

Now Clay stroked himself faster, spreading his legs and bending one knee, pushing up with his hips, using his heel for leverage. He'd never been one to wank too often, but as he thought about Ethan's smile and brown eyes twinkling in the firelight, he got harder and let out a low "Uhhh."

His heart skipped, and he tensed, the knowledge that it was weird to be wanking and thinking about Ethan thundering through him. But his prick was so bloody hard and aching, and he fucked up into his fist, working his thick shaft. He just wouldn't think about—

Ethan laughing a little too loudly. Ethan's shirt riding up when he stretched his arms overhead, his belly looking pale and ticklish. How nice his full lips were. His long fingers. How pretty he looked when Clay made him really smile. Ethan's slim, firm limbs pressed against him, their bodies colliding as they splashed around the pool playing. The sprinkling of hair across Ethan's chest that had rubbed against him as they tussled. Ethan's cheeks rosy with drink and happiness as they passed the pad back and forth, not saying anything very important, but worth being said all the same. The way the sunrise on Mission Beach had cast a pink glow over Ethan's skin.

Clay was too close now. He couldn't stop, sweet lust filling every bit of him even though he couldn't stop thinking of Ethan as he stroked. Needed to come…

Ethan was gay… What was it like to kiss another bloke? Touch his cock and—

Shouting in the still of the early morning, Clay climaxed, his balls tight as he shot his load all over his stomach. He gasped, eyes squeezed shut, the pleasure burning hotter than it had in a long, long time. He jerked himself as he spurted again, his whole body seizing. He saw stars—and Ethan.

Letting go of his half-hard, twitching prick, Clay opened his eyes, his chest heaving. *Strewth.* He stared down at himself with wonder and a pulse of horror. It was almost as though he was a stranger. There was his prick and his semen on his skin and caught in his short and curlies.

Bolting out of bed, he hurried to the bathroom and turned on the shower. But even as he scrubbed himself clean, he couldn't pretend. No two ways about it: he'd flogged himself off thinking of Ethan. Ethan, who was a bloke. Ethan, who…

Under the hot water, Clay stood motionless. He'd never had feelings like this for a bloke. He'd never wanted… He took a deep breath, the desire pulsing through him undeniable. He'd never wanted to *kiss* another bloke. He'd only ever had such tender feelings for Barb—the urge to protect and care for.

And that was there with Ethan, but it was deeper than that. A lust scratching inside him, clawing to break free even though he'd just shot his load. He had to admit his romance with Barb had never been particularly hot and heavy. They'd gotten on fine in the bedroom. Hadn't they? Maybe he was simply forgetting, but he couldn't recall desire for her ever scorching him this hot, turning him inside out.

Clay tried to make sense of it, water streaming down his back, starting to cool since the eco resort only had so much hot water. What the devil was the matter with him? He couldn't stand around all day, and he wouldn't hear his phone in the shower if Sam rang about Gilly.

He had to pack and get down to brekkie, and once they reached the mainland, it would be a long day of driving. And he had to find a chemist for Ethan's batteries.

Ethan.

Clay didn't have a clue what to think. His stomach twisted into knots. He was embarrassed, confused…

Excited.

Then the strangest memory floated up in his mind, breaking the surface like something lost to a river's current getting caught in an eddy. The name—one he hadn't thought of in decades—swirled around his mind.

Tony Taylor.

That was it—Clay apparently had a few roos loose in the top paddock. Stepping out of the shower, he wiped the condensation from the mirror and stared at himself as he brushed his teeth harder than the dentist said he should. He was strangely relieved that his reflection was familiar—as if he'd somehow expected a stranger to be looking back at him.

He managed a laugh at himself. Everything was fine. He'd keep his head down and do his job over the next couple days until they reached Sydney. It was nothing against Ethan, but Clay had made a mistake not maintaining a professional distance.

Besides, he wasn't into blokes, despite what he'd just done. Nothing wrong with it, but that wasn't him. Must have had more grog the night before than he'd reckoned. Scrambled his brains. Simple as that.

Except panic rose up in him now, along with the memory of Tony Taylor leaning over the engine of a ute, waving as Clay rode by on his bike, legs pumping as hard as his heart.

Noises in the night, headlights cutting through the darkness. That voice so thick with disgust.

"Filthy fucking queer."

Standing by the sink, gripping his toothbrush so hard he thought the plastic might snap, Clay shoved the memories back down. Leaning over, he rinsed his mouth, spitting and spitting until he was clean.

Chapter Ten

*W*HAT DID *I do wrong?*

Sitting a few rows back from the front of the bus on the left side, Ethan could just make out the side of Clay's face. He stared at Clay's arm on the steering wheel, the gold watch and reddish hair gleaming in the sunlight through the windshield. It was stupid to have sat so close—at least with Clay out of sight Ethan wasn't tempted to act like a total stalker the way he was now.

He forced himself to slide over to the window seat and watch the trees go by as they drove south.

What did I do wrong?

The question had haunted Ethan since they'd left Fraser Island and headed south to Surfers Paradise. Clay had barely spoken to him. He hadn't been rude, and he'd answered when Ethan had asked him questions about things to do in Surfers, but there was a strange chill between them, a tightness to his mouth and shoulders that hadn't been there before.

Honestly, Ethan had been hoping Clay would suggest they hang out after the group had dinner, but Clay's gaze had danced around nervously, and Ethan hadn't had the courage to ask him what was wrong.

Ethan wondered if he was feeling sick again, since when they reached the hotel, Clay had disappeared once his duties were done and hadn't appeared at dinner.

Truthfully, he *hoped* Clay was sick again, which was a dick move. But if Clay was sick, maybe that meant he wasn't pissed off at Ethan for something. Ethan had considered asking the front desk for his room number so he could check on him, but had decided it was insanely inappropriate.

Right? It is completely inappropriate. Clay was only being nice to me, and I must've freaked him out somehow. Or maybe he just doesn't like me after all. Maybe he's sick of having to repeat himself, and he has better things to do than hang out with a friendless loser lusting after him.

The loneliness gnawed at him, an endless black pit. He stared out blindly at the trees and clearings, blinking back tears. He'd fooled himself about Michael and Todd, and apparently his judgment was still completely fucked. He'd been so sure the connection he felt to Clay was real. And even though he'd known it was only temporary and that his crush was one-sided, it had brought him so much peace and joy.

What did I do wrong?

Conflicting emotions tore at Ethan when he thought of the night on Fraser Island writing notes and sharing pizza. After the awfulness of losing his batteries, Clay had somehow made it into one of the happiest days Ethan could remember in a long, long time. He'd had so much *fun* talking to Clay via pen and paper. He cursed himself again for not remembering to grab the pad when they left, wishing he could see their notes again now.

Why, so you can be even more pathetic?

Still, he wished he had some evidence that he hadn't imagined it all. Laughing together and goofing around and just…being. It had been magical, and after they'd strolled back along the boardwalk toward their rooms, Ethan's head buzzing from more beer than he was used to, Clay had squeezed his shoulder, his blunt fingertips brushing the bare skin of Ethan's neck above the collar of his tee.

Fuck, Ethan had wanted to jump him so badly, but obviously he'd restrained himself, saying goodnight and thank you, watching Clay continue along the lamp-lit boardwalk to his room about twenty feet away. He'd had to dive for his door when he realized he was still standing there like some creeper. And inside, he'd slumped back against the door and jerked himself off faster than he had since he was a teenager, even with all the beer.

He cringed now as he remembered how eager he'd been to see Clay the next morning, but how Clay had kept his head down at breakfast, sharing a table with Shiv, and then had talked to Shiv on the boat back to the mainland. He'd stopped at a drugstore for batteries as promised but had barely met Ethan's eyes, his smile strained.

They'd stopped at Steve Irwin's zoo, which had gotten Ethan's mind off obsessing over Clay's sudden coolness and of course Michael and Todd's betrayal. He hadn't thought about them the whole night on Fraser Island when he was with Clay in their own little world. Without his hearing aids all the sounds had been hushed, and it had somehow made it even more special.

He hadn't felt so connected to another person in far too long, and now Clay couldn't seem to look at him. Had he imagined it all? Was he completely delusional? He had been about his relationship with Michael. Maybe it was the same with Clay, and now Clay just wanted to do his job and not have Ethan bugging him.

It shouldn't have hurt so much, but fuck.

It did.

There was a lot of driving the last couple days of the tour, with not as many stops in between Surfers and Sydney. They stopped in a weirdly Scottish town called Maclean, where the telephone poles were all painted in different tartans.

Clay announced that it was forty-five degrees outside according to the dash thermometer, and Google told Ethan that was one-thirteen Fahrenheit. No one wanted to spend long outside, so they all agreed on a shortened break, Shiv saying something else Ethan missed but seemed to be some kind of joke.

It was like walking into an oven, and Ethan turned to say as much to Clay, hoping they could at least talk about the weather, if nothing else. But Clay was speaking to a couple from England, smiling warmly at them and gesturing toward the little town's main street, which was just around the corner from where they'd parked.

Ethan stood there about ten seconds as they talked, not able to make any of it out and feeling like he was intruding. He hurried across the street, dabbing at the sweat already wetting his hair, making sure his aids didn't get wet. It seemed like most of the group were going to a little cafe or the bakery next door, chatting to each other and smiling.

The idea of talking and listening was just too tiring, and Ethan continued down the street, wishing he'd brought his hat. The sun was brutal, and he stopped in the small grocery store for a big bottle of water and a banana. His stomach was tense and acidy, and he didn't want to eat, but he figured he should get something. He wandered the air-conditioned aisles for ten minutes before braving the heat again and returning to the bus.

Clay had it running, waiting with the AC blasting as the group straggled back. When Ethan climbed aboard, Clay glanced at him and gave him a tight smile before going back to reading something on his phone. He couldn't have been clearer that he had zero interest in any conversation, so Ethan slumped back into his seat and forced down the banana.

The really fucking sad thing was that part of him wanted to message Todd and ask for his advice. Todd had always been confident and outgoing, dating plenty of guys over the years. But now Todd and Michael were in love, and Ethan was more alone than ever.

He tried to keep his mind busy and away from the cycle of hurt and anger and shame and despair that now included Clay as well as Michael and Todd, but on the long stretches of road toward Port Macquarie it was a challenge. He read the tour notes that Clay had copied for him, which was a double-edged sword. He wanted to be distracted by learning new things, but the notes made him think of Clay.

What did I do wrong?

At least it was the last night before Sydney, and Ethan was relieved there was no organized meal in Port Macquarie. He was so freaking sick of trying to make small talk in noisy restaurants. He just wanted this tour to be over so he could…

What? Be alone in Sydney at an Airbnb? Why did I come on this trip? What was I thinking?

Breathing deeply, Ethan fought to keep his composure as they arrived just before six. Everyone else was going into the hotel, Shiv handing out room keys in the lobby. At least it was a little cooler by the ocean than it had been inland.

Throat dry, Ethan lingered as Clay started unpacking the luggage. Maybe he was a glutton for punishment, but he blurted, "Um, hey." It was stupid, but he'd really been looking forward to hearing Clay's deep, sexy voice again once he got his batteries, and now Clay had barely said more than a few overly polite words to him.

Barely glancing over as he hefted out a suitcase, Clay gave him another forced smile and said something Ethan couldn't make out since Clay's head was down.

Fuck, take a hint. Leave the guy alone.

But now he had to say *something*, so Ethan asked, "Is there somewhere good for dinner nearby? Sorry, I didn't catch every-thing Shiv said."

Clay deposited a suitcase on the concrete. He faced Ethan, but his gaze still didn't settle on him. "Yeah, there's a nice Thai place a few doors down. A seafood spot too, but it's a little greasy. Most of the places are along this street."

"Cool. Thanks. Um… Yeah. Thanks." Ethan escaped into the lobby, where Shiv was waiting to give him his key. He knew his bags would be taken up, so he just put the key in his pocket and headed back out, avoiding Clay unloading the rest of the luggage as he took a left toward the water, unsettled energy thrumming through him.

He walked along the river that emptied into the sea. The melancholy scent of wood burning wafted on the wind from time to time, plumes of smoke from a wildfire visible in the distance back inland. He kept walking, his mind chewing over how delusional he'd been about Michael and what had happened with Clay—and how Ethan had screwed it up too. Not that *it* was ever really anything.

There were large painted rocks all along the paved path beside the river, and according to a plaque there had been an art contest some years back. There were all kinds of colorful messages and drawings, and Ethan slowed to read them as he neared the ocean, the wind whipping. He stopped by one that was a family's handprints with their names scrawled beneath. He wondered how old they all were now, breathing through the painful twist of longing for his own family.

Some were memorials, which made him think of his parents, his throat thick and eyes prickling. Others were inspirational messages about valuing life and being in the moment, which sounded like cheap platitudes. Others were just painted artwork. Then he stopped at a simple painting of black letters on a cream background on the gray rock.

Lewis
Smithy
Taylor
Mulley
"The best antiques are old friends"

Standing there alone, Ethan's chest was hollow, and he felt like the wind could just sweep him away into nothing. Stupid tears spilled out of his eyes. He hadn't stayed in touch with high school friends aside from the odd Facebook or Instagram comments and likes. Todd and Michael had been his family, and now they might as well have been strangers.

They were, really. They'd lied to him every day for two years. Maybe longer. Everything he thought he'd known was garbage, and now here he was again, thinking he'd been getting to know Clay only to have the rug pulled out.

Maybe he did get to know me, and he didn't like what he found. Maybe I can't blame anyone for not wanting to be around me.

Pulling out his phone, Ethan was suddenly desperate to know if Michael and Todd had contacted him. He tapped open his Facebook messenger, almost dropping his phone onto a painted rock. He'd steadfastly ignored the red number in the corner of the app as it had climbed through the week. It was in the twenties now, and his heart was in his throat as he saw the list of names.

Michael and Todd were at the top. Followed by Uncle Chuck, Clara, and a couple of other people who were primarily Michael's friends. Ethan didn't bother scrolling down farther. With trembling fingers, the wind whistling painfully in his hearing aids, he hit Michael's thread, where there was a string of similar messages.

I know you don't want to hear from me, but I want to make sure you're okay. Are you in Cairns now? I hope the flights were all right. Have an amazing time, okay? You deserve it.

Eth, please just let me know you're okay. You haven't been reading messages. We're worried.

Please reply. I hope you're having a great time like your mom always wanted. I'm sorry for everything, I really am. I didn't want it to go down like this. I still love you.

Seriously, are you okay? We're really worried. Can you just let us know you're alive?

Okay, I know you're on the tour since I called the office to confirm. I hope it's incredible. We understand you need space right now, but we're here thinking of you when you're ready, baby.

Ethan tasted bile and was afraid he'd vomit. There were similar messages from Todd, just with more use of "dude" and "bro." But like Michael's messages, there was a lot of "we" mentioned. As he had so many times, Ethan cycled through the hurt and shame and anger.

The fear was a tremor in him, making his knees shake, and as he stood there by the water, alone as couples and families walked by, it wasn't just about Michael and Todd.

Why wouldn't Clay talk to him like he had before? What had Ethan done to mess things up? Had he been hitting on Clay too much? He hadn't meant to. He really hadn't. But maybe he'd made Clay uncomfortable by lusting after him and being way too fucking obvious.

Walking quickly, he made it back to the hotel, forcing himself to stop fucking crying. It was ridiculous that he even cared about what Clay thought of him. They'd just met, and Ethan had clearly expected too much.

He cringed as he thought of how clingy and annoying he'd probably been. Spending time with Clay had been a glorious distraction, and he'd asked far too much of a near-stranger who was just trying to do his job.

He decided to forget dinner, and got into bed even though it was still light out. Guilt nagged, and he opened the message from Uncle Chuck.

Hey, buddy. Are you okay? I talked to Michael, and he told me what happened. Probably not all of it, but enough, I guess. Kara had the baby yesterday—another girl, seven and a half pounds. We named her Lily Emma. Can you just let me know where you are and that you're okay? I know you're a grownup, but I still worry.

Ethan quickly replied that he was fine and on the tour, and congratulations, etc., etc. It was strange to think of life back home going on. It all seemed so incredibly far away. The numbness had started to lessen thanks to Clay, and now Ethan just *hurt*.

What did I do wrong?

AFTER A MORNING spent seeing a few of Sydney's sights, they trooped off the bus and gathered outside the hotel entry. They'd had a farewell dinner the night before up Sydney Tower, although Clay hadn't gone up with them. Some of the other passengers had skipped the final morning, already off to other destinations.

Ethan said his goodbyes, nodding and smiling and wishing well, then hung back as the remaining group members said goodbye to Shiv and Clay, giving them envelopes with tips inside. Ethan had his own folded into his pocket that he'd gotten from the front desk. He'd asked Violet how much passengers usually tipped on tours like this, and she'd said fifty to a hundred dollars. Even though Australia didn't have much of a tipping culture, apparently tours like this were an exception. Considering Shiv and Clay had taken care of them for ten nights and eleven days, it seemed right to give them a bonus.

Ethan had gone for a hundred. He gave one envelope to Shiv, who thanked him and pumped his hand. The engine of an arriving car drowned out what Shiv said, but Ethan guessed it was pleasantries and nodded and smiled. While Shiv went to help Violet with her luggage, Ethan stood a few feet from Clay, who had his hands shoved in his pockets, his gaze skittering around.

Fuck.

Clearly he made Clay uncomfortable now, and he had to respect that. Maybe it was the gay thing after all, and that he hadn't hidden his attraction to Clay as well as he'd hoped. Yet Ethan still flushed with regretful longing now to think of sitting there for hours under the glow of the torches that night, passing notes back and forth. He'd felt so…seen. Accepted. And the loss of it was shockingly difficult, no matter how many times he lectured himself on the fact that he and Clay had just met and he shouldn't be so upset.

Now Ethan was making it even fucking weirder by just standing there while Clay looked at his feet. Closing the distance left between them, Ethan thrust out the envelope and said, "Thank you so much for everything. It was a great tour."

Lifting his head, Clay eyed the envelope, his cheeks above his beard flushing. He swallowed hard, his Adam's apple bobbing. "No, mate. I can't take anything from you."

Yet Ethan had seen him accept tips from the others. Maybe he should have just been glad to save the money, but it felt like a punch to the gut. "Why?" He should just walk away, but he found himself finally asking it aloud. "What did I do wrong?"

Clay's face pinched, and he looked pained as he sighed heavily. "Oh, mate. No, it wasn't anything you did. Sorry if I've been…" He waved a hand through the air. "It's not you. Honestly. And you should keep the money. It just wouldn't feel right. I'm really sorry for how I've been acting."

Clay sounded so sincere and looked so sorrowful that hope exploded inside Ethan. He grabbed onto it desperately, and the idea popped into his head and came out of his mouth before he could lose his nerve. "Then let me buy you a beer, at least? I saw in the news that there's a big cricket match on this afternoon." He glanced toward the hotel, which had a more casual pub attached to it as well as a fancier restaurant. "We could just go in there. You could teach me more about the game."

"Uh…" Clay shifted uneasily. "I shouldn't. I've got to drop off the coach at the garage, and I'm sure you'll be off to explore the city."

Hot, sticky embarrassment sank through him, the hope vanishing. He'd been kidding himself again, delusional as usual.

"Right, of course. I'm sorry." He shook his head, backing up. "I totally get it. Anyway, it was good to meet you. I'll just…" His baggage was with the porter inside, and he tried not to trip over his own feet.

"Wait!"

Ethan turned back, hoping he'd heard correctly. Clay approached, glancing around as if making sure no one overheard. "The garage is only a couple blocks away. I can come back for a beer. I'm off now."

He tried to keep his cool, but Ethan's heart leapt, sweet relief flooding him. He grinned. "Yeah? Cool. I'll meet you in the pub over there."

Clay nodded, looking strangely shy. "See you in twenty."

The next twenty minutes were a freaking eternity. Ethan loitered in the lobby, struggling through a conversation with Stan and Violet, the flurry of sound from check-ins and check-outs echoing off the marble surroundings. He was relieved when their cab showed up, and after a final goodbye, he escaped into the bathroom to get his shit together. His face was stupidly red, and he splashed cold water on his cheeks, careful not to wet his hearing aids.

This isn't a date for fuck's sake. He probably just feels sorry for me and is being nice. Again.

Still, eagerness zipped through him. At least he'd be able to leave things with Clay on a better note. It shouldn't have mattered to him so much—he'd only known the guy eleven days. But it mattered. It did. *Clay* mattered, and even though Ethan would have to get over this crush sooner rather than later, he'd have a couple more hours to indulge it.

But don't be creepy. No creepiness. Just two guys having a beer together and watching a confusing sport on TV. It's nothing more.

He waited for Clay by the pub entrance. When he arrived, he'd changed out of his uniform into plaid shorts that went to his knees and a white T-shirt that showed off his hairy, freckly arms.

The sun coming through a skylight made his beard gleam copper around his lips, and Ethan wanted to kiss him so badly he—

Get. It. Together!

He managed to say hi, and they found a table near one of the TVs. Ethan insisted on getting the first round. There didn't seem to be a server, so he approached the bar and looked at the taps.

One said "XXXX Gold," so he asked the young woman behind it for two of those since he knew Clay liked it and he'd enjoyed it as well. He hoped he was remembering correctly that it was said "four X" and not "X-X-X-X." She asked something that was a soft slur of sound, background music drowning it out, along with laughing and conversation from a few people sitting at the bar. Ethan took a guess that she had asked if that was all, and said, "Yes."

She frowned, looking at him askance, and his heart sank. She asked again, and he still couldn't hear, so he said, "I'm sorry. I can't hear you."

Now she was looking at him with confusion and slight suspicion. She leaned closer. "*Mumble mumble?*"

His cheeks were hot, and they'd garnered the attention of the man sitting on the closest stool. He said loudly, "*Mumble schooner or a pint.*" Ethan was able to hear his deeper voice more clearly, but he was still completely confused. Schooner? Like a sailboat? *Huh?* He felt like everyone was staring. He was fairly sure the other word was pint, so he grasped at it and said, "Pint, please," hoping like hell that was the right answer.

Fortunately it was, and she poured two glasses from the tap. She put them in front of him and said, "*Mumble mumble room.*"

"Oh, I'll just pay for it." He pulled out his wallet and prayed that he'd filled in the correct blanks.

Apparently he had, because she turned to the register and then came back with the bill. He gave her his card, deciding to save the cash, and when she came back she handed him a pen. As he leaned over to sign, she yelled in his ear, "If you want to charge something to your room, you'd just put your name on the line at the bottom, and then it would go on your hotel bill. So you wouldn't have to pay now."

Wincing, he sighed. He wanted to tell her he wasn't an idiot—he simply hadn't heard her initial question, and he understood how it worked. But he didn't. She was probably trying to help, but she looked at him like he was stupid. At least tipping wasn't the norm in Australia so he didn't have to give her anything extra.

Back at the table, Clay thanked him, and they drank in weird silence. The cricket match hadn't started yet, and the TV was just showing some talking heads, the sound not on yet. Luckily the background music in the bar didn't seem as loud in their corner, and Ethan was able to angle his chair so his back was to the main area. He adjusted his hearing aids to filter out the sound behind him.

At the same time Ethan asked, "So, who's playing?" Clay said something as well. They laughed awkwardly, and Ethan said, "Sorry, what was that?"

"Just asked where you're staying while you're here. I think you said you've rented a spot."

"Oh, yeah. It's an Airbnb. Condo in…Darlinghurst? I think? I should probably check so I know where I'm going, huh?" He flushed to the tips of his ears, nervously adjusting his hearing aids again before pulling out his phone and opening his email.

And seeing two words that leapt out at him: *reservation* and *canceled.*

Heart seizing, he jabbed at the email to open it. There it was: a cold-blooded email saying that he'd received a refund for his canceled reservation. Of course he'd heard horror stories of hosts canceling at the last minute for whatever reason, but he'd picked a place with a Superhost and only glowing reviews!

This isn't happening.

Clay was saying something, but Ethan couldn't listen. The email was from three days ago, and he *despised* himself. Why hadn't he checked? He'd wanted to avoid all contact with Michael and Todd and the real world, but he should have fucking checked on his reservation!

Clay's hand was firm and warm on his shoulder, his rough thumb resting on the skin above Ethan's collarbone. Ethan met his worried gaze as Clay said, "Mate, what's happened? Bad news?"

It felt so good to be touched in just a simple way, and Ethan wanted to fold into Clay's arms and make everything else disappear. But he couldn't. He managed to speak, his voice sounding hoarse. "My condo reservation got canceled. I..." He swallowed hard, his mind spinning. "Maybe I can see if I can stay longer at the hotel. It's Saturday, but hopefully they aren't full."

Clay grimaced. He was still holding Ethan's shoulder. "This'll be a busy weekend in the city. There's a big music festival at Darling Harbour."

"Right. Okay. Well, I'm sure I'll find something. Somewhere." He laughed so he couldn't cry. "I should just go home. Maybe it's a sign that it's time to face all that stuff." He covered his face to keep from breaking down. "I don't know if I can, though."

For a few heartbeats, Clay didn't say anything. Then he blew out a big exhalation that ghosted over Ethan's cheek. He squeezed his fingers around Ethan's shoulder. "You can come back to mine. Sam's away for the weekend, so it's no bother."

"I..." The relief was so intense Ethan had to catch his breath. He wouldn't be alone. "Are you sure?"

After barely looking at him for the last couple of days, now Clay's blue eyes met Ethan's squarely. "I'm sure."

Chapter Eleven

THE TRAIN RATTLED along as they headed to Parramatta, the suburb where Clay and his daughter lived. Ethan attempted to keep his shit together and not get too excited that he'd be seeing Clay's home. That he'd be sleeping in Clay's home!

Yeah, but I'm not sleeping with Clay, so get a grip.

"We can pick up some groceries and stop by the bottlo after we drop off our bags."

Ethan frowned. "Stop by the what? Sorry." He'd asked Clay to sit across from him on the train so he could see his mouth clearly and hopefully get the sound straight to both ears without any interruptions in the flow.

"The bottlo." He laughed. "Sorry. Probably sounds like nonsense to Americans. The liquor store. We'll get a carton of stubbies and put our feet up."

Ethan laughed too. "Whatever you just said, it sounds great."

He had no idea why the sudden, brittle tension in Clay had eased, but he sure wasn't complaining. It was still a little tentative between them, not the completely easy rapport they'd had that night on Fraser Island, but instead of avoiding looking at Ethan altogether, Clay seemed to be sneaking glances at him now. Ethan didn't question it. Even though his crush was hopeless, he was thrilled to have his new friend back.

"What kind of food are you keen on?"

"I'm easy. Whatever you want."

"I can do some steaks on the barbie. Jacket potatoes. Some veggies too. Sam's always on about me eating more of the damn things."

He laughed. "That sounds amazing. Are you sure—"

"*Yes.*" Clay raised his eyebrows. "I'm sure it's not a hassle having you stay the weekend."

Ethan smiled gratefully. "Okay. I'll look for a place right away. I should start now, actually." He pulled out his phone.

Clay's low laughter reached him in the quiet of the train. There were only a few other people in their car. Ethan looked up as Clay said, "It'll be fine, no worries. Is this an American thing, being wound so bloody tight?"

"Maybe? Or just a me thing. I can get worked up sometimes." He shifted in his seat, glancing at the industrial area zipping by, suddenly embarrassed. "As you know from the other day."

Was that why Clay had been so standoffish? Because Ethan had freaked out about his missing batteries and been so...needy? Clay hadn't seemed to mind at the time.

He seemed unbothered now. "Well, there's no need. We'll work it all out. I'll bore you with some cricket, and you can have a nice nap."

Ethan laughed, warmth blooming in his chest—that wonderful feeling of *safety* that he couldn't quite explain. "Are you sure you're not missing too much of it?" They'd left the pub before the match was under way, only having the one drink since Ethan had been so antsy and upset.

"Nah, it's an ODI. It'll go at least six hours. Probably more. It's barely started."

"Holy shit. That's a long time."

Clay chuckled. "A test match can go five days, so not by cricket standards. Oh, and ODI means 'one day international.' There are some differences to test matches, but I won't bore you with them now."

"You'll wait until later?" Ethan teased.

"Too right."

They lapsed into silence again, and Ethan tried to think of something to say. "When do you have to drive back up to Cairns?"

"About a week and a half. I've got four full days off now, then I'll do some day trips to the Blue Mountains and whatnot. I've been doing Sydney to Cairns and back every month for almost two years now. Paid my dues, so I've been speaking to the company about staying closer to home. Next run, I'll have a new fellow shadowing me. I'll show him the ropes, and then it's all his. I tell you what, it'll be lovely to be home more with Sam and Gilly. Sam's finishing uni soon, and she'll be looking for a job as a teacher. Won't want to be living with her old man forever. She and Jase are getting fairly serious, I reckon."

"Did she take Gilly with her on her trip?"

Clay smiled, warmth in his eyes. "Yeah. Looking forward to seeing them both Monday. Had a bit of a fright earlier this week with Gilly. He was bitten by a paralysis tick. But Sam got him to the vet quick and he's fine now."

"A paralysis tick? What's that? I mean, aside from the obvious." Ethan shuddered at the thought. "Does it affect humans?"

"Not the way it does animals. Can be absolutely deadly for dogs and cats. Unless you're very young or allergic, it's more a nuisance for humans, as far as I know. Didn't have to worry about the buggers until we moved to Sydney. Only found along the East Coast. They inject a venom or whatever, and if it gets to the lungs and heart, that's it. But it was still early, and Gilly's doing well." He pulled out his phone. "Sam sent this earlier."

He passed over the phone, and Ethan smiled at the picture of Sam and Gilly. Sam's blond hair blew around her face, and Gilly's tongue was out happily, the ocean blue behind them. "Great shot." He passed the phone back.

"Yeah." Clay gazed down at the picture, practically beaming. It made Ethan's heart swell.

"Where does Gilly's name come from?"

Clay shifted in his seat, looking a little...embarrassed? "Well..."

Ethan laughed. "It's something to do with cricket, right?"

"Guilty as charged." Clay snorted. "You're going to think I'm a nutter."

"My Uncle Chuck is obsessed with the Buffalo Bills. Like, has a Bills flag on his front lawn, rewatches games regularly, and named his first daughter Kelly, after Jim Kelly. Nothing will shock me."

"Same surname I have—Kelly. He was a good player, was he? Which sport is that?"

"Oh, football. American football, I mean. Yeah, he was the quarterback for a long time, I think. He's like a god to Uncle Chuck." He smiled. "So come on, 'fess up. Who's Gilly?"

"Adam Gilchrist. He's a legend. His batting was out of this world. And he was always a solid bloke, not like Shane Warne. I mean, Warne's probably the greatest spinner ever, but he couldn't keep it in his trousers. Always sex scandals, and taking a banned substance and the like. Never had to worry about that nonsense with Gilly. He stood up for what was right." Clay grimaced, shaking his head. "And I don't even want to get into those three who tampered with the ball during a match last year. It was a disgrace to Australia. The captain was in on it! Should have banned them all for longer than they did, I tell you."

Clay's righteous indignation was freaking *adorable*. Not to mention sexy as fuck. Ethan kept his expression serious even though he wanted to smile. "Wow. That sucks that they cheated. I'm sorry."

"Yeah, well." Clay crossed his arms, his nostrils flaring. He was quiet for a few moments as he looked out the window. "Broke my heart when I heard the news. Still beggars belief. You should lose fair and square and win the same way. The blokes who wear the baggy green have always been heroes. *Should* be. To do wrong like that..." He rubbed his face, some other words lost, but Ethan didn't ask him to repeat himself.

The urge to smile at Clay's indignation had vanished as Ethan realized this was something Clay was truly upset about. "I'm so sorry that happened," he said quietly. Considering Clay had a cricket tattoo, clearly it was something he loved. It was part of his identity. "Cheating really sucks."

Visions of Michael and Todd barged into his mind, and he held his breath, cycling through the mess of emotions the memory brought before firmly refocusing on Clay, who exhaled loudly, shaking his head as he said, "Sorry, mate. Still get the shits when I think about it."

Now Ethan frowned as he tried to figure out if he'd heard correctly. "Did you say you...get the shits?"

"Yeah." Clay gazed at him with no hint of humor. Then he laughed, his eyes crinkling. "I mean I get aggro. Makes me angry. Not that I have to run to the loo."

"Oh! I get it." Ethan laughed as well, and they smiled at each other as the train arrived at Parramatta.

"Here we are," Clay said, leading the way out of the train with his small suitcase, Ethan pulling his two. "You all right walking? It's only a few blocks."

"Totally. Been sitting a lot, so a walk'll be nice."

They headed away from the train station, both putting on their sunglasses. Clay's aviators were still incredibly sexy, Ethan noted for the record as they walked. They passed by a few three-story apartment buildings and other small houses, turning onto a quiet street with dry, green-brown lawns. Clay turned onto the short walkway of a small one-story bungalow. There was red tile on the roof, white siding, gray shutters, and a separate garage farther back at the end of the driveway. On either side of the stone steps up to the door were neatly kept bushes.

At the door, Clay said something as he fit the key into the lock, and Ethan had to ask him to repeat it. Clay turned around on the top step. "Sorry. Said it's not much, but it does the job. Especially since I'm gone almost two weeks every month."

"It looks great!"

"Well, it's a rental, but it's nice enough." He led the way into the shallow foyer past the faded doormat. There was a closet on the right, and on the left was the living room with a brown leather couch, a green arm chair and ottoman, and a wooden coffee table. The walls were beige and decorated with some framed abstract art Ethan was pretty sure he recognized from IKEA. A striped area rug had a distinctly Swedish mass-produced vibe as well.

Michael would be horrified. Then another thought: *Good. Fuck him.*

"At least Sam tidied up before leaving. There's a little dining room back by the kitchen, but we rarely eat in there. Usually park ourselves in front of the telly."

"Cool. It looks really comfortable," Ethan said, shutting the door behind him. It was warm in the house, and Clay switched on the ceiling fan over the couch and opened a window.

"Like I said, it's not much."

Ethan hesitated, not sure if he'd heard correctly. "I didn't mean that as a backhanded compliment. It seriously looks so comfy. I'm used to form over function. Michael—" He broke off, grimacing. "You know what? It doesn't matter." He stood his suitcases inside the door. "Time for your cricket. If you tell me where the store is, I can go get the beer and whatever groceries you need."

"No, no, mate. I'll take my ute. Pickup truck, I mean. It's in the garage. I'll just peek at the score. You can make yourself at home. Put your feet up." He motioned to the armchair.

"I'd actually like to come to the store. It's weird, but I like grocery shopping. In Maclean I spent twenty minutes wandering around that tiny store. I love looking at the different stuff."

Clay smiled. "Suit yourself."

"But you're sure you wouldn't rather go to the pub to watch the game?"

"Nah. I'll go from time to time, but haven't really found a local here. Not like in the Curry. Sam's always saying I should make the effort to make more mates, but I dunno. It's strange at this age. Most of my life I knew the same people. Here, everyone's a stranger but her and the people from work. Shiv and the other guides."

"Right. If you're sure…"

"Absolutely. Besides, you'll hear better here, won't you? How will I bore the shit out of you if you can't hear me yammering on?"

Ethan grinned, warmth in his chest that Clay was concerned about him being able to hear. "Sounds like a plan."

WITH HIS BELLY full of steak and the cricket finally over, Ethan cleared their dinner plates and took them into the kitchen, despite Clay's protests. Cricket seriously went on *forever* and was still confusing, but Ethan had really enjoyed himself. Clay hadn't seemed to mind at all about putting on the captions, even though for live sports they were a little delayed and kind of annoying. Ethan still liked to hear the commentary.

There was no dishwasher, so he filled the sink with soapy water. Clay followed him, sipping from his bottle of beer in its foam insulator that had a cartoon of a drunk insect and the words

CRISSED AS A PICKET.

Ethan said over his shoulder, "Yes, I'm doing the dishes. No arguments."

Clay replied something Ethan missed as he turned back to the dishes, but he didn't seem to be arguing. A breeze came in the open window over the sink, the ceiling fans throughout the house picking it up. The extreme heat had broken, thankfully. Clay had said he'd put the air conditioning on before bed, and Ethan's dick had tingled with the thought of Clay in bed.

Don't. Be. Creepy.

He'd thought Clay had gone back into the living room, but when Ethan pulled out the stopper and wiped his hands on a dish towel, everything drying on the rack next to the sink, he turned to find Clay still standing there, leaning a hip against the counter that came out in an L-shape to separate the kitchen from the dining room. Clay watched him intently, and a shiver rippled over Ethan's skin.

"When did you first kiss another bloke?"

The words hung in the air, and Ethan was sure all the oxygen *whooshed* from his lungs. Had Clay really said… Was Ethan hearing things? "I… Sorry, what did you say?" He had to have misheard.

Now Clay's already-flushed face went darker red, his knuckles white where he gripped his beer. He looked down and opened his mouth, but then snapped it shut and raised his head, meeting Ethan's gaze. "I asked when you first kissed another bloke." He took a swallow of beer, his throat working. Then he shrugged, a jerk of his shoulder. "Just curious."

Wow. That *was* what Clay had said. And now Ethan had made it even more crazy awkward by making him say it again. His heart thumped. A minute ago, he'd been contentedly washing dishes, everything peaceful and even domestic. Now there was something new in the air that sent sparks rushing over his skin.

He tried to be normal and act like Clay had asked what time it was. *He's only curious. It's nothing.* "Oh! Sorry. Um, I was in high school. I was a junior, so I was sixteen. His name was Jaden. We were both in the GSA. We dated for a bit, but nothing serious."

Clay nodded rapidly. "Ah. Right." He took another sip of beer, his throat working. "GSA?"

"Sorry. Gay-Straight Alliance. It's a club where LGBTQ kids are supported and know they have a safe space and that everyone there is an ally."

Clay's eyebrows went up. "They have that in school? That's good."

"Yeah, I guess it can be controversial with homophobes, but most people at my school were cool. And I was out to my parents, so. Anyway, yeah. I was sixteen."

"And you already knew you were gay?"

"Oh yeah. I knew from the time I was eight or nine."

"So young." Clay drank again, apparently draining the bottle because he put it on the counter, knocking it over in the process. He laughed nervously and righted it.

Why is he so nervous?

Ethan shrugged. "I guess? My mom was really open about stuff. She said she thought maybe I was when I was little. Just a mom gut instinct or something." A memory of her telling him that one day he'd marry the boy of his dreams seized him, and his throat tightened. He forced a breath and exhaled slowly. He didn't want to think about any of that right then, not his mom dying or his non-wedding. None of it. No, he was focusing on Clay, and how nervous Clay suddenly seemed. Ethan had to be reading this wrong.

Clay's hands were at his sides, his fingers twitching. "Reckon I never considered the possibility." He laughed thinly. "Don't know why I'm talking nonsense. I'm too old to change my stripes now anyway."

Whoa. Whoooooa.

Ethan's heart thumped against his ribcage. What was happening? Was it in his head, or was there something…*happening?* Was Clay… What was Clay saying? Mouth suddenly dry, Ethan took a step toward him. Then another. Clay's gaze skittered around, and he was breathing hard, practically vibrating with…what? Tension? Excitement? Nerves?

Desire?

All of the above? Ethan was now within arm's length. He had no fucking idea what to say, so he tried to joke. "Well, if you want to kiss me to see what it's like, feel free."

Clay didn't laugh. He didn't punch Ethan either, or shove him away, or tell him it wasn't funny. He didn't do any of those things. No, with lips parted, his face and neck bright red beyond his beard, he looked Ethan square in the eye and jerked forward.

They were only inches apart now, their bare big toes grazing on the tile floor. Ethan swore he could feel an electric current through just that slight touch, and he *had* to be dreaming, because it sure as shit seemed like Clay wanted to kiss him.

Clay looked at Ethan's mouth, his brow furrowing as if he didn't know what to do. He was shaking like he was *terrified*—and excited—and Ethan took a long breath, confidence surging through him with the urge to take care of Clay and make everything okay.

Slowly, Ethan touched Clay's bare forearms, keeping his touch light as he ran his palms up to Clay's shoulders, the skin hot. His thumbs brushed the cotton of Clay's tank top. Clay breathed hard, his chest rising and falling, puffs of hot air on Ethan's mouth. They were just about the same height, and Ethan looked into Clay's eyes, making sure he knew what was coming as Ethan leaned in and brushed their dry lips together.

It was barely a kiss, but it was everything.

They both shuddered, and Clay's hands clutched Ethan's

waist. Ethan pressed his lips over Clay's now, covering them softly. Their eyes were open even though they couldn't really see each other that close. Ethan inched back, searching Clay's stunned expression.

Ethan whispered, "Do you like that?"

Clay nodded jerkily, a spasm of what looked like grief creasing his face. But then he nodded again, exhaling in a rush as he closed his eyes and kissed Ethan harder.

It was clumsy, but fuck, it really was *everything*.

Their mouths were still closed, and Ethan didn't push. They kissed like that—like kids, really—for a minute, just pressing mouths together and sucking in little breaths. Cautiously, Ethan opened his mouth a bit and licked at the seam of Clay's lips.

On a desperate groan, Clay opened his mouth, grasping Ethan closer against his body, welcoming Ethan's probing tongue. And holy shit, Clay was *hard*. Ethan's dick had stiffened as they kissed, and now it surged against Clay's through their shorts.

Ethan slid his hands up to cup Clay's head, tilting his face so he could deepen the kiss. He pressed him back against the counter, pushing his thigh between Clay's legs and rutting against him. They gasped and moaned, the wet sounds of their kissing reaching Ethan's ears.

I'm kissing Clay! This is actually happening!

He wasn't sure how any of it was possible, but Ethan ordered his brain to shut the fuck up and go with it. Their tongues pushed together, mouths fused. Clay's facial hair was rough against Ethan's face and probably giving him beard burn and it was *glorious*.

He wanted to climb Clay like a tree, and his dick was already going to explode. He'd probably break the spell if he came in his shorts, so he pulled back with a gasp, spit stringing between their lips.

He asked again, "Do you like that?" Clay clearly did, but he wanted to hear him say it.

Muttering something, Clay nodded. Ethan gripped his face. This time he wasn't apologetic. "Say that again. Clearly so I can hear you."

A shiver ran through Clay, and he croaked, "I like it."

The question entered Ethan's mind and came right out his mouth. He knew the answer, confidence filling him. "Do you want me to suck your cock?" Said cock was pushing on his hip, and Clay nodded desperately.

After kissing him again deeply and sucking on Clay's tongue, Ethan sank to his knees, which were bare on the hard tile beneath his cargo shorts. He quickly unzipped Clay's shorts and yanked them down, along with his underwear, and the fact that Clay wore black briefs sent a fresh rush of lust through Ethan.

He nuzzled the ginger pubic hair around the base of Clay's dick, the wiry hair scratching his face. Then Ethan leaned back and teased the slit on the end of Clay's cut cock with his tongue. Wrapping his palm around the base and twisting gently, he focused on the head, kissing and licking it as Clay got even harder. When Ethan finally took the head fully into his mouth, Clay groaned.

Sucking deeper, Ethan looked up, eager to see Clay watching him. But Clay's eyes were squeezed shut and he was reaching back with both hands and gripping the edge of the counter. He seemed to be holding his breath, and the rush of pleasure Ethan had from tasting him ebbed.

Does he still want this? Does he really want me *or is he just not one to turn down a blow job? He kissed me back, but...*

The voices in his head were too loud to ignore, and Ethan was probably going to ruin it all, but he had to ask. Sitting back on his heels, taking some of the pressure off his knees, he let Clay's dick slip out of his mouth. It was wet with his spit and flushed bright red, and *fuck*, Ethan wanted to suck it like there was no tomorrow.

He wanted to coax Clay over the edge and swallow his cum.

But only if Clay *really* wanted it too and wasn't just taking what he could get because Ethan had offered.

He couldn't bear to break contact all together and held onto Clay's muscular, freckled thighs. *God, those freckles. I want to lick them all.* But first he had to focus. He looked up, and after another beat, Clay opened his eyes and met his gaze, exhaling sharply.

Ethan asked, "Do you want me to stop?"

"Huh?" Clay blinked down at him.

"Do you really want this? If I'm pressuring you…"

Clay stared at him incredulously. "Are you taking the piss?"

"No, I just… You had your eyes closed and you weren't touching me at all."

"I…" His Adam's apple bobbed. "Never done this with a bloke. Not sure…"

"If you want to?"

He barked out a laugh. "Mate, does it look like I don't want to?" He motioned to his straining cock, thick and flushed red, and muttered something else. When Ethan squinted and turned his ear a bit towards Clay, Clay said more clearly, "I don't know what it's like between men."

"Pretty much the same as with a woman, I guess. I mean, generally."

"Yeah, well, Barb and I weren't too adventurous." Clay's blush crept down his neck to his chest.

Wow, if a blow job was adventurous… Ethan gave him a smile. "It's okay." Clay's thighs trembled just a bit, and Ethan stroked them slowly. *Time to take charge.* He grasped Clay's cock again with one hand and kissed the head. Still looking up, he said, "I want to suck you and taste you until you come in my mouth."

Clay groaned, his cock twitching. He muttered something that might have been "Bloody hell."

Confidence building, Ethan added, "And I want you to touch me. Watch me. Be here with me."

Clay nodded and tentatively reached for Ethan's head with his right hand, resting it there. He stroked gently with his fingertips, as if Ethan might break, but it was a start.

"That's good. Just watch my hearing aids, okay?" Ethan slowly licked down one side of Clay's shaft and back up the other before taking him fully again. He only sucked for a moment before pulling off, the sound of Clay's whimper reaching him and filling him with pride. "Do you like that? Do you like it when I suck your cock?"

Clay nodded, murmuring something too softly for Ethan to hear. Ethan couldn't remember the last time he'd been so bold during sex, but it felt *great*. Clay wanted him. Clay *needed* him. He was clearly afraid, and shit, maybe he'd been repressing this desire his whole life if it really was his first time with a guy.

Ethan was going to make this the best blow job in the history of the goddamn world.

With one hand on the base of the shaft and the other holding Clay's trembling thigh, Ethan sucked him deeply now, going back up fully on his knees so he could get closer. Hollowing his cheeks, he sucked eagerly, his own cock throbbing in his shorts and pressing against the fly.

Clay's pubes tickled Ethan's nose, and he tried to relax his throat, taking in almost all of him. He had to pull back so he didn't choke, gurgling as spit leaked out of his stretched lips. Clay's palm still rested on his head, following his movements. Ethan stroked with his hand in concert with the up and down of his mouth. He'd been concentrating, and now he looked back up at Clay.

A jolt of lust tightened his balls as their eyes met. He didn't care about the hard tile beneath his knees, or the growing ache in his jaw as he stretched his mouth to its limit. All that mattered was

Clay watching him with such wonder and warmth, as if Ethan as the most amazing thing in the world.

Clay stroked Ethan's head, pushing his fingers into his hair and sending a shiver of desire down Ethan's spine. He moaned, his mouth full, and Clay's hips jerked, panting with lips parted. He caressed Ethan's hair and scalp, still gentle, but bolder now. He was so hard in Ethan's mouth, musky and hot.

Needing to taste him fully, Ethan sucked more forcefully, sliding his left hand down to cup Clay's balls. Hair scratched his palms as he kneaded them, loving how heavy and meaty they were. Clay cried out, his hips thrusting as he came.

His fingers tightened in Ethan's hair, and he moaned loudly, emptying every drop down Ethan's throat. Ethan swallowed as much as he could, breathing desperately through his nose. When he sat back on his heels again, semen dripped out one corner of his mouth.

Chest heaving, Clay stared down at him, his dick twitching. He relaxed his fingers in Ethan's hair, but didn't take his hand away. He said something, and Ethan asked, "What?"

"I said 'Christ almighty'!" Then he laughed incredulously, and Ethan laughed too, wiping his mouth with the back of his hand and releasing Clay's spent balls with the other. Ethan grunted as he pushed to his feet, his knees feeling it, and Clay grabbed his arms, pulling him up the rest of the way and holding on tightly. He stared at Ethan in wonder and leaned in to kiss him.

Ethan pressed his hand to Clay's chest. "You'll be able to taste it." He didn't want it to freak him out since this was Clay's first time with a guy, but maybe mentioning it would freak him out more? Maybe he should have just said nothing. Maybe he was making it weird when it didn't need to be. Maybe—

He lost his train of thought as Clay took his face in his hands, his thumb brushing over Ethan's swollen lips, his gaze dropping from Ethan's eyes to his mouth, then back up again.

Ethan murmured, "But maybe you'll like tasting your cum in my mouth."

A laugh burst out of Clay. "Strewth, the things you say!"

Ethan grinned. He'd never been much of a dirty talker with Michael, or really a talker at all in bed. But something about Clay's inexperience emboldened him. It made his blood sing and his cock throb. Leaning in, Clay still holding his face, he licked across Clay's bottom lip, smiling at the groan that escaped.

Clay opened for him, and Ethan kissed him deeply, meeting his tongue. The musky aftertaste of semen was definitely still there, and Ethan passed it over wetly, stroking and exploring as Clay moaned, their bodies pressed tightly. Ethan needed to come, and he humped against Clay, not caring if he came in his shorts, the friction building, pleasure strung through his body.

He needed to gasp in a breath, pulling back from the kiss. Clay's hot exhalations brushed over his mouth. Clay looked down and said something. Then he looked back up, and Ethan squinted to indicate he hadn't heard.

"You need to get off."

Laughing, Ethan eased back enough to unzip his shorts and shove them down enough to pull out his dick. He grunted as he gave himself a hard tug. "Fuck, I really do."

Then Clay's hand was on his. "Can I?"

Ethan nodded, easing back a few inches. Clay sucked in a breath as he wrapped his callused hand around Ethan and started moving it experimentally. Holding on to Clay's shoulder, Ethan whispered, "That feels so good. I love your hands. So rough and—" He could only groan as Clay jerked him harder. "Uh-huh," Ethan murmured. "Like that. Fuck, it's not going to take long."

And it didn't. Burying his face in Clay's neck, Ethan let himself go, the sweet pressure building until he shuddered and came, crying out against Clay's warm, freckled skin. "Oh, fuck, fuck," Ethan muttered, shaking as he released over Clay's hand. Ethan leaned against him fully, Clay still holding his softening dick. They both caught their breath for a few moments.

Then the baritone of Clay's voice reached Ethan's ears and rumbled through his chest.

"What happens now?"

Chapter Twelve

ETHAN LIFTED HIS head, his weight still heavy against Clay. Clay wasn't sure if he'd heard, so he asked again, "What happens now?"

"Well, I guess you could freak out about your first time with a guy and throw me out." Ethan laughed half-heartedly, and there was a spark of fear in his eyes now. Clay hated to see it and wanted to banish it forever.

Shaking his head, he let go of Ethan's cock and pulled him into a full hug. Ethan sighed against him and slipped his arms around Clay's back, holding on tight. The urge to comfort and protect him thrummed through Clay with each heartbeat. Clay's hand was sticky, but he couldn't bear to let go of Ethan long enough to wipe it off.

As soon as he'd extended the invite earlier for Ethan to stay, it had been inevitable. Despite the flare of panic, a strange calmness had taken over. He couldn't let Ethan disappear forever with-out...*knowing*. It was more than just figuring out whether Ethan fancied him as well—because Clay did fancy him, there was no escaping it. It was *knowing* what had been locked away, deep down where the sun couldn't reach.

Now that box was burst wide open, Clay standing there with another man in his arms and their pricks out, cum drying on his hand. And he wanted it. Wanted more. He cleared his throat and said, "I was doing a bunk before, when I gave ya the cold shoulder."

Ethan lifted his head and squinted. "You were what?"

"I was an arse. The last couple days of the tour. I'm sorry."

"It's okay." He ran a hand up and down Clay's back soothingly, resting their heads together.

Clay couldn't remember the last time he'd been held in such a way. He gave Sam a kiss and hug whenever he saw her after being away and then before he left, but nothing like this. And with Barb… It seemed a very long time ago, and they'd never been ones for big displays.

He wanted to just close his eyes and breathe in Ethan, but he owed him more. He pulled back so he could look Ethan in the eye and be sure he was heard.

"It wasn't anything to do with you. I mean, it *was*…" He laughed at himself, his face going hot. Ethan waited, rubbing little circles on Clay's waist with his hands. Clay's voice was hoarse. "It's strange to talk about this."

"You don't have to."

He did, though. "I've been in a bit of a tizzy the past few days. Every time I looked at you, I didn't know what to think." He grasped for the right words, coming up empty.

"Did I do something to upset you?"

Shame took hold of Clay, giving him a rough shake in its jaws. "No, mate. It was all down to me. I…" He snorted, dropping his head before forcing his chin back up so Ethan could hear him properly. "Makes no sense after what we just did that I'm embarrassed to tell ya. I had a wank and was thinking about you. Really knocked me back. Didn't expect anything like that."

Ethan's brows drew together for a moment, and then a wide grin lit up his face, dimpling his cheeks, his teeth bright. "You thought about me while you jerked off?"

"Yep. Kind of snuck up on me, and then…"

Ethan bit his lip and moaned softly. "That is so hot."

"Is it?" Clay couldn't deny he was pleased.

"Oh, yeah. Very, very hot." He lifted a hand and caressed Clay's beard, exploring, briefly leaning in to kiss and nuzzle him. "So then you freaked out and avoided me. I get it."

"It was a shit thing to do."

"It's okay. Thank you for telling me. I admit—" He broke off, rolling his eyes and shrugging. "I admit I was upset. I couldn't figure out what I'd done wrong. I thought maybe my raging crush on you was too obvious."

"You didn't do anything wrong. And it wasn't that obvious. I thought maybe, but I didn't really have a clue. You'll find that's a recurring theme. My kids'll tell you—" His stomach knotted with a surge of acid. "You're not much older than they are. And we're…" He waved a hand in the few inches between their chests.

"I know. But I'm a grown man. I know what I'm doing. I know what I want. We don't have to worry about anyone else right now, or what they might think."

Of course now it was all Clay could imagine—what the devil would Sam and Pete and Barb make of this? He shuddered, icy fear digging into him. He couldn't breathe, a horrible pressure in his chest as he pictured their disgust and disappointment and betrayal. *Will they hate me?*

"Hey, hey." Ethan took Clay's face between his hands. "Look at me. Don't freak out about anyone else right now. One step at a time. No one else matters right now but you and me. Here. Together. I'm here. You're not alone. Breathe."

Clay did, forcing his lungs to expand and contract, the drum of panic receding. He looked into Ethan's kind brown eyes and clung to his waist. Ethan kissed him softly. "It's just you and me here. Nothing else matters right now." He smiled briefly. "You know, when you wouldn't take my tip, I figured I'd *really* offended you."

Clay groaned, remembering how crushed Ethan had looked, holding out that envelope. He'd felt like such an arsehole. "I'd thought it was for the best, but seeing you looking so gutted, I couldn't bear it. You're smart and thoughtful and—" He had to suck in a breath. "And bloody nice to look at. You're a real corker, and I don't ever want you to be sad. To think that you might have been miserable because I was a coward was just too much. I'm so sorry."

His words hung there between them, and Ethan's eyes widened before his face went soft. His Adam's apple bobbed, and he whispered, "Thank you." Leaning in, he kissed Clay gently, his full lips warm and lovely.

Yet even though Ethan didn't have a beard, his face wasn't smooth like a woman's, the stubble there providing friction against Clay's beard. Kissing him, Clay knew he was kissing a man.

He. Was. Kissing. A. Man.

The words filled his mind, but sounded like a foreign language even as Ethan licked into Clay's mouth and Clay heard a moan. He also felt the vibration in his throat, which meant *he* was the one moaning. It was as if he were outside his body, marveling in wonder, yet more alive in every inch of him than he'd ever been.

When they separated to gulp in air, Ethan smiled crookedly. "I feel so good being with you. I never dreamed… But here we are."

"We are," Clay agreed. They *were*, and it was the strangest and most wonderful thing Clay could imagine. "I don't know what to make of it. This is all new. I don't understand where it's come from. But…" He had to suck in a breath. "It feels…true." Yet as soon as the words were out, doubt dug its rusty hooks into him. "I shouldn't be doing this, though." He fought down another burst of fear.

"Why not? We both want it. We're adults. I know it's hard to ignore the internalized homophobia that's probably shouting at you right now."

Clay mulled over the unfamiliar words. He knew what homophobia was of course, but had never thought of it as being "internalized."

Ethan added, "If there were no one else in the world—if it were just us, and you could do anything right now without being afraid, what would you want to do?"

Looking into Ethan's eyes, Clay ran his shaky hands over Ethan's sides and around his back. "Bugger, I'm getting your shirt sticky."

Ethan laughed. "I don't care." He asked again, "What would you want to do?"

Clay thought about how good it had felt to have Ethan pressed against him. He blurted, "I'd want to get our clothes off and see all of you." He barked out a laugh. "Don't reckon you'd be so keen on seeing me."

Ethan stared into Clay's eyes, holding his chin. "I am. You're so sexy." With his other hand, he rucked up Clay's shirt, slipping his hand underneath and caressing Clay's chest, sending ripples of pleasure over his skin, his nipples peaking. "I want you. I want to see you and touch you. Let's go to bed."

Clay nodded, his heart thudding. Excitement mingled with a shot of unease. "Are you keen to… You know. Do what fellas do together?" He'd never had anything stuck up his arse, and he wasn't sure he fancied it. Although as he pondered his prick inside Ethan, it twitched with interest.

"We don't have to do anything. We can just talk. I only want to be with you. Let's not rush."

"Right. Putting the cart before the horse." He exhaled in relief. *One step at a time.*

They pulled up their shorts, and as they made their way out of the kitchen and down the short hall, Clay didn't know where to look or what to do with his hands. He fidgeted with them, and Ethan grabbed one, giving it a reassuring squeeze before letting go.

Clay switched on the lamp beside his bed and made a sweep around with his arm. "Well, this is it. Not much." He flicked on the ceiling fan and gazed around nervously, imagining what Ethan was seeing.

Wood floor that was in need of some spit and polish, but the oval rug by the bed was clean, decorated with navy and green zigzags. The bed was a queen, a new one Clay had bought when they moved in, the old one he'd shared with Barb in the Curry sagging and overdue for replacement. The bed frame was a cheap job with no headboard.

The drapes over the window were navy, the walls painted the beige they'd been when he and Sam had arrived. There was a long dresser across from the foot of the bed, with odds and sods scattered on top. Not the neatest, but his clothes were folded inside the drawers and hanging in the closet, and he hadn't left any reeking socks hanging about, at least.

Ethan approached the dresser, and Clay laughed nervously. "Bit of a catch-all spot." There was some junk mail he'd been meaning to look over before ditching, an old paper he should have tossed in the bin, a pack of batteries he'd meant to return to the junk drawer in the kitchen, and a few framed pictures of the kids when they were youngsters.

Smiling absently, Ethan said, "It's great." He leaned in and gazed at the pictures of Sam and Pete, opened his mouth, but then closed it and straightened. Nodding to the framed picture over the dresser, he asked, "Where's this?"

Clay blinked at the shot of the sun sinking bright pink and orange over the red earth. "Ah, that's the Curry. Had that for years. It was a wedding present. Bit faded now. Frame could be nicer. Should probably get rid of it."

"It's gorgeous." Ethan turned back to him, smiling.

"Is that fan bothering you?" Clay craved the air on his fevered skin, and it was one of those fans that was meant to be quiet, but he wanted Ethan to be able to hear him.

"Nope. It feels great, and I don't hear anything." His face creased for a moment, as if he was concentrating on listening. "No, it's good." Then his gaze was caught by the other framed decoration in the room, which hung over the bed. He crawled onto the mattress, walking toward it on his knees across the thin blue bedspread. "Is Gilly in this? The namesake, I mean."

The sight of Ethan on his bed had Clay's lungs frozen for a moment. He coughed. "Uh, yeah. Third from the right there. That's the winning team from the Ashes in 2002-2003. The kids gave it to me for my birthday the next year. It's old too, and just a cheap thing. I should take it down."

He shoved his hands in his pockets, then realized he'd only hauled up his shorts enough to walk, and now he'd pushed them down his thighs again. He yanked them back up, wishing he'd quit being such a wally.

Ethan looked at him and grinned. "Stop apologizing. Your room's great." He looked back at the cricket team. "And I get it—baggy green is the hats, right?"

Clay blinked. "Yeah, that's right." He must've said it earlier and should've known that Ethan wouldn't understand.

Then Ethan pulled his shirt over his head, revealing his bare chest. There was a bit of dark hair scattered across his pecs, and his nipples were small and red. He was slim, but still had muscles. Clay stared, his throat dry and mind spinning.

Of course he has muscles, you drongo. All people have muscles!

But the definition of Ethan's made Clay's hands itch to touch. All he could do was try to breathe as Ethan shoved down his shorts—all the layers—and wriggled them free, tossing them to the floor before sitting back on his heels, watching Clay the whole time.

His cock was cut and thick, a thin trail of dark hair leading down to it. Clay didn't know where to look—that cock, or Ethan's nipples, or the movement of his throat, or the flash of dimples in his cheeks, or his lovely eyes, or the hair on his thighs that Clay wanted to touch and feel against him.

With a sly smile, Ethan crooked a finger, and Clay felt like his whole world was at the mercy of that one digit. "C'mere."

Feet obeying, Clay came to stand at the side of the bed. Ethan knee-walked closer, his prick bobbing and swelling. He reached out, and Clay's heart thundered, but Ethan only took hold of Clay's wrist and eased off his watch, resting it on the side table by the corked coaster with an image of Perth's black swans on it, the set a gift one Christmas from Jen.

Tension took hold. No, this wasn't the time to think about his sister, or Barb, or the kids. Of course it was like trying not to think of a pink elephant, and worry tumbled through his mind.

"Hey, hey." Ethan rubbed circles on Clay's hips, gazing up at him. "In here, it's only you and me. No judgment."

Clay nodded, exhaling. His ribs were going to be sore with all the gasping he was doing, because the next moment he couldn't breathe as Ethan pulled up Clay's shirt and leaned down to tease his bellybutton, flicking it with his tongue. There were a few moles dotted on Ethan's shoulders, and Clay touched one, leaning on Ethan so he didn't topple over as he shook with pleasure.

Ripping off his shirt and tossing it blindly, Clay stood there, trying to keep his knees from knocking. Ethan stared up at him as he licked a path up Clay's stomach. Clay squirmed, both from enjoyment and embarrassment. "Not as trim as I once was."

Ethan frowned. "Can you please repeat that?"

Now Clay felt even more foolish. "I said I'm not as trim as I once was."

The puff of Ethan's sigh tickled Clay's skin. "There's nothing wrong with your body. You're fucking *hot.* He ran his hands around Clay's middle and up his back. "You're strong and sexy." Rising up on his knees, he rubbed his cheek over Clay's pecs. "I love your hairy chest," he murmured before playfully biting at a nipple, then kissing and sucking it.

"Oh!" Clay's knees almost buckled at the intense wave of pleasure. Ethan was latched on, fingers teasing and tweaking the other nipple, and it was like fireworks were shooting right to his balls.

Grinning, Ethan glanced up, grazing the other nipple with his teeth now. "You like that?"

"Uh-huh." Clay nodded vigorously.

"Do you want to lay down with me?" He tugged questioningly at Clay's shorts, only pulling them down an inch.

Clay could only nod again, stripping off and standing naked as Ethan watched hungrily and scooted back to make room. Part of him wanted to switch off the light and hide under the covers, but no. He wanted to see Ethan, those long legs stretching out, his prick curving against his thigh.

Somehow, Ethan truly did seem keen on getting an eyeful of Clay as well, so Clay got down beside him. On their sides, they cuddled close, touching each other and kissing. Exploring.

Clay had never kissed Barb like this. Never for such a long time, for no other reason than the pleasure of it, to taste each other.

He shoved her from his mind, choking down the swell of terror, remembering what Ethan had said as he nuzzled Ethan's neck, sucking a kiss on there, loving the faint rasp of stubble under his lips. Clay had never put his hands on another bloke, and it was different in ways that excited him. The angles and firmness and hair, but then the round swell of his arse.

Jesus, Clay could touch it all day. It was only the two of them, and the rest of the world could bugger off. Maybe it was wrong, but it felt too bloody good to stop.

Ethan was half-hard, but didn't seem in a hurry to get off. He pushed himself up to sitting, his hair tousled. "I need a drink. Do you want some water?" He looked at Clay, waiting for his response.

"Forget the water. I'll take another coldie."

A smile tugged at Ethan's full lips. Lips that Clay had kissed. Lips that had been wrapped around his cock. Ethan said "I'm going to assume that whatever you just said means you want another beer."

Clay nodded, smiling himself as he watched Ethan get to his feet. Clay looked him over again from head to toe as he walked around the bed to the door. His skin was pale, his long legs and round arse especially, his arms and neck slightly tanned. There seemed to be a mole on the back of one shoulder by the blade. He was *naked* in Clay's bedroom, and it seemed like the most natural thing in the world.

There was a mirror inside the closet door on the far wall, but Clay didn't get up to look and see who he'd find staring back. Instead, he gathered the scattered pillows—he'd always kept four on his bed even though no one had slept with him since he'd moved to Sydney—and propped them against the wall, leaning back as Ethan returned with his glass of water and Clay's stubby.

Clay squeezed the foam holder as he gulped. "Ahh. That hits the spot."

Ethan sat back against his pillows as well. He drank some water and put the glass on the side table. Their arms and thighs brushed as he settled in beside Clay. The ceiling fan beat a cool breeze on their sweaty skin.

"Still with me?" Ethan asked. "Not panicking or anything?"

They were sitting there naked as the day they were born, and while Clay couldn't quite believe it yet, the last thing he felt was panic. He shook his head. "It's a strange thing."

Ethan's hand was warm on Clay's thigh. "Sorry, can you say

that again?"

"Don't be sorry. I was mumbling." He angled his face toward Ethan. "It's a strange thing, that I'm not panicking. There have been a few moments, don't get me wrong. But it feels…right. Even after years with Barb, it was…" Coming up blank for the right words, he reached up and smoothed down a piece of Ethan's hair sticking up wildly. "Nothing like this."

Ethan nodded. "You said you guys weren't very…adventurous?"

He shifted uncomfortably. "I reckon not."

"Not even in the beginning?"

"I don't know. It was a long time ago now." He thought back to those hot, dry summer nights, hanging down by the river with the mob from school. "When she decided we should date, I didn't argue. She was a nice girl, and we'd always been friendly since we were ankle biters. So then it was how it was. She was my girl-friend, and after we finished school, I was working full time with my dad, and she worked in a chemist. I reckoned she'd be a good wife, so I asked her to marry me. Most of my mates were getting hitched, and it was the thing to do. She was a good wife. We never argued much. Just went along."

"Mmm." Ethan traced his finger over Clay's thigh, sending a tingle through him. "So it wasn't ever really passionate?"

Clay knew the answer, but it felt disloyal to say it out loud. Still, it was the time now, if ever it was. "Nah. It wasn't bad, but growing up, my mates used to go on and on about girls. I never really understood the fuss." He quickly added, "Not that there was anything wrong with Barb. She's always been an attractive woman."

"Of course there's nothing wrong with her," Ethan soothed, flattening his palm. "There's nothing wrong with you either."

"Some might argue with that, mate."

"Fuck them." Ethan's tone meant business. "There's nothing

wrong with what we did."

"Even if it means I'm…" Clay couldn't seem to say the word.

"Whether you or anyone else is gay, straight, bi, trans, pan, demi, ace—it doesn't matter. There's nothing wrong with you. Or what we did together."

"Strewth, I don't know what half those things mean."

Ethan smiled. "It's okay. We can have a class in sexual identity 101 later."

"'Sexual identity,'" Clay repeated, rolling the unfamiliar words around his tongue. "Where I'm from, that's not a topic of conversation, I can tell you that much." A fleeting image of Tony Taylor bent over an engine, grease smudged on his fingers, filled his mind before he banished it.

Ethan said, "Yeah, I think a lot of people make assumptions. Not only about others, but themselves."

"Huh." Clay sipped his drink, the cold beer going down easy.

"Have you been attracted to men before?"

An instant denial sprang up, but Clay bit it back. "Honestly, I'm not sure. Sounds ridiculous, I know. How would I not be sure?"

"Years of hardcore sexual repression probably does the trick." Ethan gave him a smile, running his hand over Clay's right leg, those long fingers caressing his inner thigh. "It's amazing what our brains can do. If you locked it down a long time ago, you could just deny it to yourself. You wouldn't even have to work all that hard once it became a habit. You know what I mean? Like, when I started to go deaf? I convinced myself it was a million other things. It took me way too long to finally get it checked out." He hesitated. "Did you… When we first met, were you attracted to me?"

"I don't think so." Had that really been just a week or so ago? It didn't seem possible. "But then I got to know you. We started chatting, and… I wanted to see more of you. Started thinking about you all the time, just about." He snaked his right arm around Ethan's shoulders, loving the feel of him close.

Ethan leaned in and kissed him, a slow, wet slide of their lips and tongues. When he pulled back, he said, "You're seeing all of me now."

"That I am."

Nuzzling Clay's cheek, Ethan murmured, "Do you like what you see?"

"You know I do, mate."

Ethan smiled against Clay's face, pressing a kiss to his bearded cheek before sitting straight again. He was still cuddled under Clay's arm, and there was no place else in the world Clay wanted him to be.

"Maybe you're demi," Ethan mused.

Clay tried to figure out what it meant, but he was pretty sure "demi" meant "half," and that didn't help much. "What's that one, then?"

"Oh, demisexual is when you really only feel sexual attraction to someone when you form an emotional connection."

"Huh." Clay wasn't sure what to make of that.

"You don't need to figure it all out right this second. One step at a time." Ethan shifted onto his hip, sliding his right leg over Clay's and stroking his hand over Clay's chest and belly. He leaned in and bit at Clay's earlobe, his breath hot. "Have I mentioned how sexy you are? That night on Fraser Island? As soon as I got in my room, I had to jerk off. You made me so hard."

And apparently he was making Ethan fully hard again now, the press of his cock hot against Clay's side. *Ah, to be so young again.* Yet even in his youth, Clay couldn't remember feeling this excited, this turned on. His prick was coming to life, and he moaned when Ethan brushed over it with his hand. But then Ethan took *himself* in hand, and seeing it sent shivers through Clay.

"I was barely inside—still standing by the door. And I jerked myself, imagining you were there. Fucking me."

It sent a fiery thrill through him, and Clay shifted so he could get a good grasp on Ethan, eager to take over. Wrapping his hand around Ethan's prick again, he shuddered with a powerful wave of *want*. It was more than just lust—it felt so damn *right* in a way he'd never expected. He squeezed lightly, and Ethan moaned and rolled his hips, biting his lip.

"Feels amazing," Ethan murmured.

It truly did. To know that Ethan wanted him—to have the proof of it throbbing in his hand—had Clay shaking like a schoolboy. He'd never touched another bloke before this night, not even as a kid messing around. But now it was as if he could feel Ethan's heartbeat under his fingers, real and all for *him*. And there was only them in their world for two. No one to say it was wrong. His lungs constricted.

It was like coming home.

"Hey, it's okay." Ethan cupped Clay's face, his forehead creased. "You don't have to do anything."

"I do," Clay croaked, and he could tell Ethan hadn't understood him. He cleared his throat and grasped Ethan's prick harder, giving it a stroke. Ethan gasped, his eyes flickering shut. Clay waited until their eyes met again. Very clearly, he said, "I do. I have to do this. I want to do it all."

"Okay. You want to suck me?" He quickly added, "You don't have to."

Clay felt like he was standing on the edge of the old abandoned uranium mine near the Curry, his mates daring him to jump into the vibrantly blue-green water filling the crater. Did he want to put another bloke's willy in his mouth? The gnawing urge to *know* rose up.

He jumped.

Nodding, he wondered the best way to do it in a bed. He

didn't need to wonder long as Ethan spread his thighs and urged Clay to kneel between his long legs. Gasping in a breath, Clay ducked his head and put the tip in his mouth before he could chicken out, holding the base the way Ethan had done.

Ethan groaned as Clay sucked tentatively on the top couple inches. He was doing it. He was an official cocksucker. Inhaling through his nose, Clay lowered his head, sucking harder and taking more of Ethan into his mouth.

Ethan cried out. "Oh, fuck. That's so good. Just like that. Whatever comes naturally."

A voice hissed that it shouldn't be natural, but it *was*. He couldn't deny the release somewhere deep inside, a closed fist that was finally loosening its grip. Ethan was hard and throbbing in his mouth as Clay tried to take more of him, spit gathering. The flesh was a little spongey and tasted of sweat and salt and *Ethan*.

Just as when he'd held the power of Ethan's arousal in his hand, tasting the drops on the tip and feeling the life of him inside his mouth—knowing that Ethan felt this desire for *Clay*—was profound in a way he couldn't understand. Couldn't deny.

He licked sloppily, probably doing it all wrong, but Ethan didn't seem to mind. He ran his fingers through Clay's hair, tugging and relaxing, never too sharp. He muttered, "You're doing so good," and it thrilled Clay to hear it.

Trying to take him deeper, Clay choked and had to pull off. Ethan caressed his head and said, "It's okay. Just go as far as you can. It feels amazing. I love everything you're doing."

So Clay explored more with his tongue, his jaw aching a bit from having his mouth too full. He pressed at Ethan's thighs, opening him up, loving the scratch of leg hair under his palms.

"Oh, fuck. Can you lick my balls?"

Hearing the words sent lust spiraling through Clay. He'd never heard such outrageous things being said outside of porn, but he'd never been much for it and had never really understood why.

Maybe this is a hint, you wally.

"Yeah, lower. That's it." Ethan moaned, his head thrown back. With his long legs splayed and mouth open, he looked absolutely shameless—and beautiful. It wasn't a word Clay had associated with men before, but it was the only thing that came to mind as Ethan came, his balls slipping from Clay's mouth as they emptied.

He was nothing but beautiful stretched out with the white drops of his semen sprayed over his belly. Clay was half-hard again himself, although he knew he wouldn't be able to come again so quickly. As if reading his mind, Ethan sat up and gave Clay a long pull, kissing him slow and dirty before whispering, "We have all night."

Chapter Thirteen

ETHAN WOKE ALONE. Blinking around Clay's room, memories turned on in his mind like light switches—*flick, flick, flick, flick.* Joy and lust whipped through him, his morning wood eager for attention. The skin of his belly was tight with crusted jizz— whose, he wasn't sure. He scratched at it with a fingernail, grinning to himself.

He and Clay had kissed and kissed and kissed some more. They'd rubbed against each other, touching all over, and Clay had gotten off again. He'd seemed absolutely dazed with pleasure, and they'd finally fallen asleep curled up together, fidgeting and laughing before drifting off with Ethan as the little spoon.

They'd only just met, yet Ethan had felt so safe and warm in his arms. A little hot, actually, but he hadn't wanted to do anything to push Clay away—anything that might have been misconstrued. Although Clay was gone now, that side of the bed cool.

A knot circled Ethan's intestines and pulled tight. In the cold light of day—the yellow light of dawn shining through the gap in the curtains—would Clay regret it? Have the freak-out Ethan had been afraid of? Maybe the spell was broken, and he was sorry he'd ever asked Ethan to stay. Even though he'd been the one to invite him! It wasn't like Ethan had angled for an invite.

And Clay was the one who'd asked him about kissing. Ethan hadn't hit on him! He'd made sure over and over that Clay was consenting and was into it, and boy, had he been into it. So if he was freaking out now, that was on him.

It was fine. Ethan had barely even unpacked. He stared at his suitcases in the corner of the room. Clay had gone to get them last night so Ethan could brush his teeth and get whatever he needed, although he'd ended up sleeping naked anyway, same as Clay.

But if Clay wanted him gone, it would only take a few minutes. Maybe he should just go now and not wait for Clay to throw him out.

Stop freaking out when you haven't even talked to him! Maybe—

He stared at Clay, who'd appeared in the doorway of the bedroom. He wore shorts, flip-flops, and a black tank top that showed off his freckled arms and shoulders, a tuft of dark copper hair peeking out on his chest. For a frozen heartbeat that stretched out, their eyes met.

Then a smile brightened Clay's face, the wrinkles around his eyes crinkling, and relief flooded Ethan. Clay hadn't run away, and he was positively *beaming*. Knowing what a massive leap Clay had taken the night before—and how scary it must have been—to see him the morning after looking so peaceful and satisfied, not panicked and denying what they'd shared, Ethan was so fucking proud of him.

Clay said something, and from reading his lips, Ethan thought it was possibly "G'day."

He replied, "Good morning!" and realized from Clay's little wince that he was shouting. "Sorry. Let me get my hearing aids in." Still under the thin comforter, he stretched over for one, sitting up and putting it in, cringing at how sore his inner ear was. He'd worn his hearing aids much later than usual, determined to hear as many of Clay's gasps and moans as possible.

From the corner of his eye, he saw Clay hold up a hand, then gaze around the room. He hurried to his little suitcase and put it on its back to unzip. After rooting around, he came back with a pad of paper and pen. He flipped pages and wrote before handing the pad to Ethan.

It looks like it hurts? No need to put them in yet if you don't want to. I'm going to Macca's. What do you fancy?

Along with the flush of pleasure that Clay was concerned about his discomfort—Michael had often gotten annoyed and impatient when Ethan shouted without realizing—Ethan puzzled over what "Macca's" might be. A coffee place? Cafe? Seemed likely it was to do with breakfast. Trying to modulate the volume, he asked, "What do they have there?"

Clay's brow creased and he came to sit on the side of the bed and write on the pad again.

Reckon it's the same things they have in America. Egg McMuffins and such.

"Oh! McDonald's. Got it." They laughed, and Ethan wrote:
Bacon and egg McMuffin and a hash brown, please.
Clay responded: *Coffee black?*

Ethan hesitated, remembering that morning on Mission Beach, when he'd said he liked it black because he hadn't wanted to seem fussy since Clay was being so sweet to share with him. It had been a silly little white lie, but now he felt stupidly trapped in it, anxiety rising, his shoulders going tight. Frowning, Clay gave him a quizzical look.

Face going hot, Ethan scribbled:

Actually, I usually take a cream and half a sugar. When we were on the beach, I didn't want to seem... I don't know, ungrateful or something. So I just said I like it black.

Clay read the note, his brow furrowed even more. He gave Ethan a confused smile and wrote:

Mate, you can have your coffee however you like.

Ethan tried not to shout. "It's not like I can't drink it black!" It was such a dumb thing, but he felt so self-conscious and wound up that he'd fibbed in the first place. *Will Clay think I'm a liar? Will he think this is something I do all the time? Maybe he won't trust me. Maybe—*

Clay had written another note as Ethan's mind had spun:

I'll bring the sugar packet back so you can get it just the way you like.

He'd drawn a little smiley face after that sentence, and Ethan could only pull him near for a long, hard kiss. Clay's beard scratched pleasantly. Part of Ethan wanted to yank him closer and forget breakfast, but his stomach disagreed. Clay pulled back, running the tips of his blunt fingers over Ethan's sensitive cheek, which Ethan suspected was red with beard burn.

He gave Clay a smile and wave as he left. Ethan knew he wound himself up over nothing sometimes, but at least Clay didn't seem to mind. Ethan was still holding the notepad, which had used pages bent back over the top. He peeled them back, realizing with a shot of adrenaline and delight that this was the notepad from Fraser Island. That Clay had actually kept it, and it hadn't gone in the trash along with their pizza-stained napkins and empty beer bottles.

Clay had *kept* it.

Ethan re-read their conversation from that night, laughing in places and grinning to himself. Clay was his very favorite person in the whole world. Yes, Ethan recognized that Clay was a relative stranger, and that this was likely the glow of infatuation, and he had to be realistic about what was happening between them. It was a vacation fling. Clay experimenting with his sexuality. A rebound for Ethan after having his heart broken. Just temporary.

He duly noted each warning, yet his heart *sang*.

In the bathroom, Ethan cleaned up and pulled on his gray boxer-briefs—and discovered with delight that his chin and cheeks were indeed faint red with beard burn. He padded into the kitchen, scratching his chest and yawning, the tile worn and warm under his feet. He poured a glass of water from the pitcher in the fridge.

As he ran the tap to refill the Brita, he heard a dull thud. Was it the front door already? It hadn't taken Clay long at all. Ethan turned off the water and turned—to find a young woman standing in the kitchen archway and a mid-sized shaggy dog bounding toward him.

Gripping the plastic handle of the pitcher, he stood frozen as a thunderous expression darkened Samantha's round face.

Oh fuck. Fuuuuuuuuck!

She wore capri pants and flip-flops, a white tank top showing off her golden tan, blond waves falling around her freckled shoulders. Gilly was nudging him, looking for pets and attention, tongue wagging, but before Ethan could do or say anything, he heard the faint murmur of Samantha's words as she spat out a furious tirade, fists clenched at her sides, speaking far too quickly to read her lips.

Ethan's heart pounded as he stood there holding the pitcher like some kind of shield. She'd called Gilly back to her, and the dog could clearly sense something was wrong, barking now and taking a protective stance in front of her.

Samantha stopped talking, watching Ethan with raised eyebrows. This was the part where he was supposed to say something, but his throat was bone dry, and all he could do was sputter. She stared at him. Her next words he could read clearly since random people had asked him the same question over the years.

"Are you fucking deaf?"

With a jolt, he nodded and hoped he wasn't shouting. "Yes. I just—I need my hearing aids. I'll get dressed and…" He put the pitcher on the counter, feeling even more exposed and ridiculous standing there in Samantha Kelly's kitchen in his underwear. Belatedly, he added, "I know your dad. I didn't break in or anything."

She was still clearly pissed, face creased and nostrils flaring, shaking her head in apparent confusion. And since she was blocking the only way out of the kitchen, he had to approach. She jerked back, fists clenching again and eyes narrowed. Gilly's barking sounded like muffled claps, sharp and confused.

"I swear, I'm a friend of your dad's." He raised his hands and pointed to his ears. "I need to get my hearing aids. I can't understand you otherwise. Okay?"

Warily, she backed up into the short hall to the foyer, and he scurried away from her down the other hall to the bedrooms. Yanking on his jeans and a tee, he took shallow breaths, his heart thudding dully. He put in his hearing aids and turned them on, ignoring the soreness in his ears, then hurried back out. Skidding to a stop, he stared.

Samantha stood at the junction of the hallways with her phone in hand and Gilly by her feet, agitated but mercifully not barking. She gave him a steely look. "Can you hear me now?"

Ethan nodded, swallowing hard.

"I've only got one more number to press before I tell the police to come around." She backed up. "Now get out here and start talking."

Ethan did as he was told, and they faced off in the foyer next to the living room. The front door was open behind her. She said, "*Mumble* fuck are you and where's my dad? What are you *mumble mumble.*"

"I'm Ethan Robinson. He went to get breakfast." Those questions were easy enough. He didn't want to lie about why he was there, but it didn't feel right outing Clay to his daughter either. He guessed at what her last question was. "I, um, needed a place to stay, and your dad was helping me out. I'm visiting from the States. He was the driver on the tour I just took." Those parts were true as well.

"You're crashing on our couch?"

Ethan grabbed for the explanation like a life raft. "Right, exactly. My Airbnb canceled at the last minute and he was doing me a favor. I'm so sorry to frighten you. He wasn't expecting you back yet? He said you were down the coast? Have you ever been to the Great Ocean Road? It looks so beautiful there. I've always wanted to go. See the Twelve Apostles and everything. Although I heard there are fewer now because of erosion and there were never actually twelve to begin with?" *Stop fucking talking.*

She stared at him, her face still creased in confusion, but perhaps less fury now? It was hard to say. When she spoke, her tone was definitely calmer. "If you're sleeping on the couch, why were your clothes and stuff in my dad's room?" She glanced into the living room to her left. "And why isn't there a blanket and pillow out here?"

"I… Uh…" *Shit, shit, FUCKBALLS.*

"What the fuck is going on?" She shook her head, stiffening with another bolt of anger, her jaw clenching. "Did you do something to my dad? I'm calling the cops." Gilly started barking, and Ethan cringed at the loudness.

"No, please don't!" He held out his hands. "I didn't do anything to your dad! I'm telling the truth." Or at least part of it. "He'll be back any minute. He went to McDonald's."

And thank *fuck*, Clay appeared on the little stone walkway leading to the house from the sidewalk. He jogged the last few steps and filled the open doorway, holding a paper bag in one hand and a cardboard tray with two coffees in the other. His smile froze on his face. "Sam? What are you doing here?" Gilly raced forward, tongue wagging as he butted against Clay's legs.

"Dad, what the fuck's going on?" She pointed at Ethan, her finger jabbing the air. "Who is this?"

Clay's chest rose and fell rapidly, his eyes wide as he looked between Ethan and his daughter. "He's…" Clay opened and closed his mouth like a fish on a hook, Gilly circling him and rubbing against his legs.

Sam huffed. "What's the big secret?" As soon as the words were out of her mouth, she blinked. "Wait…" She shook her head again, closing her eyes briefly and raising her hands. "You're not…" She laughed hesitantly.

Ethan held his breath, afraid to move a muscle as Sam glanced between Ethan and Clay as if she was watching a tennis match. It was her turn to open and close her mouth, the words apparently not coming, her brain clearly working a mile a minute as it processed the evidence.

Gilly whined and barked, and Sam impatiently grabbed his collar and shepherded him to the back door and out into the little yard, closing the door behind her as she came back in, the continued barking mercifully muffled now.

Sam looked between Ethan and Clay again dubiously and said something Ethan couldn't make out.

Clay cleared his throat. "Well, we met on the last tour down the coast. Struck up a friendship. You're always saying I need more mates."

"Uh-huh." She laughed nervously. Incredulously. "Dad, is this… Are you… *Mumble mumble?*"

Still gripping the takeout, Clay stood there unmoving and eyes wide. Ethan's heart pounded, and he wanted to ask Sam to repeat herself, but decided staying silent was the wiser course of action. He assumed she'd asked if they were fucking given Clay's ashen face, the normal ruddiness drained away.

Then Clay barked out a laugh. "No! Bloody hell, what kind of crazy idea is that? He needed a place to sleep. That's all. You know I'm not—" He broke off, laughing dismissively, as if he couldn't imagine anything more ridiculous.

Even though Ethan knew Clay was terrified and in shock facing his daughter, that he was still trying to process what was happening, that he still needed to come to terms with his feelings and his very identity and was *so* not ready for this—the denial *hurt.* It cut deeper than it had any right to.

And Clay had to know it, his wild gaze cutting to Ethan. He opened his mouth again, then closed it.

"I should go," Ethan said, dropping his head, his words sounding distant, chest hollow and limbs feeling strangely light, like they weren't really attached anymore. He took a couple steps, but Clay was blocking the main hallway. And shit, Ethan needed his stuff, but in that moment he just wanted to escape before he started crying like a pathetic loser.

Still holding the McDonald's bag and drink tray, Clay stepped aside, but then moved back. "No!" Ethan lifted his head to meet Clay's sorrowful gaze. Clay shook his head. "I'm sorry." He looked to his daughter, and Ethan backed up a pace and turned to face her too. Taking a deep breath, Clay simply nodded at her, his expression achingly vulnerable.

Samantha stared at them, her brow furrowing. "Dad, what the…? You and this guy?"

Clay nodded again. "Fair dinkum."

"Well, fuck me sideways!" Her eyebrows practically disappeared into her golden hairline. She said something else Ethan didn't get over Gilly's sudden barking beyond the door.

"I'm sorry," Clay croaked, and Ethan choked down another swell of hurt. He didn't want Clay to be sorry, even though he knew he shouldn't take it personally.

The silence stretched out, broken only by Gilly's demands to be let back in.

Should I leave after all? Will I make it worse by leaving? Or worse by staying? Why aren't they saying anything else?

Ethan blurted, "Sorry. I should probably just…go?" Sam and Clay tore their gaze away from each other and focused on him.

Sam put her hands on her hips, words flying. "*Mumble mumble,* fuck *mumble?*"

He'd only picked up the "fuck" from the familiar shape her

lips made. "Um, sorry. I didn't catch all that. If you could speak more slowly, please? It's a huge pain repeating yourself over and over, I know."

"There's nothing for you to be sorry about," Clay said, his voice low and clear, sending a shiver of warmth down Ethan's spine despite everything.

Sam blew out a deep breath and spoke more calmly. "Can you hear me now?" At Ethan's nod, she went on, articulating her words carefully as if speaking to a toddler. "I said, if you and my dad are shagging, why the fuck are you running out on him? Are you spineless or what?"

"Oi!" Clay disappeared for a moment into the living room, then came back without the bag and drinks, standing next to Ethan now. "He's not spineless, and he's not stupid, either. You can talk clearly without treating him like he's slow. He's damn well not."

She opened her mouth, then snapped it shut, her jaw tight. After another deep breath, she said, "Sorry. This is all just…" She waved her hands. "Not what I was expecting this morning."

Clay's indignation evaporated, the guilty lines on his face deepening. "I'm sorry, love. I know it must be a real shock." He dropped his head and said something else Ethan didn't pick up.

"Disappointment? No." Sam shook her head incredulously. "I'll tell you it's definitely a shock." She rubbed her face. "Trying to wrap my head around it. Been a long night, and I didn't see this coming."

Clay nodded, and Ethan kept quiet, darting his gaze between them.

Sam shook her head again. "You're a real dark horse, aren't you? Thought I knew you inside and out. Yeah, I'm surprised. I'm not *disappointed*, and you don't have to be sorry. I just wish you'd've told me. I would have stopped nagging you to find a new woman if I'd known it was a bloke you were after. Saved us both a lot of strife.”

A laugh bubbled up out of Ethan, coming out in a nervous rush before he could clamp down on it. Sam and Clay stared at him, and then at each other. Matching grins creased their faces, and it was like a wave breaking on the sand as they laughed too, uncertain and ragged.

“Well. I reckon we’ve got a few things to chat about.” Sam turned to Ethan and stuck out her hand. “I’m Samantha Kelly, but everyone calls me Sam. Except my mum when she’s aggro.”

“Hi. Ethan Robinson.” He shook her hand. Unsurprisingly, her grip was firm. “It’s great to meet you.”

“It’s blowing my mind to meet you.” Her phone was still in her hand, and it rang, making her jump. “Let me just…” She swiped to answer. “Hi. Yep, I’m on my way. The doc fit you in? All right.” There were a few moments of silence. “Babe, it’ll be fine.” She rolled her eyes at Clay and turned and walked a few steps, the rest of her words a mess to Ethan.

When she hung up, she turned around. “Jase took a fall last night and knocked out his front tooth. Wasn’t even on his bike, the wally. I had to wait until I sobered up to drive back to the city for a dentist with emergency service. Going to cost a fortune, but hopefully Jase’s insurance *mumble mumble.* He’s been whinging nonstop.” She winced. “He did bang up his mouth on a rock pretty good, to be fair. *Mumble.* I just came home after I dropped him to get Gilly fed.”

Apparently Gilly heard this, because he started barking enthusiastically beyond the door. Ethan’s shoulders crept up, and he fiddled with his hearing aids. Clay touched his arm briefly—for barely a nanosecond—and nodded toward the living room, away from the barking.

Sam followed. “I’ll be back *mumble,* assuming the patient’s bucked up.” Ethan thought maybe she’d said “this arvo.” She gave Ethan a hesitant smile, and then walked a few steps to Clay, throwing her arms around his neck. She was petite, and Clay hugged her back, lifting her clean off her feet.

Which was incredibly sexy, but Ethan shut down the train of thought about how strong and protective Clay was. How tender and—

Focus, for fuck's sake.

Sam said something to Clay that Ethan didn't hear, and then turned to go. She spun back around and glared at the McDonald's takeout sitting on the coffee table. She shook her head at Clay with clear disapproval before giving Ethan an awkward wave and leaving.

Now it was Ethan and Clay alone again, but in a whole new world. Ethan was terrified to ask, but there was nothing else to do.

"What happens now?"

Chapter Fourteen

ETHAN STOOD A few feet away, and they stared at each other. After the surprising—shocking, really—ease Clay had felt since he'd woken with Ethan sprawled on his belly beside him, now it was painfully awkward. He was half convinced he'd wake up alone now and this would all be gone in a sleepy blink.

He didn't know what to think or say, so he blurted, "Reckon we should eat our brekkie before it gets too cold. Oh, let me get Gilly sorted. Go ahead and start."

Ethan nodded, and Clay hurried to let Gilly in and give him some love and food, refilling his water dish as well. Once Gilly was wolfing down his kibble, Clay returned to the living room.

Perching on the near end of the couch, Ethan hadn't touched the Macca's. He smiled at Clay anxiously, and Clay moved to sit beside him, leaving the middle cushion between them, a strange buzzing in his head and chest. At least it didn't seem like Ethan was going to do a runner at the moment.

Clay rummaged in the paper bag, eager for any kind of distraction. He pulled out his sausage McMuffin and hash brown, then slid the bag to the left toward Ethan. Then he put the coffee with the creamer on the table in front of Ethan, almost spilling both cups as he yanked one too hard from the cardboard holder. "The sugar packet's in the bag."

"Great. Thanks." Ethan gave him a half-hearted smile.

It was surreal was what it was. Clay unwrapped his sandwich and took a huge bite, filling his mouth. As he chewed, his brain tried to catch up with it all. When he'd woken in bed with Ethan breathing heavily beside him, his full pink lips parted and brown hair askew, Clay had waited for the panic to set it.

Except it hadn't.

Flushing from head to toe, he'd remembered all the things they'd done together, and he'd been happier than he could imagine possible. Peaceful. Satisfied. *Thrilled.* He'd done it. He'd done the thing he'd been thinking about since Fraser Island. He'd kissed Ethan and touched him all over, and it had been marvelous. Clay honestly hadn't realized sex could be like that.

And he wanted more of it, he couldn't deny it. Didn't *want* to deny it. From the corner of his eye, Clay glanced at Ethan as he used a plastic stick to stir the sugar into his coffee. Clay wanted more of Ethan. It was crazy, though. Wasn't it? Aside from being a bloke, Ethan was too young. Only a few years older than Sam and Pete.

A fresh spike of dread hooked into him. Sam had been there. She'd been standing right there, and she'd seen him and Ethan together, and he'd had to answer her incredulous questions honestly because aside from the momentary lapse that morning when he'd denied it, he'd never lied to her about anything that counted. (Fibs about Santa Claus being real, eating Maccas, and messaging women on dating sites didn't count.)

What he and Ethan had done counted.

Clay bit into his hash brown in the silence. Part of him still couldn't believe he'd done any of it. But that urge to *know* had clawed at him, and he didn't regret it. Couldn't. Even after seeing Sam's sweet, pretty face so stunned.

But she was a good girl. Always had been. For some reason or other, his brain spewed up a memory of one of her primary school report cards.

Samantha is friendly and kind to all students. She always speaks up for her classmate Tom if he is teased on the playground. As you know, this has at times taken an aggressive turn, but we can't fault Samantha for her compassion.

It had gone on to say that of course they didn't condone violence, referring to the time Sam had given a bully a swift kick below the belt. Tom had Down syndrome, and Clay had never understood how some of the other kids could be so cruel to the poor lad. He supposed that was kids for you. People, really. Some of them were cruel arseholes their whole lives.

But he'd always remembered the teacher's words with pride. His Sam would always kick bullies and tell off anyone who needed it. She'd never been afraid to speak her mind. And she'd hugged him so tightly before she left. As Clay and Ethan ate in silence, Clay thought of how she'd smelled faintly of vanilla and barbecue smoke, and how she'd whispered in his ear.

"Love you, Dad. No matter what."

He felt another rush of relief now. Yes, she'd have his back the way she had when Barb had announced she was leaving. Clay had been at such a loss, and Sam had made the plan for him to move down to Sydney. Said she was tired of living on campus, and renting a house together would be perfect. Even though the last thing most kids her age wanted to do was live with their old man instead of their mates. Pete had been bumming around the New Zealand ski hills and had probably been relieved to be off the hook.

What would Pete think about his dad being a…a whatever he was? And Barb? Clay couldn't even imagine what Barb would think. His gut tightened.

"Thanks for breakfast."

Clay yanked his mind back to the couch and Ethan barely an arm's length away. "Of course," he said before gulping down a mouthful of cooling coffee. Then he realized he'd been mumbling and not looking at Ethan. Taking a deep breath, he turned his head to face Ethan directly, repeating, "Of course." He added, "Sam gets on me for eating too much fried food, but sometimes it hits the spot."

Ethan smiled tentatively. "Totally." He folded his empty sandwich wrapper into a tiny square. "Are you okay?"

Clay had to laugh. "No bloody idea, mate. Reckon I'm in a bit of shock."

"I don't blame you. This is a lot to process. But Sam seems really cool. Whether or not you decide you're…" He seemed to be trying to find the right words. "Whether you're just experimenting, or you end up, you know…officially coming out? It seems like she'll be supportive. Which is awesome."

Coming out.

The words loomed large and strange. He took another gulp of coffee. "Feels like more than experimenting. All those names you were ticking off last night—gay, bisexual, demi, and the rest—it's all new to me. I mean, of course I knew there were gay people about. Just seems that it's much more open now."

"Right. It's being destigmatized. I think people are able to be more open about their identity than they could be in the past. There's still a long way to go, though."

Clay rolled the new word around in his mind, repeating it. "Destigmatized. Huh."

Gilly bounded into the living room, eager for attention. Clay and Ethan both scratched him for a minute, then Clay pointed to the doggy bed in the corner. Gilly obediently went and curled up.

Clay cleared his throat. "Anyway, growing up, all this stuff just wasn't talked about. At least not that I remember. I'd see Peter Allen on the telly sometimes when I was little. He was always flashy, but it just never crossed my mind. I remember my dad wasn't keen on him, but Mum loved that song 'Tenterfield Saddler.' She had the old record. It's a good one, that. Tugs on the heartstrings. She still likes to listen to it. It's amazing how even with dementia, songs are somehow hardwired into the brain. She can still sing along to all her old favorites even when she can't recall my name."

"Really? Wow. That's amazing." He smiled softly. "At least you can still share music with her."

"Yeah, we'll listen for hours. Peter Allen had another one called 'I Still Call Australia Home' that's brilliant." Clay laughed ruefully. "I've never even been as far as Tassie and it chokes me up."

Ethan smiled. "I'll have to look those up."

"Qantas did a good commercial with 'I Still Call Australia Home' about twenty years ago with kids singing it and all these shots of places around the world and then around Australia. I tell you what, you'll never see a pub full of blokey blokes get so teary as when that advert came on."

"Not even when Australia wins The Ashes?" Ethan teased.

Clay laughed, a thread of tension in him unraveling. "Well, perhaps it's a draw." He smiled at Ethan, able to breathe a bit deeper. He let the words come on a shaky exhalation. "I really liked being with you last night."

That felt like a lie, and he quickly corrected it, because Ethan deserved it. "More than 'liked.' I loved it, didn't I? But with Sam showing up like that, I'm all over the shop. I hope she wasn't too aggro with you?"

Ethan laughed uncertainly. "I don't blame her. She sure wasn't expecting to come home and find a strange guy in her kitchen in his underwear."

"Strewth. Well, at least you weren't in the nuddy, eh?"

"Yeah, that's something at least." Ethan laughed again, a little breathy and nervous, still perched on the edge of the couch and clutching his sandwich wrapper square. Clay was suddenly aware of how far apart they were, and how much he hated it.

He shifted closer, reaching for Ethan's hand. "Sorry about the upset. You certainly got more than you bargained for. Wouldn't blame you if you left." He squeezed Ethan's fist. "But I don't want you to go, just so we're clear."

With a shaky exhalation, Ethan relaxed a few degrees, unclenching his hand and turning his palm up to thread his fingers with Clay's. The wrapper was now wedged between their palms, and they laughed. Ethan tossed it on the table and held Clay's hand.

"I don't want to go, so I think we're on the same page? I really like you a lot."

Clay's heart sang, and he tried to keep his cool. "Same here."

"Last night was incredible. And I know your head must be spinning from all of this. Sam's too." He grimaced. "I know what it's like to get a huge shock that changes your life. I'm sure you weren't ready to talk about all this with your daughter so soon."

Clay smiled ruefully. "Wasn't on the agenda, no." He pondered the expression of pain that had just crossed Ethan's face like a clap of thunder and took a guess what it was about. "What happened with your fiancé? If you don't mind me asking."

The pained look returned, and Ethan shifted on the couch, the tension zapping back through him. But he still held Clay's hand. Even if it was a bit too tight, he hadn't let go. Clay said, "Mate, we can leave it off. I'm sorry."

"No. I should talk about it. I think I need to, if that makes any sense." He rolled his shoulders, still sitting upright on the edge of the couch. He looked toward the window, but his gaze was distant, like he was seeing something else entirely. "The short version is that the day before Michael and I were supposed to get married, I walked in on him fucking Todd, my best friend."

Clay sucked in a breath, fury quick on the heels of his horror. Oh, to get in a room alone with those two arseholes. He'd pack a wallop. "I'm sorry." Ethan wasn't looking at him, but it seemed like he'd heard in the silence of the room.

Adam's apple bobbing, Ethan nodded. "Yeah. It was the worst, basically. I guess the long version's pretty much the same. I just couldn't believe my eyes, you know? I didn't see it coming. I probably should have, but I didn't. I ignored the clues, and all the signs that things with Michael weren't right. I was in complete denial."

"Oi." Clay squeezed Ethan's fingers. "It's not your fault. They were the cheaters."

Ethan gave him a watery smile. "Yeah." He stared back to the window, and Clay glanced over. There was a fluffy white cloud in a blue sky visible. Below the window, Gilly had fallen asleep, curled peacefully. Clay waited in the quiet for Ethan to go on.

"When I met Michael in college, he was really exciting. Even though he was from Buffalo like me, he seemed…sophisticated. So cool. And even though we didn't have a ton in common, we had enough. I mean, it was college. We didn't even know who we were yet, and we really liked each other. We were attracted to each other. The sex was great. We had a lot of fun. I mean, it was really, really hard losing my parents and my grandmother when I was a teenager. But I was getting through it. The grief was still there—still is, but it…evolves. You know what I mean?"

"Yeah. Life has to go on."

"Right. So I was focusing on school and Michael and living life. Partying. I think part of it was trying to deny my grief. I threw myself into *fun* with this almost sort of…aggression."

"Makes sense."

"I didn't want to be the sad orphan, you know? Then this happened." Ethan motioned to one of his hearing aids. "And I changed. On top of losing my parents it was too much. It's like, you take some hits and you manage to stay on your feet, but then another punch comes, and *bam*. I really had to deal with my grief. For my family, and for my old life."

In the silence, Clay said clearly, "That's understandable. Not your fault."

Ethan sighed, squeezing Clay's fingers. "I know. But I did change. And Michael didn't leave me. He and Todd were so supportive. After I lost my hearing and I was so depressed, they were determined to bring me out of it. And maybe that was more for them than for me. Because they wanted the old, fun Ethan back." He sighed again. "That's probably not fair. Michael really did stick by me for a long time when I was miserable."

"That's what someone who loves you is supposed to do. Sticks around through thick and thin."

Ethan squinted at him. "Through what?"

"Thick and thin."

"Oh, right. And I think that's how this happened. Michael and Todd sincerely wanted to help me. And they got in so deep. We all moved to the city, and before I lost my hearing I probably would have loved it too. But it's so crowded and loud, and honestly? I hate it. The traffic and honking and construction. Those noises are amplified in my hearing aids and it's constantly painful. And I know other places can be noisy too." He shrugged. "It's just never felt like home. But I couldn't expect them to stay in Buffalo. That wouldn't have been fair to them. So I went, and that was my choice."

Their clasped hands were sweaty now, but Clay didn't lessen his grip a millimeter. He waited.

Ethan said, "So there we were in New York, and Michael and I lucked into this apartment in Brooklyn, and he and Todd thrived. They made new friends, and they loved going out to bars and clubs. Those places are just full of frustration for me now. And it took me a long time to get a job. I was still so depressed. My inheritance went to paying my student loans, so I had no money for therapy or meds. And I didn't want to talk to a shrink. I just wanted to hole up and play video games and not face the world. I didn't want to have sex. I didn't want to party. More and more, it was Michael and Todd who had things in common."

"Still, that doesn't give them the right to—" Clay broke off before he said it.

"No. And I'm angry, don't get me wrong." Ethan's eyes filled with tears. "I'm really fucking angry. But the thing is, Michael and I should have broken up a long time ago. We trapped ourselves. He didn't feel like he could leave me when I was so down. But I think he started to resent me. And I was the only person who could get me out of my depression. I just had to work through it. I had to wallow in my grief and anger until I'd had enough. Then I could start to accept that I'll never hear the way I used to, and my life has changed permanently."

Ethan swiped at his eyes with his free hand and laughed softly. "It's weird saying this all out loud. I guess it's been simmering and now it might as well boil over."

"It's the day for that," Clay agreed, giving him a smile. Seeing Ethan cry was like blows to his kidneys. He ached, wanting to haul Ethan into his arms and kiss the tears away. But he reckoned Ethan still had a few things to say.

Ethan smiled. "I guess it is. Anyway, when I finally came out of that fog I'd been in for years, Michael and I were in too deep. And I think I knew that our relationship didn't work anymore, but I told myself he'd been so loyal. I thought we could fix it. I threw myself into being the best boyfriend. I did all the things he wanted to do even if I hated them. I tried not to argue with him about anything, even when he was being a dick. Jesus, then I asked him to marry me." He shook his head. "I really was delusional. I'd always wanted to get married, and I told myself Michael was obviously the one after all we'd been through together. It was like… I didn't even *think* about the possibility of anyone else out there being a much better fit."

Clay laughed ruefully. "Sounds familiar."

Ethan looked at him. He smiled faintly. "I guess so. I hadn't thought about the parallel."

"We're a fine pair, aren't we?" And a voice in his head answered, *we are.* Excitement and affection surged through him even as another voice warned that he and Ethan barely knew each other. And that Clay had to sort out who he was. But as Ethan's cheeks dimpled, his brown eyes warm as he smiled, it was tough to listen.

Clay blurted, "Why were you so keen on getting hitched? Doesn't seem like most people your age are nowadays. At least not my kids. Pete's busy breaking hearts around the world, and Sam's in no rush."

The thought of Pete brought another stab of fear between his ribs. They'd always butted heads a bit, but didn't most fathers and sons? Pete had been Barb's pet, and Sam had been Clay's. But of course he and Barb loved them both something fierce. Pete and Sam were their kids. Of course they loved them. It would surely be a shock to Pete, but he'd come round in the end. He always did. And Barb…

Clay shoved the thought in a box and threw away the key for the time being. He couldn't worry about that, not when Ethan's eyes were wet again.

Ethan's cheeks puffed as he blew out a noisy breath. "So, when I came out to my mom, I was thirteen. I had a crush on this guy on my soccer team. Tanner. He was the goalie, and he was so hot. And he had a birthday party and didn't invite me. Which was fine—we'd barely even spoken aside from saying 'good game' and high-fiving. He went to a different school, and he only invited a few guys from the team. But fuck, I was devastated. It was ridiculous. And I was bawling my eyes out, and my mom had this way of getting stuff out of me. You know how moms are."

Clay smiled. "Yeah."

"Anyway, I finally blurted out that I was in love with him."

He laughed and rolled his eyes. "So dramatic. But I was heartbroken. And my mom just hugged me and let me cry for a long time. And then she told me about how she'd been in love with a boy named John. How she'd wanted to marry him so badly, but he wouldn't commit. They were still young, but I guess it was typical in Switzerland to get married fairly young. Small town."

Ethan was quiet a few moments, his gaze distant again, his sweaty fingers clutching Clay's. Finally, Ethan said, "Mom told me she was wrong, and that John wasn't good enough for her. That she'd finally met the boy of her dreams in Buffalo, New York, when a young man stopped to help push her car out of a snowbank. Dad carried cat litter and a shovel in his trunk in the winter." At Clay's clear bafflement, Ethan added, "To sprinkle on the snow so the tires can grip. The point was that Dad was always prepared, and Mom realized responsibility was the sexiest thing in the world." He smiled softly to himself. "That's what she always said."

"Good to be prepared," Clay agreed, hoping Ethan found it sexy too.

"So, Mom told me that one day she knew I'd marry the boy of my dreams, and that it would be beautiful, and she'd be so proud. That *I* was beautiful just the way I was, and she and Dad and Oma and the whole family loved me." He chuckled. "I guess they'd already suspected, and I'd thought it was such a massive secret. That maybe they'd hate me. I should have known not to be afraid to tell them. They were nothing but loving."

Clay flinched, and the fist inside him tightened, his insides squeezing like sausages between its merciless fingers. And bloody hell, why was he thinking about Tony Taylor in the driveway and his crooked smile and grease-black hands as he waved to Clay going by?

"Hey," Ethan said, leaning closer and ducking his head to meet Clay's gaze. "Are you okay? You look like you're going to be sick." Ethan held Clay's palm and scooted closer, reaching up and smoothing his free hand over Clay's head, sending a trickle of warmth through him.

"It's that damn Macca's!" Clay forced his lungs to exhale. "Sam's right. Shouldn't eat that garbage." He was able to smile genuinely, focusing on Ethan and forgetting the past. "But I'm all right. Just had a funny turn."

"Are you sure?" Ethan frowned.

"Absolutely. You were telling me about your mum and dad. They sound lovely."

"They were. I'm really lucky I had them."

"And that's why you were so keen on getting married? Because of what your mum said that day?"

Ethan huffed out a laugh, his free hand sliding down to Clay's neck, his fingers drawing soothing patterns. "Stupid, right? I mean, it hadn't even been this big thing. It wasn't like she went on and on about my future wedding. But I always remembered it. How accepting she'd been. And I told myself I'd marry the boy of my dreams and make her proud even if she wasn't here to see it. I convinced myself marrying Michael would fix everything. And he was already fucking Todd when I asked, and he felt too guilty to say no to me—but not guilty enough to come clean. I guess they kept telling themselves they'd do it, but there was never a good time."

"Well, there isn't bound to be, is there? You've just got to man up and do it!" Clay had never clapped eyes on this Michael and Todd, but he hated them. "Cowards is what they are. You deserve better."

"You know what?" Ethan nodded. "I think I do. And if they're happy together partying and being polyamorous, they can go to town."

"Poly what?"

"Polyamorous. Where there's multiple people in a relationship. Or someone has more than one separate relationship. Like, after I walked in on them? Michael said he loved both of us, and he wanted to be with me *and* be with Todd."

Clay couldn't believe his ears. "He expected you to agree to that? So he could have his cake and eat it too? Crikey."

"For some people it works great. If everyone's consenting, I have no problem with it, but everyone has to be on board from the start. That's a pretty key factor."

"I reckon so, mate."

Ethan laughed, dragging his hand down to Clay's chest and scraping his nails through the hair poking out of Clay's singlet. He let go of Clay's hand, but Clay didn't have time to protest since Ethan was scooting closer, tucking his feet under him and running his damp palm up Clay's arm.

Ethan said, "Thank you for listening. It was good to say that all out loud. I feel like you really hear me. Not just literally, but… You know what I mean?"

Clay knew exactly that he meant, and he nodded, very aware of Ethan's hands touching him, not forceful or with intent, but just there and solid.

Ethan looked down and swallowed hard before meeting Clay's gaze. "Do you still want to do this? Us?" He huffed out a laugh and quickly added, "Not that there's really an *us* yet, and I know this is all new and confusing." He lifted his hands and motioned back toward the front door with one. "And crazy stressful with Sam coming home. So if you want to press pause, I totally get it. I don't want to pressure you. I can get a hotel."

What Clay wanted was Ethan's hands back on him. Grounding him. "I don't want you to go anywhere." It occurred to him with a nasty jolt that Ethan would be going back to the other side of the world in less than a week's time.

He took hold of Ethan's shoulders. "I want you here with me. Teaching me new words. Amongst other things. You've got your work cut out for you. You know what they say about old dogs and new tricks."

A grin brightened Ethan's face, and it was like the roof was gone and the sun was beaming straight down. "You're not that old, and I'll teach you everything I've got."

Then he kissed Clay soundly, and Clay's hands came up to frame his face, breathing him in. They tasted like fried brekkie and bitter coffee, and it was marvelous. Ethan pushed his tongue into Clay's mouth, gasping, and Clay hauled him over his lap so Ethan's legs straddled his, knees tucked beside Clay's hips.

The need to touch sparked in Clay like wildfire in the brush, sweeping over the red dirt. They rubbed against each other, getting hard through their clothes. He loved the feel of Ethan in his arms, safe on his lap and far away from the cowards who'd hurt him.

He knew there were other things he needed to sort, like talking more to Sam and figuring out what was going on inside him, but in that moment all Clay wanted was to hold onto Ethan and make him sigh and moan, dry his tears completely, and make him feel good the way he deserved. Everything else could wait, couldn't it?

They broke apart to gasp for breath, Ethan's jeans undone now and Clay's shorts tugged as low as he could get them without dislodging Ethan. Ethan's pale face was reddened again, and Clay lightly caressed along his chin.

"Going to give you more pash rash."

Ethan drew his eyebrows close. "Did you say 'pash rash'?" Then he laughed delightedly, his cheeks dimpling and making Clay's heart squeeze. "Does pashing mean kissing?" At Clay's nod, he added, "Then you sure are." He waggled his brows. "And I love it. Amongst other things. This is on the list too." He rolled his hips, and they both groaned.

Then he caught Clay's lips with his, and they kissed and kissed, and Clay loved so many things about Ethan and how he made him feel that he didn't have a clue where to start counting.

Chapter Fifteen

T HE LAZY, WONDERFUL looseness in Clay's limbs evaporated as his phone rang and Sam's beautiful face appeared on the screen. Clay and Ethan were sitting in the shade of a wide awning in the yard talking about Buffalo winters—which sounded like torture—with Gilly by their feet gnawing on a rubber toy.

Throat dry, Clay answered, trying to sound as normal as possible. "Hiya, love. How's Jase?" Ethan gave his knee a squeeze and threw Gilly's toy across the grass, Gilly eagerly bounding after it, Ethan following.

Sam groaned. "Not great. Tooth is fixed up, but they had to give him laughing gas and he spewed all over my feet in the parking lot. He's feeling pretty crook. I'm going to stay over."

"Poor bloke. And right, of course. Makes sense to stay with him." *Is that the real reason? Or does she not want to see me now?*

"I'm not staying away because of you, Dad."

He had to laugh. "How do you always read my mind?"

"Years of experience, mate. Although apparently I haven't been doing such a bang-up job." She laughed awkwardly. "Didn't spot this, and I reckon I should have. All teasing about you being madly in love with Adam Gilchrist aside."

He laughed. "Maybe there was something to it after all. But I didn't spot it either, if you can believe that."

She was quiet a moment, and Clay watched Ethan and Gilly playing across the yard, Ethan laughing joyfully and rubbing Gilly's belly. Then Sam said, "Is that true? You didn't know you were into blokes until now?"

Tony Taylor's face flickered through his mind, and his lungs seized. He rasped, "Sounds mental, doesn't it?" He managed a breath. "I don't really understand it yet. But I…"

She was quiet before prompting, "What, Dad? Whatever it is, it won't change anything with us."

"I fancy Ethan." His neck prickled, and he gripped the phone so hard he thought it might snap. "Quite a lot."

"He's really cute. Seems nice. So he's part deaf? Not that it matters."

"Yeah. Hard of hearing is the right phrase."

"Right, okay. That's cool. He's…" She laughed. "Well, he's very young, isn't he? You sly dog. Didn't think you had it in you."

Face hot, Clay shifted in his creaky lawn chair, tearing his gaze away from the way Ethan's T-shirt lifted up and showed his belly as he stretched his arms overhead in celebration as Gilly jumped and caught the toy on the fly. "He's twenty-seven. I know, it's quite a gap. People won't like it."

"People can get stuffed. If you're keen on each other, that's all that matters."

"You really think that?" His chest tightened. He loved her so damn much he could hardly stand it sometimes.

"Of course. I want you to be happy. That's why I've been on you so much to try dating. When Mum did a runner with that wanker Bazza and everything changed, you did too. I figured you missed her. Missed the company."

"I reckon I did a bit, even if… Well, even if there were never fireworks with your mum. I still loved her, of course. Always will."

"I know. You both deserve to be happy. Properly happy. She was a right bitch for what she did to you, but maybe it was for the best."

"Oi! Don't talk about your mum like that. You know better."

She laughed dryly. "All right. Sorry. Look, you know I love Mum. It was just a real shock when she decided to up and leave. Obviously. I mean, we've talked about this a hundred times."

He sighed. "I know. It was a shock to me too. But it was for the best. It really was." Thinking of Barb, he tensed. "You haven't mentioned this to her, have you?"

She huffed, and he could imagine the eye roll. "Sure, Dad. First thing I did was ring Mum and tell her all about it. Who do you take me for? Pete?"

Clay barked out a laugh, and Sam joined him. "And no, haven't told Pete either. Or Auntie Jen or Nan. Not that Nan would remember it thirty seconds after you told her. Regardless, that's all up to you. I mean, you'll have to do it eventually, but it's been about five minutes. Reckon we can let this settle in for a bit."

"Yeah. Suppose this business today was a surprise." He tried to laugh. "To both of us."

"My head's spinning, that's for sure. Need a good drink."

"Was just thinking it was time to grab a stubby."

"Surprised you've waited this long. It's past noon and it's your day off, mate. Speaking of which, when are you working again?"

"Thursday. Doing day trips to the Blue Mountains the rest of the week. Then a couple two-nighters to the Great Ocean Road next week." The reminder that Ethan would be gone by then lodged in his throat like a stone.

"Look, maybe I should stay with Jase this week. Give you and Ethan some time to yourselves. You reckon?"

"Well…" He blew out a long breath. "Yeah, that would be good, love. You sure?"

"Positive. And it's not because I'm running away from you."

"I know. Thanks."

"All right, the patient's calling. Love ya, Dad."

"You too, sweetheart."

Clay hung up and watched Ethan and Gilly playing tug-of-war with the rubber chicken. Ethan's face was flushed pink, and Clay wanted to press him back against the grass and kiss him. Then kiss him some more.

And more.

He was glancing around, wondering if the neighbors would be able to see, when Ethan returned, flopping down into the chair next to Clay, a little out of breath. Gilly had followed, butting his head against Ethan's legs.

"Such a fickle beast," Clay said. "I'm yesterday's news." He reached over and gave Gilly a pat. Gilly was torn between them, tongue wagging, head going back and forth.

Ethan laughed. "He's awesome." To Gilly, he added, "Aren't you? Yes. Such a good boy." He scratched behind Gilly's ears while Clay petted his flanks.

"Yeah, he's a good lad. The best."

"How's Sam's boyfriend doing?"

"Bit crook. Feeling sick to his stomach after the drugs they gave him while they fixed his mouth." Clay's pulse jumped. "Sam's going to stay at his place this week. Give us some time together. Is that good by you?"

Still petting Gilly, Ethan's white teeth flashed in a smile. "Yeah. That would be great. Assuming you don't want me to find a hotel?"

"No, I want you right here with me." The words had come out sounding serious, and the air felt thicker as they looked at each other, some kind of new emotion swelling. Clay cleared his throat and added, "I don't have to work until Thursday. Can take you sightseeing the next few days."

"That would be awesome. Actually, I realized I have tickets to the opera tonight. I mean, if you hate opera, it's totally cool. We don't have to go." He laughed anxiously, his gaze dropping as he shrugged. "It's pretty lame, I guess. Michael fell asleep the one time we went to the Met. But the Opera House is iconic, so he agreed to go."

Clay enunciated very clearly, "Michael's a wanker." He honestly wondered what on earth Ethan had ever seen in him, but reckoned there must have been something.

Ethan looked over at him, laughing. "Yeah. He kind of is. For me, opera's perfect because there are subtitles, so I can understand what's going on. Or ballet, since they tell the story through dance. But Michael only ever wanted to go to off-off-off Broadway plays about the most pretentious shit. Like, we saw one that was two naked people cooking dinner and talking about their day. That was it. I'm sure it was a commentary on the meaninglessness of life or something, but it made me even more depressed. Plus I could only make out half of what they were saying."

"Never been to an opera, but I'd love to go. It's a beautiful spot on the harbor. You definitely need to see it. We can have dinner first. Find a nice quiet place. And I know a good place to park."

"Yeah?" Ethan grinned. "Okay. You're sure you want to drive down? I don't mind the train."

"Oh yeah, on a Sunday night it'll be easy. After you've driven a coach through the city during rush hour, anything else is a snap."

"Cool. It's *Turandot*. There's a really famous song in it. 'Nessun Dorma'?" Ethan started humming, and then shook his head. "Oh my God, I am butchering it. You'll know it when you hear it. I'll leave that to the professionals."

"For the best," Clay agreed seriously.

"Hey!" Ethan playfully slapped Clay's arm, and Clay tickled him back. Then they had to take it inside, because the neighbors were definitely about to get an eyeful.

SYDNEY WAS ABOUT as sleepy as it ever got as they made their way back later that night. Clay brought the ute to a stop at a red light, pointing out the view of Sydney Tower through two buildings. Ethan leaned down and craned his neck.

"Oh! Awesome." He sat back up and smiled at Clay, and Clay's heart swelled. They'd dressed up in trousers and shirts and ties. Ethan's tie was purple with a faint shimmer, and even in the ute's cab with only the streetlights and the dash, it brought out his eyes. Ethan was a beauty, he was.

And he's mine.

Gripping the steering wheel, Clay reminded himself that wasn't true. That was getting far too ahead of himself. They'd only known each other little more than a week. Only been…*involved* twenty-four hours. He was barking mad if he thought he and Ethan were a proper couple or something.

"You really liked it?" Ethan asked. "Fair dinkum?"

Clay chuckled. "Fair dinkum, mate. I may be a banana bender from the back of beyond, but I enjoy a little culture."

Ethan laughed delightedly, and Clay wanted to kiss him, but the light turned. Ethan asked, "Did you say 'banana bender'? Did I hear right?"

"Yep. It's an old term for a Queenslander. Not the most flattering."

"Also sounds super gay." Ethan grinned, reaching to run his palm over Clay's thigh.

Gay. The word rumbled around Clay's brain. The thought of that word fitting him was still foreign. "Never noticed before, but I reckon you're right." Ethan's long fingers stroked lightly back and forth over Clay's left inner thigh, sending tingles right to, well, his *banana.* "And I did enjoy the opera. Quite a spectacle. So much color. I don't know how they hit those notes. Gave me chills down my spine a few times."

"Yes! Me too. Their voices are so powerful that I can hear them really well. Like, it's not so much the volume, but the…richness. Does that make sense?"

Clay nodded. "The acoustics are something else as well. And those sets and costumes. I've only ever been to the theater once before. Took the kids to Brissie to see *Wicked*. Enjoyed it, but it never occurred to me to go once I moved down here. It was really good tonight."

Ethan rubbed Clay's thigh. "I'm so happy you liked it. The first show I ever saw was some regional production of *Rocky Horror*. I was a kid and I didn't understand half the jokes, but I knew I was totally queer."

Clay went rigid. "Oi! Don't call yourself that!" Sudden fury thrummed through him like a landmine detonating.

Beside him, Ethan's eyes were wide. He snatched his hand away from Clay's thigh. "What?"

"That's a nasty word!"

Ethan stared at him with mouth gaping. After a few beats of silence, he tightly asked, "Why are you yelling at me?"

Clay felt sick to his stomach, sweat breaking out on his forehead, his skin clammy and breath short. "That's a nasty word," he repeated in a lower voice. "Don't like you saying that about yourself." He merged onto the highway, his heart thudding too hard in his chest. Why would Ethan say that?

When he glanced over, Ethan was still staring at him, his face creased in a frown and—bugger it all—clear hurt shining in his eyes. Clay quickly said, "I'm sorry I yelled. I didn't mean to get aggro with you."

After a few moments, Ethan said, "Okay." He cleared his throat, clearly still leery.

Clay hated himself and made sure he spoke calmly. "I'm sorry. Truly." He tried to breathe evenly. Why had he flown off the handle like that? Ethan was going to think he was nuts.

After another few beats of silence, Ethan said, "Okay. So, the thing with that word is that a lot of people use it now. Not in a negative way. With pride. Like, you've heard the acronym LGBTQ? That's what the Q stands for. Queer. Well, some people might say it's 'questioning,' which is obviously fine, but in my mind it's always been queer." Ethan took a shaky breath. "Anyway. My point is that it's not a bad word to many people now."

Hearing that word again, Clay tried not to cringe. "No, I didn't realize that." His throat felt like it was full of rocks. His father's voice suddenly filled his mind as clearly as if he was squeezed into the ute between them.

"Filthy fucking queer."

"Clay? Are you okay? Shit, maybe you should pull over." Ethan reached for him again, rubbing his leg. "Breathe."

Blood rushed in Clay's ears, and for a moment the red tail-lights ahead went double. Then he gulped air, the horror receding. He grated out, "I'm all right." From the corner of his eye, he could see Ethan watching him worriedly, his hand a warm, wonderful pressure on Clay's leg.

Clay kept his eyes on the road, and they drove in silence for a minute as he concentrated on breathing. Finally, he repeated, "I'm sorry."

"It's okay. Are we almost there?"

"Not long. No traffic."

"All right. Just focus on the road."

So he did, and with Ethan's hand and kind, patient presence steadying Clay, soon enough they were home. He stopped in the driveway, his voice hoarse when he said, "If you want to hop out before I put it in the garage? It's tight in there."

Ethan did, waiting by the pathway. He followed Clay into the house. When the door was shut and the light on, Ethan said, "Are you okay?"

"Yeah." Of course he was. Why shouldn't he be? It was nonsense. "I'm sorry."

Ethan was a few feet away, fidgeting with his fingers. "It scared me when you yelled like that."

Shame punched through Clay. "Jesus, I'm sorry." He wanted to pull Ethan close, but was that the wrong thing to do? "I'm not often aggro, I swear." He grimaced. "That sounds like a load of garbage, doesn't it? That's what all the blokes who are a terror to their wives say. But I promise. On my kids' lives, that's not like me."

Ethan nodded. "I believe you."

"Yeah?" Clay was afraid to hope. "I haven't ruined everything?"

A little smile tugged at Ethan's pretty mouth. "No."

"Would you mind if I... If we..." He motioned between them.

The smile was still there. "You want to hug?"

"That would be nice."

Then Ethan was in his arms, holding Clay so tightly. Clay hadn't even realized he was shaking until Ethan soothed him, running his hands over Clay's back and murmuring, "It's okay. I'm here."

And damn it, Clay didn't want him to ever leave. Which he knew was mad. It wasn't possible, and Clay would have to say goodbye to him within the week. Ethan had said his flight was Saturday, and it was too soon. "Don't go," he said before he could stop himself.

Ethan leaned back. "Sorry. Can you say that again?"

This time, Clay only said, "Thank you. For being so good about this. I didn't realize. About that word."

"I understand. It's been reclaimed, I guess? I think some older people have a different reaction to it. It's like the F-word to them. And I don't mean 'fuck.' I hate saying that word in any context."

"Got it." Clay nodded and hugged Ethan tightly again. It felt so damn good to hold Ethan and just breathe. Like everything would be okay as long as Ethan was in his arms.

Not for long. Don't get too close.

Reluctantly, Clay pulled back. He tried a teasing smile. "And wait, are you calling me old? Cheeky."

"Never." Ethan grinned. He popped an eyebrow. "Want to go to bed?"

"Thought you'd never ask."

They laughed, and some of the tension leeched from Clay's limbs. They went to the bedroom and took off their fancy clothes, Ethan cracking a few other jokes. Clay's body hummed, eager for the release of getting off with Ethan again, rutting against him, sucking and stroking hard. Eager for the escape.

Yet when they were finally naked on the mattress, Ethan's kisses were gentle. He rolled on top of Clay, pushing their hips together, but it was easy and sweet. He seemed to worship every single freckle dotting Clay's skin. Clay held him close, careful not to knock his hearing aids.

The ceiling fan beat a breeze over their bare skin, sweat gathering where they were pressed together. The tenderness that filled Clay at each press of Ethan's lips was almost too much to bear, and bloody hell, tears pricked his eyes. What was wrong with him?

When Ethan finally took him in his mouth, Clay almost came right then. But the pleasure simmered and grew. He spread his legs for Ethan, following the silent directions of his hands. Clay's arse was practically in the air by the end. He nearly jumped out of his skin when Ethan actually *licked* it, spreading him open.

"Fuck!" Clay shouted.

Between his legs, Ethan grinned up at him with a wonderfully devilish expression that had Clay's balls drawing up. He tightened his fingers in Ethan's hair as Ethan licked him again, a long swipe from Clay's arse to his prick.

"Christ! How does that feel—" Clay gasped at the wet friction over his hole. "Like that?"

Ethan raised his head. "Sorry, I didn't catch that."

Clay wanted to say never mind and get back to it, but Ethan hated not to hear something, and Clay didn't want to upset him. He repeated himself, and the warm puff of Ethan's laughter hit his privates, sending a shiver through him.

Ethan said, "Welcome to the wonderful world of rimming."

"Whatever it's called, get back to it, would ya?"

Ethan's joyous laugh was cut off when he did just that, licking Clay's arse like it was a lolly. He began stroking Clay's shaft as well, and when the tip of his tongue pushed *inside*, Clay came so hard he saw white dots when he threw his head back, the release wringing him out like a washcloth.

His limbs were lead in the most wonderful way as he shook from the aftershocks, Ethan kissing all around him down there, then licking the milky drops from Clay's belly. The sight and blissful, cared-for sensation made Clay's spent balls twitch.

It was Ethan's turn, but Clay wasn't sure he could even make a fist. He waited to speak until Ethan straightened up, sitting back on his heels, his cock straining nearly as purple as his tie from earlier.

Clay said, "You've done me in." He reached out. "You'll have to come closer."

But Ethan only grinned. "It's okay. This'll only take a minute, trust me."

Then he was jerking himself, eyes locked with Clay's, and wanking had never been so exciting. Clay's breath was short again as he watched Ethan reach up his free hand to twist his nipples, making them stand up red. Ethan's muscles were tense, his hand flying. Then he sucked his free index finger, spitting onto it.

He reached behind himself, eyes fluttering closed on a moan as his back arched. Clay realized he was sticking his finger into his arse, and he wished desperately that he could see. Was he just going around the top like he'd done to Clay, just dipping a bit inside?

Or was he going deeper?

"Are you rooting yourself?" he blurted, surprised to hear his own words aloud.

Ethan's brow creased. "Did you ask if I'm fucking myself?" His hand was still moving behind him, his jaw clenching and the muscles in his neck and arms straining. At Clay's nod, he smiled. "Uh-huh. Trying to get just the right spot. Have you ever felt it?"

Clay shook his head. He didn't think so. Had never had anything up there except for once at the doctor's. What would it be like? And how would it feel to have *his* finger inside Ethan? Better than that, his cock?

The thought knocked the wind from him. What they were doing was already so intimate—Ethan sitting back on his heels between Clay's spread legs, their eyes locked as Ethan touched himself freely, with no embarrassment or shame.

Clay's heart swelled at the thought that Ethan trusted him enough to be so…exposed. Clay needed to touch, and he stretched down so one hand could squeeze Ethan's thigh.

"It feels amazing," Ethan moaned. "When I hit the prostate and—" His back bowed, and he spurted long, ropy strands all the way onto Clay's stomach. Gasping, Ethan kept stroking himself, getting more drops, his finger apparently still inside him and clearly in just the right place.

"Jesus," Clay mumbled, and Ethan flopped into his arms. Right where he belonged.

Until Saturday, a cruel little voice reminded him. Clay held Ethan and tried his very best to ignore it.

TONY TAYLOR.

As Clay drifted in the half-space between waking and sleep, nonsensical thoughts starting to take form, the name jolted him, appearing bold and clear.

Stubborn. Unwilling to go away this time.

He opened his eyes, his breath shuddering as dread spiraled. Dozing with his head on Clay's chest, Clay's arm anchored around his back, Ethan jerked up, blinking.

"Are you all right?" he asked far too loudly, almost shouting. Clay couldn't hide his wince, and in the moonlight, Ethan reached for his hearing aids on the side table, inserting them into his ears and turning them on. "Sorry," he said.

"No worries. Go back to sleep." Of course now they were both wide awake.

The sheet was tangled around Ethan's hips as he rolled onto his back. The fact that he was really there—naked in Clay's bed— seemed like a dream in the hush of night. Ethan gazed at him patiently. "Are you freaking out?"

Clay rolled onto his right side toward Ethan, smoothing his palm over Ethan's belly, which quivered under his touch. "I don't think so."

"Good." Ethan traced the contours of Clay's hand with his fingertips. He didn't say anything else, just waited, watching Clay, silver light glinting in his beautiful eyes.

"Can you hear me all right?"

"Uh-huh."

Still pressing his hand to Ethan's stomach, Clay finally said, "Thinking of a man I haven't in a long time. Decades."

After a silence, Ethan whispered, "Okay."

"Strange to be remembering him after all these years. We should go back to sleep."

Ethan said nothing, just continued tracing little patterns over the back of Clay's hand and along his fingers, sending a little ripple of warmth through Clay.

"I didn't even really know him."

Ethan was quiet. Still waiting. After a few moments as a confusion of memories swirled through Clay's mind, Ethan asked, "What was his name?"

"Oh, right. Anthony Taylor. Tony. Lived a few houses down from us on Doris Street. In Cloncurry, I mean. It was nothing much, Doris Street. One-story houses, a few trees that made a go of it. The odd empty lot. Lawns that were scrubby and peppered with red dirt, but people made an effort. Kept their fences straight and yards neat. No cars rusting out, or trash. A respectable street."

Ethan murmured a listening sound and waited.

"Tony worked down the mines. He was probably twenty. I was, I dunno, nine or ten. Didn't really know him at all, like I said. Jen and I would call out and wave to him if he happened to be working on his car when we rode by on our bikes. He'd be out there without a shirt, leaning over the engine for hours, tinkering away. Had a big green metal toolbox like my dad's. I wanted one too."

Taking a deep breath, Clay thought of how Tony's hands would be stained black with grease when he'd straighten up and wave to them, smudges on his chest sometimes. Tony always gave them a big smile. Once, he'd helped fix the chain on Jen's bike and given them both lollies from the glovebox of his ute.

Clay cleared his throat. "Tony still lived with his folks. Taylors had a couple other kids in high school. Mrs. Taylor stayed home like my mum, and Mr. Taylor worked down the mines as well." Clay shook his head. "I dunno why I'm thinking about all this."

After another silence, Ethan quietly asked, "What happened to Tony?"

Clay's lungs seized up, and a shudder ran through him. He slipped his hand away from Ethan's and rolled onto his back, blinking up at the ceiling. He tried to laugh it off. "Feel like someone just walked over my grave."

Of course he knew exactly what had happened to Tony—well, not *later*, but that night in the lot at the corner of Doris and Alice streets. Maybe not *exactly*, but he knew enough.

Still looking at the ceiling, Clay could feel Ethan beside him. Ethan propped himself on his elbow, probably so the flow of words from Clay's mouth would be clearer. Watching Clay, but not touching him. Waiting.

"This is such nonsense, dredging this up." Clay's heart hammered, and he felt a fool. But the pressure in his chest only grew until he forced a breath and said, "We were coming home from dinner at Auntie Marg and Uncle Ian's. They lived near Julia Creek, about an hour and a half down the track."

"So far to go for dinner."

Clay had to smile, even though the pressure in his chest hadn't eased. "In the outback, that's nothing. Anyway, my parents always played rummy for hours with them, and Jen was sleeping beside me in the backseat. I was trying to stay awake. Hated falling asleep in the car and then having to get up and go into the house and brush my teeth and put on my PJs. And I remember as we got close to our street, I was grateful we were finally home, because my eyes were getting so heavy. Then…"

He took another shallow, sharp breath. He didn't realize his hands were in fists beside him on the mattress until Ethan tentatively covered the right one with his own hand. Ethan stroked with his thumb, and Clay breathed again, still too shallow, staring at the rectangle of silver moonlight coming through the window and cast on the ceiling at an angle.

"Then I realized something was happening at the corner. There were people there. Young guys. It was a Saturday night, and I thought maybe they were drinking grog. Having a party. There was some kind of commotion, and Mum slowed the car. She always drove home from Auntie Marg and Uncle Ian's so Dad could drink all the beer he wanted."

Clay closed his eyes, seeing it all in faded snapshots. "There was someone on the ground, and the others were kicking him. Punching him. Screaming words I couldn't make out. We could see it all in the headlights."

Clay took another shallow breath through his mouth, his throat gone dry, eyes still shut. "It was Tony. And Mum slowed and said, 'What a damned shame. We should…' But she trailed off like it was a question. She always did that. Waited for Dad's verdict. And I remember how Dad barked, 'No,' with such force Jen startled awake."

Clay's heart thumped dully, seeing the headlights slash the darkness, the confusion of thrashing bodies disappearing as Mum turned the corner. "We kept driving toward our house."

Ethan held onto Clay's fist, saying nothing.

Clay exhaled. "I couldn't understand it. I said, 'It's Tony from down the street! Why aren't you stopping?' And Dad said…"

He couldn't go on, the lump in his throat too massive and unmovable. He kept his eyes squeezed shut, the pressure in his chest about to crack his ribs. But Ethan was there beside him, his hand on Clay's, comforting and patient. Steady as a rock.

Clay's lungs expanded enough to breathe, his voice like gravel. "Dad said, 'He's a filthy fucking queer. Brought it on himself.'"

Ethan sucked in a breath then, and Clay opened his eyes and turned his head on the pillow. Ethan's eyes shimmered with tears, and Clay hated the sight. He unclenched his fist, the horrible pressure that had built in his chest releasing as he threaded his fingers with Ethan's and held on tight.

Clay's voice was hoarse, but he made himself go on. "And that was that. Tony could have bloody *died*, and my dad didn't care. He'd stop on the road and pull out his shotgun if there was a roo or emu that had been hit and was suffering. Tony wasn't even worth as much as an animal."

Wordlessly, Ethan kissed Clay's knuckles and listened.

When Clay caught his breath, he went on. "Not sure how Tony got found out, but I reckon word had spread around town. When we got out of the car, I could still hear his cries and their shouts in the night. The neighbors had to have heard as well. I looked around the street, but there was no sign of anyone coming out to investigate. Not even from the Taylors'. Most of the houses were dark, and I imagined them all hiding in there, listening to his screams."

Ethan made a pained noise, like a whimper, but didn't say anything.

"And I didn't do a thing. Spineless. I just followed my parents into the house. Jen didn't know what was going on, her eyes big in the moonlight. I remember her opening her mouth to ask, but I shook my head, and she shut up."

Holding Clay's hand between them, Ethan squeezed.

"I saw him one more time, the next morning. Jen was helping Mum peel spuds for Sunday dinner. We always had mashed potatoes and roast."

Clay grabbed onto the snatch of memory. The back door banging shut behind him, Jen griping loudly that she wanted to go out too. How his bike was getting too small for him, and he had to stand up a little or else his legs would cramp. He'd taken a wide loop out of the driveway on the empty road, a bit of grit flying into his eye.

"I rode by the Taylors' on my bike, and Tony was getting into their ute. Well, his brother was pushing him up into the seat." Clay had to stop and force an inhalation before he went on.

"His face was so swollen, Tony barely looked human. His dad was behind the wheel with a stone expression. And that was the last time I ever saw Tony. The Taylors stayed there on Doris Street—still lived there as long as my parents did. Might still now if they're not dead. But all those years, Tony never came back.

Not once."

Still holding Clay's hand, damp and tight and solid as a rock, Ethan murmured, "I'm so sorry."

A strange laugh bubbled up in Clay. "And do you know what I did that morning as I passed by Tony Taylor, beaten within an inch of his life, being sent away because he was a 'filthy queer'? I *waved.*"

Christ, Clay's cheeks were wet, and he realized he was crying with a rush of shame. "What's wrong with me?" He wasn't sure if he meant then or now.

But it didn't matter, because Ethan was there, holding him close against his warm, slim body, pressing kisses to Clay's head. Not judging as he murmured, "I'm sorry," and "It's not your fault."

Clay gasped against Ethan's throat, clinging to him as the tears flowed. It was as though his brain was back in time, unearthing a series of memories seemingly at random…

A Christmas Day barbecue when his dad let him drink a stubby of XXXX, all of them roasting in the sun in the scrubby yard but wearing the paper crowns from the Christmas crackers, little Jen collecting all the paper slips with jokes on them and reading them out delightedly. "*What do you call a three-legged donkey? A wonky donkey!*"

Mum driving him and Jen into The Isa and letting them each pick out a record at the music shop, eating lollies in the ute and listening to the radio station dad couldn't stand.

Chasing Jen down the street with a snakeskin he'd found in the yard, the husk dry and crumbling in his fingers, her shrieks absolute music to his ears.

When the tears stopped and Ethan still held him close and safe, Clay wondered what it felt like to shed your skin and be reborn.

Chapter Sixteen

"*M*UMBLE MUMBLE.*"

Ethan had been looking out the window of Clay's pickup as they neared Sydney's downtown, a city bus rumbling by drowning out whatever Clay said. Ethan turned to him. "Sorry, can you please repeat that?"

Clay glanced over at him. "Just asking if you're all right? Seem quiet this morning." He was wearing his navy uniform pants and short-sleeved white button-up shirt with the DL logo on the breast pocket.

Seeing him back in uniform was both sexy and depressing. The reminder that Clay was going back to work and Ethan was leaving tomorrow weighed heavy on him. But he made himself smile as if nothing was wrong. "Yeah, of course. It's just early." And it was, not even six a.m.

"We're coming up on the first hotel. I'll drop you off while I go park and fetch the coach. It's a mini, so fits twenty guests. And there's only fourteen of ya today, plus the guide."

"Is it Shiv?"

"Nah, it's a woman called Kerry." Clay's chuckle was a little uneasy. "She doesn't know about you and me."

"Right, of course not. Don't worry." Ethan was pretty sure Clay wasn't ready for co-workers to know about their relationship.

Relationship. He scoffed at himself. Was it really? It felt like it, but soon he was going back to the other side of the world where he lived and, more importantly, worked.

Ethan added, "It's not like I'll be hitting on you during the tour. We'll keep things strictly professional." He smoothed a hand over Clay's thigh, fingertips brushing his junk. He lowered his voice. "Think about how hot it'll make it later when we're finally alone again. It'll be our little secret. When we're sitting in traffic, you can imagine how I'm going to suck your cock and swallow your cum."

Clay laughed, going redder. "Strewth, the things you say."

He uttered it with such affection that Ethan ached. He'd been tempted to say something about Clay fucking him and being inside him, but would that be too much? He hadn't wanted to push since it was all so new for Clay.

They'd touched and kissed and sucked, and gotten off too many times to count. It was the best sex of Ethan's life, hands down. God, the way Clay's big, rough hands could make him feel…

The past several days after Clay's sort-of meltdown had been blissful. Ethan had been worried he might retreat after crying himself to sleep in Ethan's arms, but the next morning he'd been good. It was cliché, but he really had seemed more relaxed and like a weight had been lifted.

Decades of ruthlessly repressing any same-sex attraction wasn't going to be "fixed" in one night, but understanding one of the big reasons he'd denied himself was huge.

He'd apologized for "getting a bit sappy," trying to shrug it off, but when Ethan had looked him in the eye and told him he never, ever needed to apologize for expressing his feelings, he'd nodded and kissed Ethan sweetly. That he'd trusted Ethan with all of it made Ethan feel incredibly special.

And I have to leave. It's not realistic to do a long-distance thing. Is it?

He watched as Clay expertly navigated the city streets, the silence easy between them in the dawn. Neither of them had brought up Ethan's imminent departure. Clay had been able to switch his Thursday shift with another driver, but no one could take the Friday, so Ethan was coming along.

They'd gone sightseeing every day. Clay insisted that he hadn't actually seen most of Sydney himself aside from inside the coach. Ethan wasn't sure if he believed him, but he loved him for it.

Loved.

The word shivered through him, secret and wonderful. Not to mention absolutely ludicrous since they had known each other barely two weeks. Was it possible to fall in love that fast? Surely he was just kidding himself again, like he had when he'd been so determined that marrying Michael would fix their fundamental problems.

This was a rebound. Right?

Ethan shoved away the flare of pain and any thoughts of Michael and Todd. If this was his last full day with Clay, he was not going to waste it.

"There's Sam," Clay said.

Gut clenching, Ethan spotted her waiting in front of the hotel, tapping on her phone. She wore denim shorts and a green tank top, her golden curls half pulled back, a few tendrils framing her face. One flip-flop was off, and she idly ran that bare foot over her other shin.

"Are you sure this is a good idea?" Ethan asked. It wouldn't *quite* be his and Clay's little secret on the tour that they were involved, but obviously Sam wouldn't say anything. Still, a million things could go wrong hanging out with her all day. "What if she hates me?"

"Impossible," Clay scoffed with such confidence Ethan wanted to kiss him. He refrained since they were coming to a stop and

Sam had noticed them. Clay added, "It was her idea, after all. The two of you can get to know each other and have a lovely time of it. You definitely need to see the Blue Mountains. Spectacular, mate. Trust me."

"Totally, yeah. Cool." He got out of the truck, giving Sam a wave and smile, which she returned before going around to hug and kiss Clay. Clay said, "Back in a tick with the coach after I grab Kerry. There are another two guests staying here, and then we'll do the other pickups." He climbed back into the ute and waved.

Oh God, don't leave!

But Ethan had to put on his big-boy pants. It was going to be fine. Sam wasn't going to push him off the spectacular Blue Mountains.

Probably.

They smiled awkwardly at each other, Ethan shoving his hands in his jeans pockets, and then restlessly tugging at the collar of his tee. Sam pointed to it and said, "Have you been? It looks cool on TV."

Ethan glanced down at his own shirt, remembering belatedly that it depicted the Santa Monica Pier and iconic Ferris wheel. "No, actually. This is from Old Navy. They do these graphic tees of all sorts of stuff."

"Oh. Cool."

"Yeah. Uh… So…" *Kill me now.*

"Can you hear me all right? Dad said to speak slowly and clearly and make sure you can see my mouth?"

Another wave of affection for Clay hit him like a two by four, and he smiled. "Yes. It's—this is perfect." He glanced around at the deserted semicircle of the hotel entrance, only a few porters chatting by the doors. "It's harder when there's background noise. Like cars or music, or a lot of people. So I might have to ask you to repeat yourself. I really appreciate it if you do. I know it's annoying, but sometimes people just say 'never mind,' and it kind of sucks."

She nodded. "Right. That makes sense."

"Um…" *Think of something to say, come on.* "Oh! How's your boyfriend doing?" There. Nice safe topic.

"Heaps better, thanks." She rolled her eyes with a laugh. "Still being a big baby, but he's healing nicely."

"Glad to hear it." Ethan nodded and tried desperately to think of something else to say. "Gilly's a great dog."

She beamed. "He is. Such a sweet thing. Not the sharpest tool in the shed, but he's all heart. I've missed him this week."

Ethan nodded again, suddenly feeling awkward since the reason she hadn't seen her dog was because Ethan was sleeping with her dad. "I guess you'll see him soon though?"

"Yeah. Going home Sunday." She smiled awkwardly. "Your flight's tomorrow night?"

"Right. Clay has to work, but he said he'll be off in time to take me to the airport since it's a late flight."

"Cool." She smiled again, and *God,* it was clearly all so awkward for both of them.

"Thanks for giving us time alone this week." Ethan's face went hot. "I mean—not that—it was just—"

"Relax. Look, I'm not going to say it isn't weird to think of you and my dad—not that I'm *thinking* about it in detail—but…" She laughed, shaking her head. "Clearly this is a strange situation for both of us. Instead of making painful small talk, let's just lay it on the table. Yes?"

His heart thudded. "Yep. Let's do it."

"Okay. You're not much older than me and you're *mumble mumble.* Who I thought was straight. Apparently *mumble.* But you've changed all that. And that's fine! More than fine, it's good. *Mumble mumble.* I want my dad to be happy."

"Uh-huh. Right. Sorry, could you speak a little more slowly?"

"Oh, right." She nodded.

"Thanks." He attempted to fill in the blanks. "Um, yeah. We've talked about it, and it's not that he was straight all along and suddenly he's gay. I think he repressed who he really is for years. Wouldn't let himself even question or think about it."

A frown creased Sam's face. "Why do you think he'd do that? I've been trying to figure it out. Sure, growing up gay in the outback isn't easy, especially back then. But was it just that? What people would say? Was it that he wanted to be 'normal' so he married Mum?"

"I think all of that played a role." He hesitated, not sure if Clay would want to tell Sam about the traumatic incident involving Tony Taylor and the response of Clay's father. "You should talk to him about it and ask why." There, that was vague enough that he wasn't betraying a confidence.

"Hmm. Yeah, I will." She glanced around, but the other guests for the tour hadn't appeared yet. "So, is this your normal thing? Shagging older blokes?"

Ethan laughed uncomfortably. "No, actually. He's the first. I dated in high school and college, but only guys my age. My only really serious relationship was the last seven years or so with my fiancé." As she jolted, he quickly added, "*Ex*-fiancé." Since they were being frank, there was no sense in sugarcoating it. "I came home early the day before our wedding and found him fucking my best friend."

Sam's jaw dropped and her eyebrows shot up. "Bloody hell. That's brutal. Sorry to hear it."

"Yeah." He forcefully shoved away the memories. "It really sucked, to say the least. But I came on the honeymoon alone and met your dad, so…" What? He couldn't say anything too ridiculous—like that he was somehow already in love with Clay—or she'd call bullshit. He finished lamely, "So that's been a silver lining."

"Right. Holiday fling after having your heart broken, eh?" She smiled, but there was tension in her jaw.

"I really care about Clay. A lot." He wanted to insist that it was already so much more than *caring*, but he was leaving tomorrow. It was unrealistic to think he and Clay could make it work.

"Oh, of course. No, you seem like a good bloke, Ethan. Just worried about him having this big breakthrough and then being alone again." She smiled. "Guess I'll have to sign him up for the gay or bisexual dating sites."

"Uh-huh," Ethan agreed, wanting to scream at the thought of Clay dating anyone else.

"Do you reckon that's what he is? Bi? My mate Lucy is. But I dunno if Dad fancies women at all. If he doesn't, it explains a lot about how he and Mum were when they were together. More like mates than a couple."

"I don't know. I think he might be demisexual as well as gay or bi. Obviously he's the one who has to figure out his own identity."

"Yeah, of course. I won't rush him or anything. Just curious."

"Totally. I get it."

She peered at him. "I know we already covered this, but you're the same age as my boyfriend. It's really weird."

"Right. It's honestly weird for me that Clay has kids who are already in their twenties. He doesn't seem old enough."

She smiled faintly. "Guess it's weird for all of us."

A man and woman approached, and Sam gave them a friendly wave and asked if they were coming on the tour. They were, and after a round of introductions, the minibus arrived. Ethan gave Clay a smile as he climbed on and sat by the window near the front on the left side of the vehicle, Sam sitting beside him.

The guide, Kerry, was middle-aged and plump, with dark hair, olive skin, and a bright smile. After chatting with the other couple and getting them settled, she stood by the front, holding on as

Clay drove to the next hotel.

"Great to meet you, Sam! Clay speaks of you often. Great to have you and your mate aboard." They nodded and agreed, and it made perfect sense that Clay had told Kerry that Ethan was Sam's friend. Still, it hurt just a bit, and Ethan told himself he was being stupid. Not to mention unfair—if Clay came out to his colleagues, he had to do it in his own time. He breathed through the pang and refocused on Kerry.

"Ethan, I have something for you." She leaned over her seat across the aisle and came back with a few stapled sheets of paper. "Clay asked me to bring an extra copy of my notes. Please let me know if you need me to repeat anything."

Ethan took the paper, any hurt vanished, affection warming him. "Thank you. This is perfect."

As they stopped at the next hotel and Clay and Kerry got off to greet a bigger group of people, Sam smiled softly and nodded to the paper. "That was nice of him."

"Yeah." Ethan grinned, making sure to keep his voice down. "He's so thoughtful and kind. He does these wonderful little things that just make me feel so special."

Sam's smile grew, and she eyed him speculatively. "Yeah. He's always been like that. I'm glad you can see it. He's a real catch, my dad."

"He is," Ethan agreed. "I'm really lucky."

"Shame you're leaving so soon." She frowned, seeming to mean it.

The warmth of happiness faded, reality returning. Ethan could only nod and try to pretend tomorrow didn't exist.

"WHAT ARE YOU in the mood for?"

In the kitchen, Clay handed Ethan a cold beer in a foam holder from Surfers Paradise. Scratching Gilly's head with his free hand, Ethan said, "Whatever you like. Thanks."

Clay added, "There's loads of takeaway options around here. Chinese, Thai, pizza, burgers—anything you fancy."

"You were the one working all day. What do you feel like?" Ethan tried to smile and keep his tone light. They'd kissed briefly in Clay's truck when they'd finally been alone together, but sitting in traffic to get back to Parramatta, Ethan had kept his hands to himself. They both seemed…off, somehow. In their own heads, maybe. Not quite connecting.

Clay said, "I'll eat anything as long as it's not too spicy."

"Right. Me too. Let me think…"

During the day, Ethan had been able to enjoy the gorgeous vistas of the Blue Mountains and hang with Sam and mostly forget that the clock was running down on his time with Clay.

Mostly.

Now it was their last night together. But did it have to be? Yes, Ethan had to go home and go back to work, and they lived on opposite sides of the globe in different time zones, and it's not as if they could even meet up on weekends, and…

He sighed. Reality was so depressing.

"None of those strike your fancy?" Clay took out his phone and tapped. "There are heaps more, don't worry. Let me see…"

"No, no, any of those are fine." Then he blurted, "I can't believe I'm leaving tomorrow."

Clay gave him a half-hearted smile. "Time flies, doesn't it?" Gilly had come to his feet, rubbing against Clay's uniform pants. Clay petted him. "I'm sorry I can't get the day off. If the tour wasn't full, you could come along to the Blue Mountains again. Although you probably had your fill today."

"No, it was amazing. It really is so beautiful. You can see for miles from the lookouts. The Three Sisters are so iconic. It was wonderful to see them in person." God, he'd already said that in the truck, like, three times.

"Couldn't have asked for better weather either. Barely a cloud today. A little hot, but not too bad, eh?"

"No, and I had my hat. Thanks to you."

They smiled at each other, and God, it all felt so stilted and wrong, talking about the fucking weather.

Clay said, "I'll be back in plenty of time to drive you to the airport, though."

"Thanks. I… I wish I didn't have to go." He smiled weakly. "But I've used up all my vacation time. And money. So I need to make more of that."

Clay smiled back, but it didn't reach his eyes. "Right. Of course you do." He hesitated. "It's not as if… Well, we've only just met, and I reckon I've got plenty to sort out."

"Right. Totally." He moved his hand between them, words tripping out of his mouth. "And this was great. It was what we both needed. A vacation fling or whatever."

Clay dropped his head, rubbing at the back of his neck. "*Mumble mumble.*"

"Pardon?" Ethan's stomach clenched. *Please say this wasn't just a fling.*

When Clay lifted his head, he said, "Perhaps you could visit again. Or I could go to America. I know it's not cheap, and who knows when we could manage it. Need at least two weeks of vacation time, and even then it would be tight. But we could think about it."

Nodding eagerly, Ethan said, "Absolutely." Yet he couldn't help but think it wasn't realistic. Once he was gone and they were both back in their busy, everyday routines… Would this connection hold? They were probably fooling themselves to think it could.

Ethan was on the rebound, and Clay was just coming out. He should probably date other men instead of settling down with the first one he hooked up with. Besides, everyone knew long-distance relationships rarely worked. They'd only been together a week. Maybe it was good to slow down. Maybe…

Ethan added, "We can definitely stay in touch, right? FaceTime and WhatsApp. It's something, at least."

Clay smiled softly. "I'd like that. Very much."

"Me too. So we'll do that, and I guess we'll see what happens? And in the meantime…"

"Reckon you've got unfinished business with your ex-fiancé."

Ugh, thoughts of Michael and Todd exploded in his mind, and Ethan grimaced. "Yeah. I guess so." He shuddered, trying to shove that particular reality far away.

And fuck, Ethan needed to find an apartment. He'd been letting himself spend the week in fantasyland with Clay, and he had to face the facts. Even if he wasn't going to stay in New York permanently, he'd spent a shit-ton of money on this trip and was in no position to quit his job. His credit card bill was going to be massive.

"Sorry to bring it up. Back to the real world and all that. I'm doing a couple runs down the Great Ocean Road next week. Then heading up to Cairns again. Back to the grind."

"Yeah. It's… This has been amazing, though. I had the best time this week." *Understatement of the century.*

"Me too, mate." Clay opened his mouth, then closed it.

They watched each other for a moment, the air thick with what Ethan imagined was longing. What he *hoped* was longing.

Clay took a gulp of beer. "Anyway, we can have a quick spot of dinner tomorrow before I drop you off."

"Right. Great!" Ethan forced a smile. "I'll have fun hanging with Gilly tomorrow. Need to pack too. Might do some laundry if that's okay?"

"Yeah, of course. We can order dinner now, and I'll show you how the washer works. Don't have a dryer, but there's a line outside. Everything dries in no time."

"Great." Wonderful. Terrific. Were they going to spend their last night together being polite and awkward and talking about fabric softener?

Clay looked at his phone. "Let's see. Do you want something Latin, or maybe—"

"I want you to fuck me."

Fumbling his phone, Clay dropped it on the counter beside his beer. Gilly butted against him for more pets, and Clay muttered something Ethan missed before getting Gilly's bag of food from the pantry and filling his bowl in the little dining nook.

Pulse jumping, Ethan waited. Maybe Clay didn't want to? Not all guys liked anal sex, and obviously that was totally fine. They probably should have talked about it before Ethan blurted it out in the kitchen the night before he was leaving the country.

When Clay was across from him again, a few feet away, Ethan said, "No pressure, though. If you're not ready, or you don't want to, or whatever. It's totally cool. We should just order dinner. I didn't mean to make things weird."

Rubbing his face, Clay said something. When Ethan squinted and turned his head a bit, Clay dropped his hand. "Sorry. I said things are already weird, aren't they?"

"Uh-huh. But if this is our last night together, let's just pretend it's not."

"Right. We can do that. Could get hit by a truck tomorrow. Have to live in the now. That's what Pete always says."

Ethan nodded. "I'm still here. You're here. We're both here." He laughed too loudly. "I'm the master of observation."

Adam's apple bobbing, Clay asked, "When you say 'fuck,' do you mean…"

"Your cock in my ass."

Clay blushed pink, and it was so fucking adorable Ethan had to grin. Fuck awkwardness. Fuck reality. They were still together, and they were going to make the most of it.

He closed the distance between them, taking Clay's face in his hands and kissing him deeply, his fingers stroking the soft hair of Clay's beard. Clay kissed him back, wrapping his arms around Ethan's back, their tongues meeting.

Their little gasps and moans and the smack of their lips were loud in Ethan's hearing aids, and he loved it. Then Gilly started barking, and he had to break the kiss and wince.

Flushed, his lips red and wet, Clay gave Ethan a smile. "Hold that thought." He ushered Gilly outside and closed the door, turning and leaning against it. "He always likes to go outside after dinner and have a nap on Sam's lounger."

"Cool. So we're good?"

"We're marvelous." Clay grinned.

Ethan smiled back. "Tomorrow doesn't exist. Okay?"

Clay nodded, his lips parted, breathing shallowly. "So…how…?"

"Let's go to bed." Ethan held out his hand, and Clay eagerly came and took it, his palm a little sweaty. Ethan squeezed and led the way.

Chapter Seventeen

A	S ETHAN STRIPPED off his clothes, Clay fumbled with his own, his heart in his throat. He wasn't sure why this seemed so momentous since they'd already done so much with their mouths and hands, but…it did.

Ethan gently batted Clay's hands away from the buttons on his uniform shirt. He undid them deftly, pressing kisses to Clay's lips as he worked. After he pulled the shirt down over Clay's arms and tossed it on the chair in the corner, he tugged up the hem of Clay's undershirt.

Clay lifted his arms over his head, and the singlet flew toward the chair as well. Biting his full bottom lip, Ethan ran his hands over Clay's hairy chest and murmured, "I love your body."

"Not as fit as I was," Clay muttered, sucking in his soft belly. Ethan frowned, turning his head and jutting his chin forward the way he did when he couldn't hear. Laughing self-consciously, Clay repeated himself.

Ethan didn't laugh. Looking at Clay evenly, he said again, "I. Love. Your. Body." His hands dipped lower, around Clay's middle and up his back. He pressed his lips to Clay's collarbone. "I love your freckles, and your big, strong shoulders."

He walked around Clay, his hands firm so Clay didn't turn with him. His lips traced the ridges of Clay's back and spine, then over the tattoo. From behind, he unzipped Clay's trousers and pulled them down with his briefs. Clay stepped out of them and gave them a blind kick.

Ethan's hands dipped lower, those long, beautiful fingers tracing the crack of Clay's arse. His mouth followed, kissing lightly, and Clay's knees trembled, his prick swelling. Ethan kissed the back of Clay's thighs, his fingers drawing nameless patterns.

When Ethan came around to stand in front of Clay, cock flushed and straining, he kissed Clay's mouth again and whispered, "See how hard you make me without even being touched?"

Clay could only moan and draw him close for another long kiss, diving his tongue into Ethan's mouth, swallowing the gorgeous little whimpers he made.

They were both breathing hard when Ethan asked, "Do you want to fuck me?"

He made sure not to mutter. "Yes."

"So, I bought condoms the other day, just in case. Because I really want you inside me. If you want that."

He gave Ethan a smile. "Sounds like a good idea to me." He tingled with excitement. Sex with Barb had never done much for him, but the idea of being inside Ethan like that… Well, inside him in a bit of a different way, but Clay imagined the mechanics were similar.

Ethan licked his lips. "Okay. Cool."

It was still so new and exciting and hard to believe that he *had* Ethan. *Want to make him mine forever.* There was that deep, primal instinct again, and Clay told it to zip up. He'd surely frighten Ethan away if he started talking about forever.

Tomorrow doesn't exist.

"Okay," Ethan repeated, breathing quickly, his eyes bright and eager. "And I want to make sure you're comfortable with it, so if it's too much at some point, or you don't like it, we can stop. Obviously." He'd been speaking in a rush, and he broke off. "I'll stop babbling now."

"I like it."

"The idea of fucking me, or my babbling?"

Clay grinned, lust simmering through him along with a rush of affection. "Both." He added, "I like everything about you," because it was the plain truth.

That earned him a deep kiss, Ethan throwing his arms around Clay. They rutted against each other, their hard cocks meeting. Groaning, Ethan broke free, his lips shiny with spit.

"Don't want to come yet." Holding Clay's hand, he backed up to the bed, letting go to rifle through his smaller suitcase, then crawl onto the mattress. He stretched out on his back, dropping a foil packet and bottle beside him. Clay felt like the luckiest bloke in the world that he got to have this.

Ethan lifted his hand. "I want to see you while you're inside me."

"We can do it like that?" He shook his head, laughing. "I'm clueless, aren't I?"

But Ethan didn't laugh at him. "I'll show you. C'mere."

Heart like a drum, Clay moved on top of him. He reveled in the sensation of Ethan's body hair rubbing against him, of his lean, firm limbs and chest. "Love your body too," Clay said.

He knew Ethan liked to have his nipples touched, so he dipped his head to suck them, feeling victorious when he scraped his teeth across one and Ethan arched his back on a high moan.

The ceiling fan was on, beating a steady rhythm, the air ghosting over Clay's hot skin. Sweat gathered at the nape of his neck, and Ethan's fingers worked through Clay's hair as Clay nipped and scraped his nipples until they were red and peaked.

"Here," Ethan panted, easing Clay's head up and passing him the bottle. "Get your fingers slick. Take your watch off first." He smiled, face flushed. "Don't want to get it lube-y."

While Clay squirted the gel onto his right index and middle

fingers, Ethan wriggled beneath him, drawing his spread legs up so his knees were practically to his shoulders. Clay sat up to give him more room.

"You're sure I won't hurt you like this?" Mouth dry, he eyed Ethan's arse, deliciously exposed.

"I'm very bendy. I want to see your face." He drew Clay near for a kiss, then whispered, "Ease one finger inside me."

Nodding, Clay circled Ethan's hole with his index finger, getting the whorls of hair there goopy with lube. Ethan didn't seem to mind, urging him on until the tip of Clay's finger was pushing into him.

"Like that, uh-huh," Ethan muttered. "More. Stretch me. Get me ready for your cock. Need all of it."

They were really doing this, and the thought of his cock fitting into the tight heat clamping his finger was both impossible and irresistible. Clay pushed a little harder, and his whole finger slid in.

"God, that's it," Ethan moaned. "Crook your finger. Find the little—" He nearly came off the bed as he cried out. "Yes, right there."

Ethan's cock was leaking, and Clay leaned forward to catch the drops on his tongue. Ethan groaned and demanded, "Push another finger in."

Again, it seemed impossible, yet Ethan's arse stretched to take him in. It must have damn well hurt, and sure enough, Ethan squeezed his eyes shut, grimacing. But when Clay started to ease out, Ethan's eyes popped open.

"No. It's so good. Please."

So Clay kept his fingers inside, licking at Ethan's balls, the trimmed hair scratching his nose. But Ethan had said he didn't want to come too soon, and the way he was panting, Clay had a feeling he was close.

Clay drew back, inching out his fingers and reaching for the lube again. He asked, "You ready for me?"

Ethan's eyes had closed, and he refocused on Clay. "Sorry. Can you say that again?"

Feeling silly at saying it again, Clay's cheeks got hot. "Asked if you were ready for me."

"Am I ready to be plowed with your big, hot cock?" He grinned mischievously. "Was that the question?"

Clay laughed, relaxing a few degrees. "Yes, you bugger. That was the question."

"My tight ass is so ready to be buggered."

Trying not to shake with the adrenaline pumping through him, Clay ripped open the foil and rolled the condom on, slicking it with lube. Ethan pulled Clay closer, kissing him and reaching down to line up Clay's cock with his arse. He wriggled again, tilting his hips even more.

The head of Clay's prick nudged at Ethan's arse, and now neither of them were laughing. Nodding, Ethan urged Clay's hands to his bent thighs. "Keep me open. Push inside."

Clay did as he was told, wincing as he felt the resistance inside Ethan. "What does it feel like?"

"It burns, but you feel so good. It'll be worth it. Just a bit farther, and then—yes!" Ethan dropped his head back, groaning as Clay pushed all the way into him.

"Jesus!" Clay exclaimed, the heat gripping him better than anything he'd ever felt. Because it was *Ethan.* Clay was actually inside him. Yeah, he'd been in Ethan's mouth, but this was different. He was seated in him right at his very core.

He was actually fucking another bloke. And not just any bloke—Ethan. The best bloke there was. That they were sharing this made Clay want to shout for joy and cry at the thought of Ethan leaving. But tomorrow didn't exist, so he refocused on the now.

Ethan's throat worked, and Clay wanted to lick his Adam's

apple, but he didn't have a chance. Ethan raised his head, squeezing around Clay with his inner muscles and making him shudder.

Ethan grasped at Clay's hips. "Move. Please. Need more."

"Right." Clay inched back and rocked in gently. "God, you feel incredible."

"You're so hot inside me. The stretch is…" He broke off on a moan. Sweat dripped into the hollow of Ethan's throat, and Clay did lean down now and lick, loving the burst of salt on his tongue.

Ethan tugged Clay's hair roughly and demanded a kiss as Clay fucked into him with shallow thrusts. "Harder," he panted. "Please." He pulled back so their eyes met, his pupils almost black with lust. "You won't hurt me. I promise."

Muscles tensing, Clay pulled halfway out and slammed back in, his balls slapping against Ethan's arse cheeks. They both moaned, and Clay asked, "You like that, sweetheart?"

But Ethan didn't hear him over his own grunts and cries, and it seemed pretty darn clear that yes, Ethan liked that. A lot. He was so tight and warm and perfect, and Clay lost himself in him, fucking Ethan until he knew he was going to spill.

Ethan wrapped his long legs around Clay's waist, his eyes glazed as he panted. When Clay reached between them to jack him off, Ethan gasped, his prick like iron in Clay's grasp. It only took a few strokes before he spurted, his mouth open and eyes shut.

Ethan shook with his release, and he squeezed down on Clay, the pressure so hot and right. Taking Clay's face in his hands, Ethan ordered, "Come inside me. Imagine there's no condom and you're going to fill me up until your cum's dripping out."

"Bloody hell," Clay muttered, slamming into Ethan again before his orgasm crashed through him like a cyclone. He shuddered, deep inside Ethan, Ethan's legs tight around him. Ethan held him there as Clay trembled through the aftershocks.

He buried his face in Ethan's neck, gasping against his skin.

When he finally lifted his head, he eased out his softening prick and tossed the condom. It was wet and messy down between them, but Clay was in no rush to clean up. He nuzzled Ethan's flushed cheek. "It felt good, did it?" he couldn't resist asking just to make sure it hadn't hurt too much.

Ethan grinned. "It sure did. If you want to try it sometime…" He burst out laughing. "I can already feel you clenching your ass at the thought."

Clay laughed too. "Not sure I'm ready for that tonight." *Even though tomorrow doesn't exist.*

Ethan smiled and kissed him gently. "That's okay. Meanwhile, rest up. Because you are definitely fucking me again tonight."

"Can we order dinner first?" Clay teased.

"I suppose I'll allow it."

"Have to get my energy up after that." He frowned. "You're sure it won't hurt too much?"

"I want to feel you tomorrow."

There it was, the reminder that tomorrow *did* exist, and time was slipping away. They both knew it, but they stopped talking and kissed instead, trying to forget for just a little while longer.

OF COURSE TOMORROW arrived, the bastard.

They'd stayed up long past midnight, and Ethan barely stirred when Clay dragged himself from the cocoon of their bed before dawn. Ethan's arse had to be sore after he'd ridden Clay's cock like a cowboy on a bull. Clay's chest hair was caked with dried semen, and he smiled to himself as he quickly scrubbed in the shower.

Oh, how he wished he could chuck a sickie, but he'd be leaving twenty people high and dry on their holiday, not to mention the company wouldn't be best pleased, to say the least.

When Clay pressed a kiss to Ethan's tousled head, Ethan murmured, but didn't wake. Clay had been tiptoeing around the room as he got ready, and realized belatedly that he needn't have since Ethan didn't have his hearing aids in and was far away in dreamland. If only Clay could join him.

He gave himself a shake. Time to get going and stop wishing for what couldn't be. Gilly barked and whined when Clay left, and guilt tugged. But Ethan would be taking him for a walk soon, and they'd have a nice day together.

Clay let himself mope on the drive into Sydney, but once he had the coach and passengers, he forced a smile. He had a job to do.

Hours later, after an accident closed two lanes and made Clay perilously late fetching Ethan—and taking away the time they'd had for dinner—Clay stood off to the side as Ethan checked his bags in at the ticket counter. Clay had changed into his customary shorts and T-shirt. He slipped his foot in and out of his thong, fiddling with it anxiously, his hands in his pockets.

It had all been a rush, and they hadn't spoken much on the drive, both tense. Now here they were, and soon Ethan would have to go through security, and that would be it. Sure, they could text and FaceTime, have a chat. But they had separate lives. They had to be realistic.

Didn't they?

With each passing second as Clay watched Ethan at the ticket counter, cupping his hand behind his ear, the woman not speaking clearly enough, a word echoed through Clay. It grew stronger with each dull thud of his heart.

No.

No.

No.

When Ethan approached, Clay led him close to the wall in the long, narrow departures hall, as far away from the noise as possible even though they were still out in the open. Clay's head was light, his body thrumming with a strange energy. He stared at Ethan— at this brave, beautiful man who had burst into Clay's life and changed it forever. Clay hadn't even known how lost he was, but being found was more profound than he ever could have imagined.

Reality could bugger itself.

Ethan frowned at him questioningly, clear concern shining in his eyes. "Clay?"

"I don't want you to go." The words were barely a whisper, his throat too dry.

His frown deepening, Ethan fiddled with his hearing aids and moved so his back was to the departures hall. "I'm sorry, could you repeat that?"

Yes, he certainly could. Clearing his throat, Clay spoke clearly. "I don't want you to go." He shook his head. "I don't care if we've only just met. I don't care if it's foolish. Don't go."

Face lighting up, Ethan grasped Clay's hand, threading their fingers together tightly. "I don't want to go either. I know we're supposed to be mature and reasonable, and realistic, and all that shit. And I know we just met, and you're discovering who you are, and you should probably date other people—"

"Bugger that." Clay took a shaky breath, squeezing Ethan's fingers. He glanced around at the people walking by or waiting in lines to see if anyone was in earshot, but then shook his head. "I don't care who knows it. I'm a queer. This is who I am." Clay pondered it for a moment. "Is that the way people say it? Or is it just 'queer'?"

Ethan's cheeks dimpled, and he reached for Clay's other hand, gripping it. "Usually just 'queer,' but you can identify yourself however you want. Or not. You get to decide."

"Well, I'm not sure about the rest of it, but I know I'm not straight. Because I've never fancied anyone the way I do you. I don't want to date other people. Not those women on Sam's websites, or any other blokes. You're the one."

If Clay was going to *know* these truths—own them—he was going all-in. His voice was hoarse, but he tried to speak clearly, drawing Ethan closer so the tips of their shoes touched. "For years, I didn't know myself. I just went along and did the thing I reckoned I was supposed to. If I do what I'm supposed to now, then I'll say hoo-roo and you'll go back to America. And we'll probably never see each other again, and people will say that's how it should be because this was just a holiday fling, and there's too much of a gap between us since you're barely older than my kids."

Ethan's hands trembled in Clay's. "Right. And I'm on the rebound, and we don't have enough in common, and how will I get a job down here? We'd have to figure out my visa, and what if things don't work out?"

"All valid points, I reckon." His heart hammered so hard he could hear it. He shook his head, blurting, "And I don't give a stuff about any of it! I'm bloody falling in love with you. Might already be there." Shit, he'd said it.

And he *knew* it was true.

But Ethan frowned, and Clay's stomach dropped and twisted. He'd gone too far and buggered it up, hadn't he? He'd frightened Ethan off and—

"Sorry, you have to say that again." Ethan glared at a group of people passing by with their luggage trolleys, laughing and whooping it up. "More slowly? I didn't get any of it." He squeezed Clay's hands, giving him a nervous smile.

Taking a deep breath, Clay spoke clearly, his heart still pounding as he sliced open his chest and laid it bare. "I said I don't give a stuff about doing what we're supposed to. Don't give a stuff what other people think. Don't give a stuff that I'm too old for you. I love you, Ethan."

Ethan stared at him for endless seconds. "You… You love

me?"

"Yes. Can you still not hear me?" He glanced around, looking for a spot, but there were people all over. "Hell, what if we go to the loo? Should be quieter in there?"

"No, no, I heard you this time." Ethan's eyes were glistening, and his smile quivered. "I just wanted to make sure it was real."

"It's real." Clay clutched Ethan's hands. "I know it."

"I love you too. I don't care if it's too fast."

Clay could have flapped his arms and flown to the ceiling, pure joy bursting in him. "Can you say it again? Wouldn't mind hearing it twice."

Bouncing on his toes, Ethan grinned. "I'm in love with you, Clay Kelly."

Clay yanked Ethan into his arms, hugging him like his life depended on it. Because it did. It really did. Ethan clutched him, and Clay was about to pull back and kiss him when he spotted a family walking by, the parents frowning and muttering something, the kids gawking.

He suddenly felt like everyone was looking, so he skipped the kiss, easing back from the hug. They weren't doing anything wrong, but his face was hot, skin itching with the stares of people nearby.

Ethan's brow creased, and he glanced around. He smiled softly. "It's okay. PDA takes a while to get used to."

"Shouldn't let them bother me, I know."

"One step at a time." Ethan gave him another sweet, understanding smile.

"You've been so patient. You sure you want to put up with me?"

Ethan grinned now. "I'm a hundred percent sure."

"Yeah?" Clay's heart was ready to burst. "Why should we end things when they're just getting started, right?"

"Exactly. Why should we do what we're 'supposed' to do? I

already tried that. Thought I'd fix everything in my life by marrying Michael and doing what we were supposed to. Fuck it. I don't want to go. I mean, I have to go tonight because I can't quit my job without notice. But I want to come back. I want to be with you. Are we crazy?"

"Reckon there's only one way to find out."

"Right." Ethan shrugged, grinning. "What's the worst thing that can happen? It doesn't work out, and I end up going back to the States. Or staying here if I have a job. I think it's an acceptable risk."

Pulse racing, Clay said, "I'll help pay for your flight back. You'll move in with me. Sam's probably ready to live with Jase. We'll figure it out. I'll talk to my boss and tell him I can't do the long hauls anymore. Whatever it takes, we'll make this happen."

"We will. Fuck the real world. We're going to make it our bitch." He lifted his hand for a high five, and Clay slapped his palm, laughing.

If the real world didn't like it, it could get stuffed along with everyone else.

Chapter Eighteen

FIFTY-THREE DAYS.

It was March, and the last time Ethan had climbed these stairs had been fifty-three days ago. He glared at the flickering second-floor light for old time's sake and continued slowly to the third floor, step by step.

The walk was surreally familiar—the alarming creak of the second-last step, the dent in the pipe running up to the roof. The thud of the door behind him as he exited the stairwell. The ten steps or so to his front door on the old, stained carpet.

No, *Michael's* door. This would never be Ethan's home again. And along with the bittersweet pang of all he'd lost was the rush of relief and anticipation. He'd been dreading this moment ever since he'd landed back in New York and put his plan into motion.

Time to close this book.

It felt odd to knock, but he did, although the jagged metal of the key dug into his other palm. The door opened, and there was Michael in his customary black pants and shirt, staring back at Ethan with a strained smile.

"Hey," Michael said. "Um…" He stepped back. "Come in."

Part of Ethan wanted to refuse and tell him to just stack the boxes in the hall, but no. He could do this. He *needed* to do this. When he walked in, he almost automatically unzipped his spring jacket and hung it on one of the hooks. Keeping it on, he stuffed his hands in his jeans pockets.

Todd appeared at the end of the little entryway, wearing the classic Asteroids T-shirt Ethan had bought him for his birthday a few years ago. He smiled nervously. "Hey, Eth. So good to see you, man."

And fuck, it *was* good to see him. And Michael. They'd been everything to Ethan for so long, and for a horrible moment he was afraid he'd burst into humiliating tears.

He didn't.

Head high, he nodded to Todd. "Hey. Thanks for coming."

"Of course. We really want to talk to you." He backed up, and they shuffled into the living room.

Through the open bedroom door, Ethan could glimpse the bed. He let himself remember the sight of Todd on top of Michael, taking his cock. He let himself remember the betrayal, experiencing the emotions—hurt, fury, shame, despair—and coming out the other side.

Acceptance.

No, Ethan was not going to cry, and he wasn't going to shout. It was over, and his life would be better for it. So. Much. Better. He smiled to himself as he thought of Clay finishing his last East Coast tour, and the picture he'd texted at the beginning of the week from the amazingly pink sunrise at Mission Beach.

Only thing it's missing is you.

"Um, Eth?"

Blinking back to the present, Ethan watched as Michael and Todd exchanged leery glances. They were probably afraid he was about to completely lose it, what with the smiling.

"Yeah." He glanced around at his former home—all cool shades and fashionably sharp edges. Moving boxes were stacked by one wall. Not many, probably ten, neatly labeled in Michael's script, since he knew how much Ethan liked organization.

Bathroom stuff
Books
Misc.
Mementos
Clothes

Most were clothes, presumably the contents of his dresser drawers. A few bulging garment bags hung from the top of the bookcase.

"Uncle Chuck's downstairs with his van," Ethan said.

"Okay," Michael replied. "We can help bring it all down." He shifted from foot to foot, a habit when he was nervous. He said something else Ethan missed, but it didn't matter.

"Just put it in the hall. We can do it."

Todd blurted, "Eth, please talk to us. We know we fucked up big time, but—"

"I am going to talk. And you're both going to listen." He waited a few beats as they glanced at each other. "I'll never forgive you for lying to me like that. And for so long. I might have been able to forgive you two falling in love, but not this." He zeroed his gaze on Michael. "Not fucking in our bed the day before our wedding."

Michael exhaled a shaky breath, his eyes on his feet. "I know. I'm sorry."

Ethan looked at Todd. "You were my best friend."

Swallowing hard, Todd managed to keep Ethan's gaze. "I'm sorry. I—"

"It doesn't matter. The truth is, Michael and I should have broken up years ago. It's over, and it has been for a long time when it comes down to it. We were young. We made bad choices. All of us. I chose to move here with you guys, and when I hated it, I chose to stay. And now I'm leaving."

They stood a little straighter, sharing another glance. Michael asked, "Where are you going?"

"Australia. I'm transferring to the firm's Sydney office. I already did international work, and it's in demand and specialized. They didn't want to lose me, so they're sponsoring my work permit."

Michael gaped. "Are you serious? You're moving to the other side of the world? For how long?"

"Who knows. Maybe forever. I guess I should thank you for being lying cheaters. Going on the honeymoon alone was the best thing that ever happened to me. I met my own version of Crocodile Dundee. We're going to make a go of it and see what happens."

"*Mumble mumble.*" Michael was speaking far too quickly, his hands slicing through the air in agitation.

"Wait, who is this guy?" Todd asked, frowning.

"None of your business," Ethan replied calmly. "This relationship, this friendship?" He motioned between himself and them. "It's over. For good. I'm deleting my social media accounts. I'm going to Australia and I'm starting fresh. New me, new Instagram."

"But wait," Michael implored. "I still love you, baby." He reached out. "Don't you love me at all anymore?"

Ethan's throat tightened, and years of memories unspooled in a rush through his mind, too blurry to focus on, more the sensations of warmth and affection and passion and laughter that had faded too long ago. "The last few years, we were going through the motions. You were lying to me, and I was depressed, and then when I came out of it, I was pretending that everything could still work. That getting married would fix it all." Tears burned his eyes, but he fought them back. "I loved you both, and part of me always will. But this is goodbye."

Todd shook his head. "Come on, man. Don't uproot your whole life for some dude in Australia you barely know. There has to be a way for us to work through this. To at least be friends again. I know it'll take time, but—"

Ethan turned and strode calmly to the hanging garment bags, piling them over one arm. They were heavy, but he didn't let it show. He glanced over his shoulder for a last look at the two people he'd loved most in the whole world watching him in silent dismay.

"I hope you and whoever else are happy together. Because I'm going to be." He thought of Clay and smiled. "I'm going to be happy as hell."

As that ruddy, gorgeous face filled the phone screen, Ethan's heart swelled. He wished he could kiss Clay and feel his beard against his face. "Hey," Ethan said. "How was the drive into Sydney?"

"A little traffic, but not too bad." He paused. "How did it go with—" He cut off. "Uh, Michael?"

"You were going to say 'shithead,' weren't you?"

Clay laughed. "Guilty as charged."

Ethan exhaled and leaned back against the headboard. The room wasn't particularly fancy, but it was clean and new, and airport hotels at least had reasonable rates. "Anyway, it went fine. It was what it was."

"Meaning?" Clay frowned. "Did they do anything to upset you? I mean aside from what they already did."

"You going to fly over here and kick their asses if they did?" Ethan teased, secretly loving it.

"Too right, I am."

Ethan tried not to swoon too much, failing miserably. "My knight in shining armor. But there's no need. They didn't do anything. I mean, it was tough seeing them again and being back at the apartment. But I needed to do it. It was good closure. I sent a message to Michael's sister Clara and a few other people before I deleted my Facebook account. Sat in the back of Uncle Chuck's van and went through the boxes of stuff. Most of it he's putting in storage for me."

"He's a good bloke."

"He really is. It's at least thirteen hours roundtrip to Cheektowaga, and he still dropped me off at Newark before he left. We're not super close or anything, but it's nice to know I do still have some family."

"Of course."

"So yeah. It went okay. I'd been dreading it, but it feels good to have it done." He swallowed hard over the swell of emotion. "Feels right." He laughed shakily. "Sorry. Don't know why I'm getting all choked up now."

"It's all right, love."

Ethan's breath hitched at the casual endearment. Looking at Clay's face and hearing the steady reassurance of his low voice filled Ethan with such peace. He managed a real smile. "Yeah. It is. Oh, how did Sam's move go?"

"Great. Put most of her stuff in the back of the ute since Jase has furniture already. She's thrilled to be living with him, although poor Gilly's less pleased. We're going to make sure he gets to spend a couple days with her every week."

"I can't wait to see Gilly again. Think he'll remember me?"

"Course he will. You're unforgettable."

Ethan blushed at the compliment, and how Clay delivered it with such sweet sincerity. "I like myself so much more when I'm with you." He laughed. "Does that sound stupid?"

"Nope."

"All those years when I was depressed… I really hated myself sometimes. And I finally came to terms with everything, and I felt a lot better. I did. But now? I've never been this confident. No matter what happens, I'm a stronger man now because of you."

"Nothing's going to happen, mate. Well, nothing and everything. You know what I mean?"

"Yeah." Ethan sighed happily. "I know exactly what you mean." He hesitated, not wanting to ask, but feeling like he had to. "Have you spoken to Barb?"

Tension creased Clay's face. "Going to ring her tomorrow. She and Baz are finally back from their holiday to Milford Sound. Looks gorgeous, by the way. We should plan a trip."

"I'd love that. I'll google it tonight. I don't know when I'll be able to get time off, but hopefully by the end of the year."

"No rush, mate. We can take our time and research. It'll be fun to plan it together."

Ethan nodded. It would be *everything*. "I can't wait to see you again." His flight to LA was earlier this time, but he didn't mind the longer layover. Anything to just get on the move and away from New York City.

Clay grinned. "Me either. I know we've spoken every day, but this month has been torture." He laughed. "Sam says I should play it cool, but that's just not me, mate. I miss you so damn much."

And Ethan loved him for it. "Miss you too. So…" He couldn't resist a mischievous little smile. "Are you going to be thinking about me and…" He waggled his eyebrows suggestively.

The blush on Clay's cheeks was clear even via the small screen of the phone. "Strewth, the things you say."

"Or I could help you out now. Show you a little bit of what you're missing until I get back." He'd never had phone sex, let alone FaceTime sex, but shit, he missed Clay so much. He burned to see him come—to know it was because of him.

But Clay's eyes bugged out, and he looked adorably scandalized. "Mate, what if someone's watching? Hackers or something? Don't know how safe these transmissions are. No, it'll be worth the wait when I see you in the flesh."

Ethan chuckled. "Yeah, okay. But I'll definitely be thinking about you when I jerk off. Like always. For the record."

Clay's teeth flashed in a grin, his eyes crinkling. "Ditto. I think about you all the time. For the record."

His heart was going to burst, and Ethan could only grin like an idiot. "See you soon. In the flesh."

Chapter Nineteen

"HIYA, MR. KELLY. How ya going?" Barb's voice was warm and familiar, and the rush of fondness in Clay helped him exhale.

"Hiya." He paced the small kitchen, the worn tiles warm beneath his feet. He'd put Gilly in the yard after lots of scratches and kisses, then changed out of his uniform. "Finished my last run down the coast this morning after doing the Sydney sights."

"Ah, congrats! Must be a relief. They've agreed to let you stay closer to home?"

"Yeah. Blue Mountains, Great Ocean Road, Hunter Valley. Canberra and Melbourne. I'll be gone for a night or two sometimes, but it'll mostly be day trips to the Hunter and Blue Mountains."

"Brilliant. You never miss working on that old mine machinery?"

"Not a damn bit."

"Did Pete tell you he's gotten a job?"

"Yep. Sent a picture of himself in uniform behind the bar to prove it."

She laughed. "Sent me the same. Let's hope he didn't borrow a mate's uniform to stage it." She laughed again. "Nah, he'd have to ask for more money if he hadn't got a job."

"True."

"How's Sam?"

"She's good. Not calling about the kids, actually." His breath came short and shallow, and he gripped his mobile where he held it up to his ear. "There's something I have to tell you."

All traces of laughter vanished from Barb's voice. "What's happened? Is it your mum? Or Jen?"

"No, no, everyone's fine. It's about me. I…" His mouth was bone dry, and he cleared his throat.

"Bloody hell, what is it? Are you ill?" Her voice was tight and reedy.

"No, nothing like that." At least he hoped she wouldn't think there was anything wrong with him once he told her the truth. And of course this truth was about more than him. It was about the life they'd shared together.

She exhaled noisily. "Nearly gave me a heart attack, you mongrel. What is it, then?"

His heart pounded, feeling like it was about to explode. "I've met someone," he spit out.

Barb whooped delightedly. "You've finally got a girlfriend? About time. You've spent long enough pining for me, Mr. Kelly," she joked.

Head light, he couldn't breathe, much less respond.

Barb's chuckle was uncertain now. "Come on, you haven't *really* been pining for me."

"No," he managed. After gulping a mouthful of water and dropping the glass back down on the counter too hard with a shaky hand, he added, "I haven't been pining for you."

She laughed. "Had me worried there for a minute, mate. But what aren't you saying? Come on. Better out than in."

Clay had to smile. Same old no-nonsense Barb. It was one of the reasons they'd got on so well for so long, even if there'd never been passion between them. She was a good woman, solid and dependable. Well, until she'd fallen in love with another bloke, but she was still a good woman. She'd deserved more than Clay could give her. The thought of losing her regard, of hurting her with his truth, had him gripping the counter, knees knocking.

"What, is she some sweet young thing with perky tits? I won't be cross. As long as you're happy, it's fine by me."

He half laughed, half groaned. *Better out than in* had a whole new meaning now. With a deep breath, he blurted, "It's not a she. And he is younger. Twenty-seven, so not *that* young, but young enough."

In the silence, he couldn't hear Barb even breathe. Finally she exhaled. "I… Did you say a he?"

"Yeah." Clay's jaw was so tight it might snap. "I reckon it'll be a shock. Sorry."

After a few more beats of silence, Barb muttered, "Strewth. You're…" She was silent again, before saying, "Is this why…? You're saying you like blokes? All this time?" She sputtered for a moment. "Why didn't you bloody well tell me?"

"I'm so sorry," he rasped.

Her tone hardened. "You could have at least fessed up when I told you I was leaving."

"I didn't realize it then." He winced at how foolish that sounded, his belly clenching. "I know that probably sounds like a load of nonsense, but I really didn't. I would have told you, I swear. I was in denial. Since I was a boy, I reckon. Locked it all away and tossed the key. Then I met this bloke, and he sent my head spinning."

In the silence, Clay thought of Ethan—the dimples in his cheeks, the touch of his long fingers, the press of his body, those legs wrapped so tightly as Clay came inside him. His kisses of all sorts—sweet and soft, deep and demanding, teasing, sleepy. The warmth and joy Clay felt simply from sitting beside him watching a flick or cricket, sharing in the simplest things.

He could breathe again.

Maybe Clay was fooling himself and it would all fall apart once Ethan was back and the shine wore off, but… No. He knew it was right, being with Ethan. He knew it in his bones.

When she spoke, Barb's voice was still tense, but it softened a few degrees. "So in all these years, you've never fancied another fellow? Aside from Adam Gilchrist, but you're not alone in that man crush."

Clay managed a little laugh. "Nah. Not that I was aware of, really. But with Ethan, I got to know him, and… It's different with him. I think… I do fancy blokes, and him in particular." Saying it aloud to Barb, he knew it was the absolute truth, and his shoulders inched down from his ears a few degrees.

"Well."

After too long of a silence, he asked, heart in his throat, "Are you still there?"

"Yeah. Just taking it in."

He exhaled. "Right. I understand."

She was quiet a few moments before asking, "So, you're not keen on women at all?"

"No, don't reckon I am. Should have realized it, but I never gave it much thought. Suppose it scared me to consider it. Because if I thought about that, I'd have to deal with the rest of it." He swallowed thickly and whispered, "The truth is, I was frightened. Something happened when I was young, and I hid it all away. Even from myself."

He could hear the frown in her voice. And the concern, which made his heart clench. "What happened?"

"You remember Tony Taylor? He lived up the street from me."

"Yeah, I think so. There was some sort of nasty business with him before he moved away. I remember Mum and Dad whispering about it."

Clay swallowed thickly. *Better out than in.* "He was gay. Run out of town. I saw the mob that nearly beat him to death. And—" He squeezed his eyes shut on the memories flooding him, acid in his belly. "Dad said he deserved it."

She inhaled sharply. "He was a piece of work, your dad." Then she sighed. "He had his good points, to be fair. But what a thing to say."

"Yeah. Can't imagine what he'd think if I told him about all this."

Barb whistled. "Don't reckon it would go down well."

"No. Not very." Sweat prickled the back of Clay's neck at the thought of Dad knowing about him. He'd loved his father—of course he had. But he had to admit he wasn't sorry to not have to face him now. He tried to joke, "Guess it's a good thing he's gone and Mum won't really understand if I tell her."

"And what is it you'd tell? Exactly?"

He swallowed hard. Better out than in, right? "I'm gay."

She was silent so long he whispered, "Hello?"

Barb exhaled noisily. "I'm here."

"I never meant to deceive you. Or waste so many years of your life. Or mine."

"Ah, now, we got two brilliant kids out of it. And you were a good husband. Maybe not in the bedroom, but in most ways." She was quiet a moment. "Look, I won't say it doesn't sting. It bloody does. It's going to take more than a few minutes to wrap my head 'round it. But I'm not hanging up on you. Okay?"

"Yeah. Ta."

"Do the kids know?"

"Sam's been lovely. Couldn't ask for better."

"Well, that's no surprise." Barb's voice was a mix of affection with a trace of resentment. "Always a daddy's girl. And she's a great person, our Sam. Always accepting of others. Pete too. Reckon you haven't told him yet, or I'd have heard about it."

Clay smirked. "Always a mum's boy. And no, not yet. I'd really rather speak to him than do it by text, but you know he hates talking on the phone."

"That's kids for you. If the bludger won't pick up, just send a text. He won't mind."

"About texting, or…what I'm telling him?"

"Either. He's always been open-minded, and you know Pete. It's no skin off his nose, is it? He's been off doing his own thing for ages now. In his own world."

"Aside from needing our money."

She laughed sharply. "Yep, aside from that."

Talking about Sam and Pete, they'd slipped into a familiar ease. Now Barb was silent again, but Clay could hear her breathing. He waited, stomach knotting again.

She asked, "So who's this bloke?"

"Ethan." Clay gave her a quick rundown on how they met. "There's just something special about him. I know we don't have much in common, but we get on so well." He paced the kitchen, laughing at himself. "Of course it's only been a week or two we've actually been together in person. He's been back in the States the past month getting everything sorted so he can come back. Suppose I shouldn't put the cart before the horse. Still, he laughs at my terrible jokes and is trying to understand cricket. We can sit and talk for hours about all sorts. It's…peaceful between us."

"You're mad about him. I can hear it plain as day."

His face went hot. "Reckon I am."

She laughed dryly. "Looking back, it explains a few things. You never panted after me the way I wanted. Even when we were young. I thought I must have done something wrong."

He groaned, guilt twisting up his guts. "There was nothing wrong with you. It was all me—it was my fault. I'm sorry. Wasn't fair to you. I had my head too far up my own arse."

"When really you wanted it up another bloke's."

Clay barked out a laugh, breathing a little easier. "That's one way to put it."

Barb laughed too. "I've always had a way with words. It's one of my charms."

"'Tis indeed. Barb, I never meant to do wrong."

She sighed. "I know. You wouldn't, would you? You were always a good sort. I never meant to either. Didn't plan on meeting Barry, but here we are. And now there's Ethan. Life's a funny thing. You said he's American?"

"Yeah." Clay's stomach tightened again, his body tensing down to his toes. Until he had Ethan in his arms again, he worried that something would go wrong. "He's on his way back now. Transferring to the Sydney office of the company he works for."

"That's good, then. You can give it a real go. Long distance isn't the same, really. Lucky for me, Barry and I have a lovely time together. Hopefully it'll be the same with your Ethan."

My Ethan. The truth slipped out again. "Bloody hell, I'll be gutted if it doesn't work out." He tried to laugh when he wanted to cry. "Shouldn't care so much."

"There's no 'should' when it comes to caring."

"People will say he's too young and that we're rushing into it."

"People can get stuffed."

Laughter warmed Clay's chest. "That's what Sam said."

"Of course she did. She's a smart girl. Like her mother." Barb sighed again. "Look, I didn't cover myself in glory when I left you. People said all sorts of things and called me all kinds of nasty names. I don't blame them, but I had to do what was right for me. We only get one shot at this. Have to make the most of it."

"That we do." Clay thought of Ethan in the air, flying closer. He smiled to himself.

"Barry's calling me for tea. Reckon I'm going to crack open a stubby instead. Could use a few drinks right about now."

Affection and gratitude swirled through him, smoothing out a few of the sharper edges. "Same here."

"Talk soon." She paused. "It takes guts, what you're doing. I'm proud of ya."

Bugger, now he really was going to cry, tears already slipping from the corners of his eyes. He had to sniff before he could say, "Ta."

"Now don't go blubbering on me, Mr. Kelly."

He laughed, swiping at his cheeks. "I'll try not to—" He hesitated before adding, "Mrs. Wallingford. Enjoy the beer."

They said goodbye, and Clay stood there a minute, letting the mixed emotions wash over him. Then he went to the fridge and popped the top on a stubby. He'd done it, and he toasted himself and drank before he let Gilly back in, kneeling and letting Gilly give him sloppy kisses. No matter what happened, he had his family.

"DAD, YOU'RE WEARING a hole in the floor."

Clay jolted to a stop where he'd been pacing. "Right. Sorry."

Sam chuckled. "No need to be sorry. But no need to be nervous either. He'll be here any minute. And everything will be great. Right?" She elbowed Jase, who stood a head taller than her and had a mop of hair he wore up in one of those ridiculous man-buns.

Jase glanced up from his phone. "No worries, Mr. K. Just an hour delay. Happens all the time on flights."

"I know, but..." Clay didn't have anything reasonable to say. He *did* know that it was an ordinary delay, and there was nothing Ethan could do about it, and that it didn't mean Ethan was changing his mind at the last second.

But when he had Ethan warm in his arms again, he'd relax.

His phone buzzed, and he eagerly pulled it out. The plane had finally landed, so perhaps Ethan was texting. But it was Pete, and Clay's heart skipped. Then he laughed as he read the message, relief easing a few tense knots of muscle.

Sam nudged him. "What?"

"Your brother." He showed her the screen.

Hey Dad. Fine with me if you're into blokes. After all, Mum's into Bazza and we've accepted that.

PS. Think you can send me a couple hundred bucks? Just this one time.

Sam rolled her eyes with a laugh. "Say no or you'll be sending him a couple hundred when he's fifty." Then she smiled softly. "And see? Told ya he'd be okay with it."

"Yes, you're always right," he joked.

"I'm glad you're finally catching on, Dad." She eyed Jase. "See? I'm always right."

"Hmm?" Jase tapped at his phone. "Yep, babe."

"This is how I win most arguments," she whispered to Clay. "He gets distracted by work."

"So he goes to the office like that?" Clay eyed Jase's hair.

"He does. You see more and more blokes in suits and man-buns these days. If you can pick stocks the way Jase can, the company won't care. He—" She broke off, squinting toward the arrivals gate. "Oh! This might be his flight."

Clay's pulse shot through the roof, and he craned his neck, impatiently peering at the people trickling out of the main doors. More people were gathering in the waiting area, all doing the same, eager to see their loved ones.

And Clay did love Ethan. He knew it down to his toes.

Then Ethan appeared, and Clay almost leapt for joy at the sight of him. Sure, he'd seen him via the phone screen, but now he was striding toward Clay in the flesh, a beautiful smile splitting his face. His big suitcases kept rolling a few feet as he let go and launched himself into Clay's arms.

They clung to each other, and Ethan whispered in Clay's ear a little too loudly, "I missed you so fucking much." Then he stepped back, glancing nervously at Sam and Jase, and then around at the crowd of people.

Taking a deep breath, Clay didn't hesitate as he cupped Ethan's face in his hands and kissed him soundly. Ethan's grin when they separated was worth every sideways glance from strangers who didn't matter.

"Hi," Clay said, even though he had so much more to say.

"Hi," Ethan replied. "I can barely hear you. Can we get out of here?"

Clay looked to Sam and Jase, who wore matching grins and offered Ethan hugs even though it was only the second time Sam was meeting him and Jase's first. In that moment, Clay was so proud of his girl and her boyfriend. They'd insisted on coming to the airport to give Ethan a warm welcome, and Clay loved them both. Man-bun and all.

When Sam and Jase were headed back into Sydney and Ethan's cases were secured in the back of the ute, Clay and Ethan climbed into the cab. They were finally alone, and Clay had so much to say he didn't know where to start.

Fortunately with all the kissing, there was no need for words. It was all Clay could do not to get Ethan naked and under him right there.

Panting softly, his lips wet and swollen already, Ethan said, "I can't wait to shower and get out of these clothes." He grinned devilishly. "And stay naked with you for days."

Clay turned the key in the ignition with a matching grin. "Why didn't you say so, mate? Let's get home."

Epilogue

Six years later

"N̲o!" The anguished cry rose up in unison around the yard as Australia lost a wicket to England. Beside Ethan on the outdoor sofa, Clay groaned. In the faint glow of the white Christmas lights they'd strung up for their backyard wedding and never taken down, Clay's cheeks were ruddy with a bit too much sun and beer.

Ethan squeezed Clay's thigh. "It's okay. Still a lot of game left." The heat of the day lingered even though the stars blinked faintly above the light of Mullaloo, the quiet seaside Perth suburb where he and Clay had settled in their own little house. His shoulder pressed against Clay's, and he nudged him slightly. Sitting on their feet, Gilly happily chewed a rubber kangaroo.

Clay nudged back and gave him a smile. "Would just be nice to have them win on my birthday." He looked back at the big screen Pete had set up in the yard, wincing at the replay.

Sam leaned on the sofa arm, a hand on her rounding belly. "Whatever happens, you've already scored a half-century for Australia, Dad."

The people around them laughed, and Ethan missed what Sam said next, but by the looks of the teasing smile she gave Clay, it was something else about turning fifty. Clay laughed good-naturedly.

As the cricket came back on, everyone's attention returned to the large screen. Pete had rigged it so his laptop was getting the TV feed from inside, so they had captions and everything. He'd also set up speakers, and though Ethan worried it was too loud, the neighbors didn't seem to mind since he'd invited them all to the party.

They'd been barbecuing since mid-afternoon, and Ethan sipped his beer, his stomach pleasantly full. He made sure he didn't drink too much, since he had another birthday surprise for Clay later.

The yard was packed with lawn chairs, their friends and family showing up from all over. Pete and his girlfriend had flown in from Bali, Sam and Jase had come from Sydney, and even Barb and Barry—still Baz to everyone else, although Ethan thought they said it with affection now—had come from Christchurch.

Clay's sister, Jen, and her husband and kids were all there of course, along with a few grandkids. It still blew Ethan's mind that Clay was soon to be a grandfather himself, but he supposed that's what happened when you married young.

Sitting nearby in the armchair Ethan and Jase had wrestled out of the living room was Sally, Clay's mom. Ethan freaking *loved* Sally. And she loved him. Sure, he had to tell her his name every time he saw her, but it didn't matter.

Taking his beer, Ethan kissed Clay's cheek and got up, scratching Gilly's head when he barked to protest Ethan daring to move from under his furry heat.

Kneeling by Sally's chair, Ethan adjusted his hearing aids to try and block out the sound behind him and said, "Hey, Sal. Having a good time?" She was small and plump, wearing her usual capri pants and flowered T-shirt. Her graying curls were still highlighted copper.

She beamed at him. "I am." Sometimes she was cranky and

could be a real handful, but other times she was content and peaceful. Ethan was grateful tonight was one of those days. She said something he missed, and then added, "I like this movie."

"Yeah. It's a good one. It's The Ashes."

She was quiet for a minute, watching the cricket. Then, glancing around the yard, she asked, "Are we at a wedding?"

"No, but you did come to a wedding here a few years ago. When I married Clay." His heart swelled at the memory. "It was a night just like this. Warm and breezy, but not too hot. Here, I'll show you." He pulled out his phone and scrolled to his favorite photo.

He and Clay wore tan linen pants and white short-sleeved shirts open at the collar, Clay with a blue belt and Ethan with red. They were in this yard, the sun setting across the sky in swathes of pink-orange. Not quite as good as a Mission Beach sunrise, but Perth sunsets were a joy all their own, and since they'd gone to Mission Beach for their honeymoon, they'd had the best of both worlds.

Ethan held up the screen so Sally could see. "This is me and Clay on our wedding day. Right here." They'd rented a flower-covered archway for the little ceremony, and they were standing under it for photos afterward. But this wasn't one the hired photographer took. It was a snap Sam had caught after someone made a joke, and Ethan and Clay were looking at whoever had said it.

They were holding hands and laughing, and in the split second captured forever, their joy and love were plain to see. It was perfect. Ethan liked that picture more than any of the posed ones.

Sally blinked at the screen. "Doesn't my Clay look handsome?"

"He does. Always." Ethan went to another pic. "And here you are in this one. That's my aunt and uncle, and there's Jen, and Sam, and Pete."

"That looks like a lovely wedding."

"It was." Ethan's chest tightened with a pang of longing. "My parents would have loved it. Especially my mom."

Ethan showed her a few more pictures, then kissed her soft cheek, ducking inside the house when Sam beckoned. She said something, but a cheer from outside drowned it out. Ethan squinted, and she repeated herself.

"Should we do the cake? Jen said the little ones have to get home to bed soon."

"Yeah, good idea."

They'd hidden the massive slab cake in a cooler and carefully pulled it out now. Sam tied back her blonde curls. "All right, fifty candles." She handed Ethan a lighter and picked up another.

"Let's do this." Ethan gave her a fist bump.

As they worked, Sam asked, "Business is going well? Yours, I mean. I know his is. Brilliant that he got number one on TripAdvisor for small tours."

Ethan grinned, pride swelling. "He's worked so hard. He signed a deal for a fourth minibus. And of course he can do all the mechanic work himself, so that saves on overhead. He hires great drivers and guides too."

She winced and whipped her hand back, apparently having gotten too close to a flame. "I'm damn proud of him. And you! A consultant now. Charging big bucks to those rich companies?"

"You know it. And I get to work from home where it's nice and quiet." The candles were almost all lit now, the heat from them making Ethan sweat. "Okay, we almost got it."

"Three, two..." Sam lit the final one. "Okay, go, go! Jase! Get the door and mute the TV!" she bellowed, and Ethan cringed away from the sound, laughing.

He and Sam each carried an end, walking slowly, wax melting all over the blue and yellow frosting. They laughed into "Happy Birthday," and everyone joined in, including a howling Gilly, Clay laughing and shaking his head at the amount of fire coming toward him. It was a mess of noise, but it was joyous.

Clay stood, and Barb said, "Make a wish for the next fifty years, Mr. Kelly."

Looking at Ethan, Clay smiled softly and said nothing. Then he leaned over to blow, Ethan and Sam helping him in the end, laughter all around them.

Later, while Clay had a quick shower before bed, Ethan changed into his other little surprise. The traditional white uniform pants hugged his slim legs. He'd gone with a smaller size so they'd be a little tighter than normal. It wasn't like he was going to play cricket in them.

Or keep them on very long.

The white, long-sleeved shirt fit perfectly, and he adjusted the baggy green cap on his head. Ethan quickly checked himself in the mirrored closet door and grinned at his reflection. Yes. Clay was going to like his birthday surprise.

Ethan realized he hadn't planned out where to wait. Lounging on the bed? Standing by the bed? Sitting on the bed? Or should he be by the door? He could stand by the massive framed photo of a perfectly pink Mission Beach that decorated one wall. Or in the middle of the floor? Maybe—

Through the half-open door to the adjoining bathroom, he thought he heard the water shut off. Tiptoeing closer, he strained, listening. Then the door opened, and all he could do was stand there and try to look sexy.

Clay jolted to a stop in the doorway, a towel slung around his hips, water clinging to his chest hair. He was still muscular and fucking *gorgeous*. His gold wedding band gleamed on his finger. He stared at Ethan in wonder.

Ethan cocked an eyebrow and went for a cricket pun. "Did I *bowl* you over?"

Bursting out laughing, Clay strode the few steps between them and hauled Ethan into his arms, his skin damp and warm. He lifted Ethan clear off his feet before putting him down and giving him a delighted grin.

"Too right you did. *Strewth*, you look incredible. I don't know where to start." He leaned back, his eyes roaming over Ethan's body and hands following.

"Lose the towel, for starters."

Giving him a smoldering glance, his blue eyes hooded, Clay did. Then he pushed Ethan backwards until Ethan met the high bed frame, a solid, rustic gumtree. He leaned against it as Clay dropped to his knees and yanked at the fly on Ethan's uniform pants.

Ethan threaded his fingers through Clay's hair, which shone a burnished copper, the overhead light also catching Ethan's gold band. "Happy birthday. You can pretend I'm Adam Gilchrist." He grinned when Clay looked up.

But Clay shook his head, speaking slowly and clearly. "Don't need him. Only you. Always you."

Then Clay took him in his mouth, and Ethan moaned, sweet pleasure and affection flowing through his veins. He'd married the man of his dreams, and their honeymoon went on and on.

THE END

About the Author

Keira aims for the perfect mix of character, plot, and heat in her M/M romances. She writes everything from swashbuckling pirates to heartwarming holiday escapism. Her fave tropes are enemies to lovers, age gaps, forced proximity, and passionate virgins. Although she loves delicious angst along the way, Keira guarantees happy endings!

Discover more at:
KeiraAndrews.com